KINGDOM
WARS II

TARTARUS

JACK CAVANAUGH

HOWARD
Fiction
A DIVISION OF SIMON & SCHUSTER
New York   London   Toronto   Sydney

Our purpose at Howard Books is to:

- *Increase faith* in the hearts of growing Christians
- *Inspire holiness* in the lives of believers
- *Instill hope* in the hearts of struggling people everywhere

Because He's coming again!

 Published by Howard Books, a division of Simon & Schuster, Inc.,
1230 Avenue of the Americas, New York, NY 10020,
www.howardpublishing.com

Tartarus © 2008 by Jack Cavanaugh

In association with Steve Laube Literary Agency.

Library of Congress Cataloging-in-Publication Data
Cavanaugh, Jack, date.
  Tartarus / Jack Cavanaugh
    p. cm. —(Kingdom wars ; 2)
  1. Good and evil—Fiction. 2. Angels—Fiction. 3. Manuscripts—Fiction. I. Title.
  PS3553.A965T37 2008
  813'.54—dc22
                          2008005019

ISBN-13: 978-1-4165-4387-9
ISBN-10:   1-4165-4387-2

10 9 8 7 6 5 4 3 2 1

Manufactured in the United States of America

For information regarding special discounts for bulk purchases,
please contact Simon & Schuster Special Sales at 1-800-456-6798
or business@simonandschuster.com.

Edited by David Lambert and Lissa Halls Johnson
Cover design by Kirk DouPonce, www.DogEaredDesign.com
Interior design by Jaime Putorti

ACKNOWLEDGMENTS

To Ramona Tucker for the late-night hours you spent whipping the manuscript into shape. You are not only a talented editor, you are a special lady.

To editor Dave Lambert and the team at Howard Publishing and Simon & Schuster, Inc.: Always professional, you make me appear to be a better author than I am.

And, as always, special thanks to my agent, Steve Laube.

Our most fatal tendency is the belief
that the here and now is all there is.
—ALLAN BLOOM

Our generation is overwhelmingly naturalistic. . . .
If we are not careful, even though we say
we are biblical Christians and supernaturalists,
nevertheless the naturalism of our generation
tends to come in upon us. It may infiltrate our thinking
without our recognizing its coming.
—FRANCIS SCHAEFFER

For if God did not spare angels when they sinned,
but sent them to Tartarus . . . the Lord knows how
to hold the unrighteous for the day of judgment,
while continuing their punishment.
—HOLY BIBLE

Woe to the earth and the sea,
because the Devil has gone down to you.
He is filled with fury
because he knows his time is short.
—HOLY BIBLE

Six days angelic choirs sang in rapturous praise
As new worlds cooled within the Father's calloused hands.
The seventh dawned with trumpets stilled, a day of rest.
In muted awe all heaven's host beneath the stars
Reclined; at peace, content, enthralled. Save one.

Cursing, sputtering, muttering threats, a shadow figure
Slipped unseen into the fields of time.
One hand clutched a bag of tares; the other freely sowed
Discord among harmony,
Chaos among peace.
Rocks were planted in the grass,
Flowers hosted weeds.
Clouds reflected in the mud,
Flesh would know disease.
Thus did Lucifer despoil all creation's glory,
Warping it in likeness own, perverting heaven's story.

On morning eight the angels woke with joyful hearts,
The terror sown the night before unknown to them.

His work not done, the black-winged foe flew down to earth,
And slithered in the garden grass one final tare to throw.
While Father God prepared a Seed of flesh to sow.
—ABDIEL, SERAPH OF HEAVEN

TARTARUS

PROLOGUE

The screams were getting louder. The curses. The pleas for mercy. The clanging swords.

Unnerved by the violence, Zelek ben Judah waded elbow-deep into a mound of scrolls, frantic to find the misplaced manuscript. He cursed the incompetence of his subordinates. How many times had he lectured them? A disorganized library is worse than no library at all. To misplace a scroll is to destroy it, for who can read words that cannot be found?

Sweat ran into his eyes as he searched. He dared not lift a hand to wipe it away. Sifting through a stack of scrolls was like digging in the sand. If he pulled out now, the scrolls would tumble in and he'd have to start over. With an angry grunt, he wiped the sweat from his eye with the sleeve of his shoulder.

An ungodly shriek from the central room startled him, the dying cry of a man put to the sword. What made it worse, Zelek recognized the voice. Orosius. Only this morning the two of them had discussed the sophist Polemon of Laodikeia while eating figs.

Zelek's heart rose to his throat. He'd spent his life hunched over manuscripts. His were hands that wielded pens, not swords. Paunchy, slow, and aging, his only chance of surviving was to find that scroll. He continued searching with greater intensity.

A tall clay jar sat at his feet. It held two scrolls with room for a third.

"Ah!" Zelek said.

In triumph he hoisted the missing manuscript. Unrolling it, he read to make certain he had the right one. A scowl wrinkled his brow. It was indeed the scroll he'd been instructed to save. But why this scroll? The two in the jar, yes. But this one?

There were worthier scrolls and codices and sacred texts. Works by Plato and Socrates. Euclid's *Elements*. Eratosthenes' calculations of the size of the earth. Archimedes' invention of the screw-shaped water pump. The *Septuagint*. Irreplaceable originals. Rare copies. Works that would be lost forever. To place this nothing of a scroll in the jar with the other two manuscripts was wrong.

Zelek checked the door. His escort had not yet arrived.

Did he dare?

Laying aside the third scroll, he chose a more suitable work and placed it in the jar instead. He capped the jar with a lid and stood, satisfied with the exchange. For good measure he sealed it with wax to keep them from discovering the deception.

He donned his cap. Using both hands, he picked up the clay jar and pressed it to his chest. He was ready.

Outside the chamber chaos awaited him. A cacophony of shouts and screams, smashed shelves, and—he sniffed the air—fire. To his horror, smoke crawled across the ceiling like a legion of demons. Every nerve within him jolted as though struck by lightning. Fire was a librarian's greatest fear.

Save one, Zelek corrected himself. *Death is greater.*

He checked the doorway again. Where was the escort he'd been promised?

The room was filling with smoke, choking him. Zelek's feet danced nervously as he began to cough.

Were they waiting for him outside? He took a step toward the doorway. Another life-ending wail stopped him. It was nearby. Death was at hand. Zelek whimpered.

He clutched the jar against his chest. He was finding it difficult to breathe.

He looked at the jar.

The third scroll! They knew. They hadn't come for him because they knew he'd switched scrolls.

Dropping to his knees, he pulled a small knife from his waistband and cut into the wax seal. Prying the lid from the jar, he pulled out the substitute scroll and replaced it with the original third scroll.

At that instant two men with swords appeared in the doorway, tall men with broad shoulders and strong jaws. They stood serene in spotless white robes. No one would mistake them for marauders.

"I'm ready," Zelek wheezed, the smoke strangling his voice.

His armed escorts turned toward the central room.

With fumbling hands Zelek fitted the lid on the jar, grabbed a leather pouch, slinging its strap over his head, hugged the clay jar, and ran to catch up with his escort.

The room that opened up before him was a familiar one, the domed palatial expanse of the central library. Hallways branched off in many directions leading to lecture halls, study rooms, dining areas, gardens, and an astronomical observatory.

For centuries the great library of Alexandria had been a repository of human knowledge, with hundreds of thousands of

documents and records collected from every corner of the
known world, the sum of mankind's learning preserved on papyrus, vellum, and clay tablets. Now it was a battlefield. Its
shelves were on fire, and its floor was littered with the dead
and dying.

Their path through the carnage was arrow-straight. In order
to keep close to his escort, Zelek was forced to step over bodies.
Midstep he recognized Orosius, his chest slashed, his eyes staring in disbelief at the terror he had seen. The mouth that had
earlier tasted figs gaped open in death.

Zelek swallowed hard, forcing back an eruption of bile.

Pairs of marauders trolled the room, looking for victims and
torching shelves. Zelek's escorts showed no concern or fear.
Their swords drawn, they strode almost casually through the
vaulted library.

Two marauders spied them. Then two more. And two more.
A moment later six filthy, screaming, sweating, wild-eyed men
were charging toward them.

Zelek's escorts did not break stride.

Even though Zelek knew something about his escorts that
the marauders didn't know, a man doesn't watch six armed attackers with a taste for blood charge at him without experienc-
ing fear. A scream erupted from his throat.

The marauders closed.

Zelek's escorts raised their weapons.

The swords shimmered, then burst into flame with a pulse of
light that knocked the marauders off their feet and sent them
flying backward.

Zelek's scream turned to giddy laughter. His feet tapped
with joy. Borrowing from Scripture, he sang lustily, "My God
sent his angel, and he shut the mouths of the lions!"

Once outside they crossed the library grounds with its statues, lush gardens, and pools, leaving behind a pillar of black smoke. They traversed the poorer section of Alexandria without incident. And upon reaching the Mound of Shards, Zelek's escorts disappeared.

"What?" he shouted at the sky. "You would leave me now?"

He stood at the base of a stone stairway that led up to a limestone portico. One of Alexandria's greatest works of architecture, the Mound of Shards rivaled the legendary lighthouse in the bay for its grandeur. It was remarkable for its vast intricately decorated rooms cut out of solid rock.

But despite its legendary beauty, Zelek couldn't get past the fact that it was three levels of catacombs. A city built for the dead. Zelek despised anything that was associated with death.

With the city's attention focused on the burning library, it wasn't surprising to Zelek that he had the catacombs to himself. Given the number of corpses he'd stepped over, business would be brisk tomorrow.

Still clutching the clay jar to his chest, Zelek ascended the steps. To one side of the stairway there was a mountain of broken pottery, terra-cotta containers that had been discarded. It was the quantity of the refuse that had given the catacombs their name. The shattered containers had once carried the food and wine of those traveling great distances to visit the site. Not wanting to carry the empty jars home, they discarded them here.

At the top of the steps Zelek passed between pillars to the underground entrance. A feeling of dread passed over him as he stepped out of the light and into the stone-cold rooms.

The first level boasted a vestibule and a large banquet hall, complete with rotunda and extensive mosaic flooring. Rectangular limestone slabs served as tables flanked by stone couches. It disgusted Zelek to think that dining clubs regularly used this facility for entertainment. What sort of people held banquets in the catacombs?

He crossed to a spiral staircase with a central shaft six meters in diameter. The shaft not only provided light for the stairway but was used to lower bodies to the second and third levels.

At the top of the stairway Zelek hesitated. The first step down was a small one. The builders had designed it so the height of the steps decreased near the top to make it easier for people as they approached the surface. There were ninety-nine steps in all. Perspiring heavily, Zelek took a deep breath and started down.

At the second level he ran out of natural light. Torches were available for visitors. He took one and lit it.

As he turned, his heart seized and he nearly dropped the clay jar. Inches from his face was a writhing serpent, carved in stone and flanking the doorway. The flickering of the torch had brought it to life.

Unlike those in Rome's catacombs, the images on these walls were Egyptian, not Christian.

Having caught his breath, Zelek continued downward to the third level, where he found a central hallway intersected by a series of connecting corridors. The dense humidity at this depth made it seem darker than the second level, and Zelek fought a strong urge to turn back. He tried not to think what lay beyond the reach of his torchlight.

Following his instructions, Zelek counted the connecting corridors as he passed them. At the ninth corridor he turned right and proceeded to the end, where he encountered solid rock. This was where his instructions ran out.

His torch flickering, the walls dripping, his heart pounding, Zelek waited for whatever was to happen next. Initially, when he was told of the plan to rescue the scrolls, the description of the massacre in the library had so frightened him that waiting alone in the catacombs seemed a minor thing. It didn't seem so minor now. He stood alone in the dark, deep underground, with his only escape a hallway of row after row of rotting corpses.

"I'm here," he said with a shaky voice.

His eyes strained at the corridor entrance, alternately wanting someone to appear and fearing someone would appear.

Then the rock wall behind him shuddered.

He jumped away from it.

It shuddered again, as did the stone floor.

Zelek's eyes bulged with fear.

He turned to run, but as he did the rock floor tilted, throwing him against a slick wall. He managed to spin just in time so that his shoulder, and not the clay jar, took the brunt of the force.

The rock underfoot rippled like waves. To keep from falling over, Zelek sank to the floor, his back against the wall. He watched in fearful wonder as a fissure opened at the closed end of the corridor, large enough for a man to walk through.

The quaking stopped. Everything was still again. Still and silent as rock was meant to be.

A light appeared through the fissure. Soft at first, then increasing to blinding brilliance.

Inching himself up the side of the wall Zelek managed to get to his feet. He approached the fissure, clay jar in hand. He left the torch behind, for it was no longer needed.

Shielding his eyes, Zelek stepped through the fissure. An exquisite radiance awaited him.

"Gabriel!" Zelek fell to his knees and offered the jar. "I have done everything you have asked of me."

The angel stared down at him. "Seal the jar."

The angel's voice resonated within Zelek's chest like the music of a thousand instruments in perfect harmony. The feeling was pleasant to the point of distraction.

"I . . . I . . . brought the wax," Zelek managed to say.

He shrugged the strap of the pouch over his head and retrieved the tools he needed to seal the jar. Under heaven's gaze, Zelek ben Judah took pains to make certain the container was properly sealed. Then he placed it with several other jars that had already been deposited in the cave.

The angel nodded his approval.

Zelek sighed with relief. He had done it. He'd faced his greatest fear and preserved a pair of invaluable scrolls. Now all he had to do was climb out of this wretched hole of death.

Beaming, he said, "God willing, in the future I will tell my grandchildren of the day the angel Gabriel dispatched two of his own to guide me safely through the valley of death."

"You would tell them a lie?" the angel asked.

The smile on Zelek's face vanished. "A lie? I don't understand."

"You have never met Gabriel."

"Then who?"

The brightness of the angel increased dramatically. His voice boomed off the walls of the small subterranean cave. "I am Semyaza. Tremble before me."

Zelek recognized the name. "You are Satan's man!"

Terror animated him. He lunged for the fissure, but it had already begun to close. Desperate to get out, he stretched a hand to the other side. But who was there to rescue him? There were only corpses there. And soon he would add to their number.

The fissure continued to close. Zelek had no choice but to retract his arm to keep it from being crushed. His back against the rock, he turned toward his captor, who pulsed with heavenly radiance.

Zelek's gaze fell on the clay jar. He understood now. "The third scroll."

He picked up a sizable rock and lifted it over his head. "Let me out, or I'll destroy the jar."

Semyaza's expression remained unchanged. He did not acknowledge the threat.

Zelek protested, "You promised—"

"—to keep you safe from the marauders. I have kept that promise."

His arms trembling with exertion, blinking back the sweat that stung his eyes, Zelek said, "You deceived me."

"Would you expect any less from Lucifer's lieutenant?"

Zelek had but one move left. He lifted the rock to smash the jar.

His arms froze in place, held back by an unseen force. Crying out in frustration, he strained against it with all his might, to no avail.

The ground beneath him trembled. The cave shuddered. From the domed ceiling rocks pelted him like meteors. He collapsed onto the floor. Semyaza, untouched by the rocks and appearing as beautiful as ever, looked down on him without pity.

A second fissure opened. This one on the opposite side of the cave. The sea rushed in, crashing against the rocks and Zelek.

The cave filled quickly. Zelek ben Judah remained alive long enough to know he'd been entombed in seawater, and long enough to watch the clay jars settle gently against the ocean floor.

The last thing he saw before he died was the glory of Semyaza shining against the black dome of the cave ceiling while a thousand flecks of sand glistened like stars in the sky.

CHAPTER

I

A heavenly glory blazed directly in my path. Shielding my eyes, I fought to keep them open. To close them now meant almost certain death. I hated driving east at this time of morning.

As if Southern California freeways weren't dangerous enough, the sun hovered at just the right inclination to make seeing nearly impossible. Through the thinnest of eye slits I saw the cars ahead of me begin to stack up at the Second Street off-ramp. I slowed, maneuvering into the queue.

For some reason my mind flashed back to an elementary-school assembly. Instead of going to the auditorium we carried our chairs out to the playground, and as we sweltered on the blacktop, a man who called himself Mr. Science taught us about the sun.

"Never look directly at the sun," he said.

To demonstrate what would happen if we failed to heed his warning, Mr. Science pointed a telescope at the sun. Then he held a grape with a pair of pliers close to the eyepiece. The grape was supposed to be our eye. We slid to the edge of our chairs in anticipation.

At first nothing happened, but Mr. Science assured us that even though we couldn't see anything yet, the sun was cooking the retina of the substitute eye, causing permanent damage. Seconds later, when the focused sunlight burned through the skin, hot juice squirted out of the grape, eliciting squeals of disgust from the girls and howls of delight from the boys. Not only did Mr. Science make his point, but he inspired all manner of shenanigans with grapes-as-eyeballs at lunch.

A wave of taillights rippled toward me. I braked. Traffic came to a standstill. I turned my head, using the pause in the action to give my eyes a rest.

As bright as the sun was, I'd seen brighter, on top of the Emerald Plaza tower in the middle of the night. Let me tell you, the sun's a dim bulb compared to the light of two dozen angry angels. If Mr. Science ever demonstrates what happened to me that night, he'll place a grape on the ground and squish it under his heel.

It's hard to believe that was a month ago, or that it's been that long since President Douglas was assassinated. I haven't seen a single angel since. At least that I'm aware. I mean, when they take human form, who can tell? I lived with one every day for four years and never knew he was an angel.

But then I suppose all that will change soon. Professor Forsythe had that Paul Revere tone in his voice when he called.

The angels are coming! The angels are coming!

He didn't actually say it. He didn't have to. Believe me, it takes a lot to drag me away from my cheese Danish and coffee in the morning.

When I finally arrived at Heritage College, the parking lot was full. Likewise, the area streets were lined with cars. If the universe is expanding like scientists say, why is it I can never find a parking place?

I ended up a quarter of a mile from the college. I must have looked like one of those Olympic walkers as I hurried toward the campus.

My cell phone rang. It was my publisher. I considered letting the answering service take the call. I wasn't sure I was ready to talk to him yet.

I flipped open the phone.

"Grant? Higgins. Have you read the contract?"

"My agent faxed it to me this morning," I told him. "I haven't had time to go over it yet."

"Whatever problems you have with it, I'm sure we can work them out," he said. "I don't mind telling you that I'm getting a lot of pressure from above on this one."

I grinned. Pressure from above. Little did he know.

"I told you, I haven't had time to look at it yet."

"Can I at least tell them you're interested?"

Of course I was interested. I needed the money.

The publisher came to me on this one. They wanted a tell-all book documenting how the Douglas administration had systematically deceived me while I was researching President Douglas's biography. It would begin with an eyewitness account of the assassination and then detail subsequent events that uncovered the web of lies that concealed the truth from the American public.

My agent said the publisher was anxious to save face after printing the president's story. And frankly, my career could use some damage control, since I was the expert researcher who had been duped.

"We want you to show that things aren't always as they seem," Higgins pressed. "After reading this book John Q Public will never take a White House statement at face value again. They'll always wonder what's really going on behind the scenes."

"This isn't the world you think it is," I mused.

"Exactly! So you're in? Grant, I want you to know that I went to the mat for you on the advance money."

It was an impressive amount. Nearly double what they'd offered me for the biography. My agent told me not to let the amount give me a swelled head, that it reflected the publisher's desperation more than their assessment of me as an author. He was right.

"Shouldn't you be talking to my agent?"

Higgins mumbled something about desperate times and desperate measures. We both knew that his end run around my agent was unethical.

"How much leeway will I be given on the project?" I asked. "If I do it, I want to do it my way."

"That's what we want!" Higgins insisted. "Your frustration. Your outrage. How you felt when you first realized you were being led down a garden path."

That wasn't what I meant. I wanted to write about what I saw in the sky the day of the assassination. I wanted to reveal to the world the supernatural forces behind the plot. But I knew if I started talking about angels and the war in heaven my publisher would pull the contract off the table in a human heartbeat.

I'd reached the stairs that led from the parking lot to the campus.

"Listen, Higgins, I'll need to get back to you."

"You sound winded."

"I'm late for a meeting."

"A meeting? Grant, you're not meeting with another publisher, are you? Let me get back to my boss. I can get you more money."

"I'll have to call you back."

"When? Grant, the pressure on me is incredible. Don't leave me hanging."

"Soon. I'll get back to you soon."

"How soon?"

I'd reached the top of the steps. My breathing was labored, and it was difficult to talk. "I'll call you as soon as I have an answer." I snapped the phone closed. For good measure I turned off the ringer.

The first thing I noticed about the campus was that there were more students milling about than usual. Someone or something had poked the hive. The place was abuzz with conversation.

The professor had told me to meet him in the library. It was our usual meeting place. As I wove my way in that direction some of the students recognized me from recent events. They fell silent and stared as I passed them.

I opened the library door and had stepped aside for some coeds who were trailing behind me when Sue Ling grabbed me.

"You're late," she said by way of greeting. She pulled me away from the door.

"I couldn't find a parking place."

"This way."

Her pace was urgent. Her expression serious. Something was wrong.

"The professor, is he—"

She plowed ahead. "He's waiting for you."

Small, with dark hair and brown eyes that shimmer with intelligence, Sue Ling is the most devoted person I know. As his personal assistant she serves the professor with passionate loyalty, with an emphasis on passionate. Just once I'd like to know what it feels like to have a woman look at me the way she looks at the professor.

"Talk to me, Sue Ling. Tell me what's going on."

"You'll learn soon enough."

Did I tell you she was stubborn? So am I.

I put on the brakes. Sue Ling's momentum carried her several steps before she realized she was walking alone.

"Grant!" she protested. "We don't have time—"

Fifty feet ahead of us the door to the administration offices swung open. Seated in his wheelchair, the professor held the door open with one arm.

"Miss Ling, I told you to bring him the moment he arrived!" the professor said, clearly exasperated.

From the expression on her face it was evident his words stung. Sue Ling prided herself on her efficiency.

I stepped between them. "Professor, it's not her fault. I—"

But the professor wasn't listening. His arm looked like a windmill in a gale as he motioned toward me. "Come, come—"

I half-ran toward him. Sue Ling didn't follow. When I looked over my shoulder, she had turned and was walking away.

"We need your help," the professor said, pulling me inside.

CHAPTER

2

"C lose the door."

Jana Torres did as she was instructed. She took a seat opposite the producer of the KTSD news, who sat hunched behind a desk that served as the bedrock for a mountain of papers. Matt Gabra was a short, sinewy man with more energy than any man Jana had ever known. During the station's annual blood drive the joke around the office was that the San Diego Blood Bank sold the producer's contribution as a substitute for an energy drink.

"New York called," Gabra said. "The network is offering you a contract. You impressed their high-priced socks off with your report from the bridge."

The thrill that shot through Jana was so strong it nearly lifted her off her chair. This was what every television news reporter dreamed of. And for someone as young as she was to be offered a position with the networks . . . she could hardly contain herself.

Gabra didn't share her excitement and for good reason. The networks were always raiding the best talent from the local stations. It was the bane of local producers. The moment local personalities boosted ratings, the networks snatched them away.

"Look, Jana"—the producer came from behind his desk and stood in front of her—"I can't match the kind of money they'll throw at you. Just tell me what it'll take to get you to stay."

The timing couldn't have been better. Jana's contract was coming up for renewal and, for the last couple of months, Gabra had been moaning that while he liked her work, the budget being the way it was, she might have to take a reduction in her salary package if she wanted to stay.

"You have what it takes," Gabra continued. "No surprise there. And it was inevitable you'd catch the eye of the networks. But consider this—now might not be the best time for you to make the move. Let me tell you what'll happen. You'll make the move to New York, thinking that within a year or two you'll be anchoring the six-o'clock news. But reality is, you're going to be the low man on the totem pole. You'll be the reporter standing in a frozen field in Idaho in January reporting on the potato blight, or hanging on to a lamppost in Florida to keep from being blown away by hurricane winds. Stay here, and you'll have your choice of assignments. All the big stories. The network will always be there for you, and with a little more seasoning and a track record of impressive ratings, you'll be able to write your own ticket."

Jana stood. "I'm sorry, Matt."

She didn't fault him for trying to talk her into staying. It was his job. But this was the networks! The big time! This was her chance!

Her cell phone began vibrating against her hip. Jana checked the display.

Grant Austin.

His timing was a few minutes off. She wanted to snatch up the phone and scream, *Grant, guess what? I'm going to New York!* But celebrating a job offer in front of a producer would be in bad taste.

"Sleep on it," Gabra said, not giving up. "Let me make some phone calls and see what I can do to sweeten the pot."

Two raps on the door and it flew open.

Jay Ostermann barged into the room. A throwback to an earlier generation, Ostermann always wore a bow tie. Middle-aged, he'd worked all of his professional career at KTSD, mostly doing research. He occasionally made it on the air when there was a science or history story that nobody else wanted to do. He clutched a fax in his hand.

"This just came in. It's big, Matt. It's really big." He thrust the page at the producer.

Apparently there had been similar barging incidents in the past, because Gabra wasn't quick to take the page. Science reporters and producers don't often share excitement over the same stories.

"Ostermann, we're in the middle of something," Gabra said.

The bow tie wasn't about to be put off. "No, sir . . . this . . . this . . . is something you're going to want to see. The networks are going to be all over this, and we have a local connection."

Jana craned her neck to see what was on the sheet. Ostermann frowned and angled it away from her.

Gabra took the page. His eyebrows raised.

"They're having a press conference at Heritage College in an hour," Ostermann said.

Gabra was nodding now. The more he read, the larger his nod. By the time he'd finished, he was saying, "Yes . . . yes . . ."

"Didn't I tell you it was big?"

"Bigger than *Da Vinci Code*," the producer said.

Ostermann corrected him. *"The Da Vinci Code* was fiction."

"Yeah? Tell that to all the tourists who are flocking to Saint-Sulpice and Rosslyn Chapel."

"Which reminds me," Ostermann said as an aside, "did you get the brochure?"

Gabra nodded. "Sherri booked us reservations for July." He handed the fax back to Ostermann. "Let's run with this. Get it to—"

"Let me do the story!" Ostermann begged. "Please. I'll never ask you for anything else."

The producer mulled for a moment. "All right. Get a camera crew."

Ostermann thanked him profusely and bolted out the door.

No sooner had he gone when Gabra turned his attention back to Jana. "Where were we?"

"Give it to me," Jana said.

Gabra's face broke into a wide grin. The man recognized a bargaining chip when he saw one. "What do you know about this? It's big, isn't it? It would have to be the story of a lifetime for you to pass up a chance at the networks."

"Here's the deal," Jana replied. "I get my choice of stories and an unlimited expense account."

Gabra laughed. "In your dreams. Double your current expense account."

"Deal."

Standing to one side of the president's office I flipped closed my phone after leaving a somewhat disjointed message on Jana's answering machine. When she didn't answer, my mind had wandered back to the projections on the walls.

"Incredible," I muttered.

I was staring at images of manuscripts that no man had seen for centuries.

"Is she coming?" the professor asked.

He and the president of Heritage College, an elderly man with thinning white hair, sat facing each other in front of the president's desk.

From the moment I entered the office the president had looked at me as if I were a refugee from a carnival freak show. Either I'd grown a second head since shaving this morning or the professor had told him of my angel parentage. When the president shook my hand he squeezed it repeatedly as though he expected something other than flesh.

It was the professor who had suggested we keep my angel heritage a secret. I readily agreed. Apparently, he felt it necessary to tell the president.

"I left a message on Jana's cell phone," I said.

"Did you try the station number?" The professor's tone had an edge to it, understandable considering what was at stake.

Turning aside I dialed information to get the station's number. The operator connected me. The conversation was brief.

"She's in a meeting," I reported. "I left a—"

"Did you tell them it was urgent?"

"They said they'd get word to her."

The professor pursed his lips. "Not good enough. Keep trying. Right now we need friends in the media."

With the press conference fifteen minutes away as a final row of chairs was set up in the gym, I flipped open my cell phone and tried Jana's personal number again. This time she answered.

"I've been trying to reach you," I said.

"I know."

"Are you still in your meeting?"

"No."

"Can you talk?"

"Sure."

This didn't sound like Jana. Normally she is two snowflakes away from being an avalanche of chatter. However, since time was short, I launched into the purpose of my call.

"Here's the deal. There's a press conference I think you'd be interested in."

"The archeological find in Alexandria."

I blinked. She was one step ahead of me. "Um, yeah— anyway, it's at—"

"Heritage College and it starts at ten o'clock."

I don't know why I was surprised. This was news. Jana was a newswoman. "OK, you know about it. Is your station going to send someone to cover it? And if they are, is there any way you could do the story?"

She didn't reply.

"I know what I'm asking. But if the station manager has already given it to someone else, is there any possibility that you could switch assignments or something? You have an edge. You know some of the key players. The professor, for one. He specifically asked me to call you."

The other end of the phone was silent.

"Look—I hope I'm not putting you in a difficult position. But tell your manager that the professor is willing to give you an exclusive interview."

Still no answer.

"Jana?"

I looked at the display. We were still connected.

"Jana? Can you hear me?"

I felt a poke in my back. It was Jana.

"Of course I can hear you," she said, amused at having startled me.

"You're here," I said, still talking into the phone.

Her cameraman and another reporter began setting up their equipment. I recognized the reporter. He always wore a bow tie. While I couldn't remember his name, I remembered watching him report a story from in front of the Reuben H. Fleet science museum. I think it was on an eclipse.

"I have news!" Jana said.

Jana Torres is one of those women who can light up a room with her smile. When she's really excited—as she was now—her smile can melt the human male heart.

"I've been offered a promotion!" She paused for effect. "By the network!"

"Jana! The network? That's the big leagues!"

Just then Sue Ling approached us. "What's this about the big leagues?"

Jana repeated her news, and Sue Ling, who is the epitome of decorum, squealed with delight. She hugged her former college roommate.

"I'm so happy for you," she said, "though I can't say I'm surprised. You're the best reporter on the West Coast."

Watching the two friends celebrate I remembered a quotation, something to the effect that the hardest thing for a friend to do is to be happy for another friend's success. Whoever said that didn't have friends like Sue and Jana.

"When do you leave?" I asked. "I assume you'll be going to New York."

Jana took a deep breath. "I turned them down."

"What?" Sue and I said in unison.

Before Jana had a chance to explain, the press conference began. School personnel filed onto a platform behind the podium. The professor was among them, wheeling himself up a ramp.

"That man! He was supposed to wait for me." Sue touched Jana's arm. "Don't leave until you explain yourself." Then she ran to assist the professor the rest of the way up the ramp.

Once they were onstage Sue took a seat next to the rest of the faculty members.

"What's she doing up there?" Jana asked.

"Assisting the professor."

"Assisting him with what? She has no books, no papers. Normally, she stands in the wings."

Leaving the question hanging in the air, Jana joined her team. I took a seat in the back row.

Whoever had arranged for the press conference had anticipated a much larger media response. There were chairs for at least a hundred people. At best there were twenty people in the gym, not including the personalities on the platform. Many—like me—were associated with the school in some capacity.

I had to chuckle. Typical academics. They assume the rest of the world will be as excited about their findings as they are. I had an English professor, a pompous curmudgeon, who once held a press conference to announce that he had conclusive proof that Shakespeare's plays had in fact been written by Christopher Marlowe. It was his contention that Marlowe had staged his death in order to escape debtors. My English professor claimed to have discovered a confession by Lord Burghley, who had assisted in the ruse by delivering the body of one John Penry, a nonconformist Puritan preacher executed a few days before, to the queen's coroner, claiming that it was Marlowe's body.

The press conference had been held on the steps of the library in anticipation of a great crowd. Three representatives of the press had showed up. One was a freshman writing his first article for the school paper.

It turned out to be just as well, though. Lord Burghley's confession was a fake. The professor had been set up by the other professors in his department. Nobody liked him.

I wondered if the people who had organized this press conference really thought it would be the lead story on *Entertainment Tonight*.

The president of Heritage College made his way to the podium. He gripped it with familiarity, like a preacher about to deliver a sermon.

"Good morning and thank you for coming," he said in a deep speaking voice. "My name is Dr. Marvin Whitson, and I am the president of Heritage College."

Cameras recorded the introduction while reporters scratched the information on pads of paper.

"For seven summers Heritage College has teamed with Texas A&M University to explore archeological sites of biblical significance. Each year two or three select students participate in the program as partial fulfillment of their academic degree. This summer one of our students had the unique privilege of working in association with the Institute of Nautical Archeology on a site in Northern Africa, specifically Alexandria, Egypt. To say that she was a participant in a finding of historic proportions is an understatement. Her discovery of two scrolls in an undersea cave rivals that of the Dead Sea Scrolls."

A buzz swept through the crowd, as small as it was.

"Mr. Dutton, if you please."

Whitson motioned to a student seated at a table laden with projection equipment. The boy pecked at a laptop computer

keyboard and moments later images of ancient manuscripts illuminated two flanking screens.

Dr. Whitson turned to the screen on his left. "What you see on
this screen is a manuscript unseen by human eyes for over sixteen
hundred years, since the day it was placed in the underground
cave. The manuscript itself—though its dating has yet to be confirmed—is believed to be older than any of the Dead Sea Scrolls.
At present, we estimate it to be approximately 2,230 years old."

Dr. Whitson turned toward the front and spoke to the cameras directly.

"But it's not the age of the manuscript that fascinates us.
What makes both of these manuscripts worthy of a press conference is that they are copies of books that have been lost to us
for centuries, books that are mentioned by name in the Bible."

He pointed to the projections. First one, then the other.

"Ladies and gentlemen, on my left you are looking at the
Book of Jasher. And on my right, the Book of the Wars of the
Lord."

A chill went down my spine even though I'd already seen the
projections in the president's office. Dr. Whitson himself was
likewise caught up in the emotion of the moment. I turned to
see if the reporters shared our feelings. They didn't. But neither
were they uninterested. They took notes dutifully.

Dr. Whitson went on to describe each of the books.

"The Book of Jasher is a sacred songbook, the national an-
thology of the ancient Israelites. A collection of verse, it describes great events in the history of Israel and is mentioned in
the Book of Joshua. It includes the Song of the Bow, David's
lament over the deaths of Saul and Jonathan.

"The Book of the Wars of the Lord is a collection of odes
dating back to the time of Moses himself. It is a celebration of
the glorious acts of the Lord among the Israelites.

"As you might imagine, Heritage College is humbled to be part of an archeological find of this magnitude. Now, allow me to introduce you to the student who made the actual discovery, our very own Tiffany Sproul."

There was a smattering of applause, from the assembled representatives of the college, not the media.

An unassuming young lady moved to the lectern. She wore a simple print dress. Straight brown hair fell to her shoulders. At first impression she appeared unsophisticated, but that was misleading. Her eyes flashed intelligence and her speech was articulate. But there was no enthusiasm in her voice. She'd been thrust into the national spotlight and she spoke as though she didn't want to be here.

She didn't. Having been briefed ahead of time, I knew that for a fact. I also knew why she'd agreed to make an appearance and I admired her for her courage.

"Louder! We can't hear you!" one of the reporters shouted.

Miss Sproul leaned closer to the microphone and began again.

"One of the requirements to be selected to the team was the ability to scuba dive. I have been a certified diver for five years. Because I was a summer intern, my assignment was to gather pottery shards on the periphery of the site, an area that had already been explored and mapped."

A map of the Northern African coastline appeared on the left screen with a red crusader's cross marking the location of the city of Alexandria.

The same reporter who had complained she wasn't speaking loudly enough interrupted her a second time. "Are we going to be given a copy of that map?"

Miss Sproul stepped aside so that Dr. Whitson could field the question.

"Press packets have been compiled for you with everything that you see here this morning. They will be made available to you at the end of the press conference. Please hold all questions until the end."

"Why can't we have them now?" the reporter complained. "We always get press packets before the start of a conference."

Exhibiting the patience of a host, Dr. Whitson said politely but firmly, "Today you will be getting them at the conclusion of the press conference. Now if you'll—"

"Is there a reason you're keeping them from us?" the reporter persisted.

"Please," Dr. Whitson said, his patience growing thin, "hold all questions and comments to the end."

He motioned for Miss Sproul to continue. She took a deep breath and once again approached the microphone. She began softly, glanced at the pesky reporter, and spoke louder.

"My pouch—a net I used to collect the shards—was getting full and I was about to swim to the surface when I noticed some plants waving, which isn't unusual given the swirling currents in the area, but these were at the base of a rock formation and were waving steadily in a direction different from all the other plants."

Her eyes had a distant look to them. She was reliving the experience.

"When I swam down to investigate I could feel an underground stream coming from a fissure in the rocks. When I explored further—"

She hesitated. Her eyes darted side to side. She was envisioning the rock formation.

"—it was like Aladdin's cave, you know? All I did was touch it and it crumbled open, as if it were magic."

As she relived the moment, excitement crept into her face and voice. Then she caught herself and the thrill faded.

"My instructions were that if I were to find anything of significance, I was to notify my supervisor immediately." She shrugged innocently. "But how was I to know if the finding was significant. I had to look inside, didn't I?"

Her playfulness made me grin.

"When the water cleared I found a cave roughly ten meters in diameter. Shards from what we have since concluded were the remains of at least five jars littered the floor. One jar remained intact. The jar containing the manuscripts."

A color photo of the vessel appeared on the screen. It was cylindrical, about two meters tall with a lid. On the second screen there appeared a picture of the interior of the cave. Miss Sproul pointed to where she had found the unbroken jar.

She continued, "Of course at the time I didn't know what was in the jar. I suspected manuscripts, but it could have been a government census or a grain inventory or a scientific or philosophical treatise. I alerted my supervisor and the experts took over from there."

Miss Sproul glanced over at Dr. Whitson to signal she was finished. The president thanked her and she left the platform. She'd agreed to give a statement only after the president promised her she wouldn't have to field any questions.

To cover her departure Whitson expounded on the historical and theological significance of the lost manuscripts. The preacher in him surfaced and when he concluded I almost expected him to give an invitation to those who had experienced a conversion experience. Instead, he called for questions.

The obnoxious reporter was the first to speak. "What was in the other five vessels?"

"We'll never know, will we?" Dr. Whitson replied. "Once their seal was broken the contents were exposed to the sea. They disintegrated centuries ago."

"Other than the jars," the reporter asked by way of follow-up, "were there any other artifacts in the cave? Any human remains?"

"No, and again, understandably so. While we wouldn't expect to find human remains in the cave, had there been any, they wouldn't have lasted long."

Jana raised her hand to ask a question.

"Yes, Miss Torres," Dr. Whitson said, obviously pleased to call on a friendly representative of the press.

"Wasn't there a third manuscript in the jar?" she asked.

To a person, the expressions onstage soured.

Whitson glanced at the professor before answering. "Yes, well—" He took a moment to formulate his reply. "As with the other two manuscripts, it is being examined with the utmost care. However, compared to the magnitude of finding the Book of Jasher and the Book of the Wars, the third manuscript is not worth commenting on at this time. Are there any other questions?"

Without waiting to be called on, Jana followed up. "Dr. Whitson, I'm afraid the Supreme Council of Antiquities in Egypt disagrees with you."

Standing beside her, Ostermann handed her a sheet of paper from which she read.

"According to Dr. Zahin Pasha, general director of the Museum of Egyptian Antiquities in Cairo, Egypt, 'Of the three manuscripts, while the two have great significance in the field of ancient history, the third manuscript is most intriguing and may prove to be the most significant.' Would you care to comment now?"

She looked to Dr. Whitson for a response.

Whitson's eyes narrowed defensively. The professor was frowning. Sue Ling silently implored Jana to back off with subtle but urgent shakes of her head.

"I assure you, Miss Torres," Dr. Whitson said, adopting a fatherly tone, "the third manuscript is nonsense. Its authorship is uncertain, and its content appears to be little more than bizarre ramblings. If anything, it will give us insight into ancient humor. And while any manuscript discovered in Alexandria merits close academic study, to give this manuscript equal time with the other two manuscripts is sacrilegious. Any other questions?"

Jana took a couple steps closer to the platform.

"Dr. Whitson," she pressed, "obviously, the person who placed the third manuscript in the jar thought it comparable in value with the other two."

"Miss Torres," Whitson countered, "while I cannot speak for the man who placed the scrolls in the jar, I can tell you with the utmost assurance that in time the third manuscript will prove to be nothing more than an amusement."

"Exactly what is it about the third manuscript that frightens you?"

"That's enough!" the professor said.

He wheeled to the edge of the platform. His outburst startled everyone in the room, including President Whitson.

Glaring at Jana, he said, "This press conference is over."

But Jana wasn't finished asking questions. Again, Ostermann fed her ammunition. "Dr. Whitson, correct me if I'm wrong, but according to my sources, the Museum of Egyptian Antiquities has carbon-dated the manuscripts and found that the papyrus of the Book of Jasher and the Book of Wars dates back to sometime in the third century. Yet you say that they record events that occurred centuries earlier."

"That is correct," Whitson said, somewhat distracted by the professor, who continued to glare at Jana. "Given the fragile nature of the writing materials it is unlikely we will ever find one of the original manuscripts. What we found in Alexandria is a copy. But that is also true for all the books of the Bible. All we have are copies. We do not have the originals. That said, the copies we have are sufficient for us to be confident that the text in our Bibles is an accurate representation of the originals."

Jana consulted her sheet. "And yet this third manuscript may very well be an original, not a copy. Is it true that the carbon-testing dates the third manuscript to the early second century?"

"That is my understanding."

"Which would place it where? In the early what? Hundreds?"

"One hundred to 125. C.E."

"C.E.?"

"Common Era. It used to be A.D."

"So then, this third manuscript was written around the time the Gospels and the rest of the New Testament were written?"

"Correct. The New Testament writings date roughly from 50 to 100 C.E."

Jana smiled. "So that explains why Professor Forsythe, a New Testament professor, is on the platform for a press conference about two manuscripts that are linked to the Old Testament."

A murmur rippled through the assembled press corps. They scribbled furiously on their notepads.

The professor and Jana squared off across the room, gazes locked.

"Dr. Forsythe is here at my request," Whitson said, "as a representative of the faculty."

"Do you have any further questions, Miss Torres?" the professor snapped.

His statement was not a question, but a challenge.

Jana didn't back down. "Are you familiar with the content of the third manuscript?"

"No comment. Any further questions?"

Behind the professor Sue Ling had abandoned her attempts to motion Jana to back down. Instead, she directed her efforts at me. There was an urgency in her eyes that bordered on panic.

What did she expect me to do? Put my hand over Jana's mouth and drag her out of the room?

I stood, though I don't know why.

Up to this point Jana had been a bulldog. She faltered with the next question.

"Why is Sue Ling on the platform?" she asked.

A couple of questions arose from the press corps. "Which one is Sue Ling?" "How do you spell her name?"

Jana ignored them. "Is it because she's a doctoral student at the University of San Diego, specializing in the study of particle physics?"

Dr. Whitson's face turned beet red. He was on the verge of losing control.

Jana took another step forward. "Is it because there are references to scientific findings in the third manuscript that had not yet been discovered? References to things like the Doppler Effect, DNA, dark matter, bosons, wormholes—"

"This press conference is over!" Dr. Whitson pronounced.

"—black holes, neutrinos, entanglement, and quantum teleportation?" Jana shouted. "Miss Ling, do you care to comment?"

"I said, this press conference is over!" Whitson repeated.

"And why is he here?" Jana pointed at me with her pen. "Why would you need the services of a—"

When she looked at me, she stopped midsentence. She knew my secret. And she knew I wanted it kept a secret.

"A what?" the pesky reporter prompted.

"A Pulitzer Prize–winning biographer," I answered for her.

Jana let it go at that.

This time the press conference was over. Sue Ling was wheeling the professor down the ramp with Dr. Whitson on her heels. They ignored the barrage of questions coming from the press.

Students cradling armloads of press packets appeared at the doorways.

CHAPTER

3

W hat was that all about?"

Jana finished jotting down a note on her pad before answering me. "What do you mean?"

"What do you mean, What do I mean? Why did you attack them like that?"

She frowned. "I didn't attack them. I was just doing my job."

"Jana, I've attended enough press conferences to know an attack when I see one."

She shook her head and laughed. "I was being aggressive. That's what network-level reporters do. They were hiding something. I wanted to know why. That's how the game is played."

"But Sue and the professor are your friends."

"Exactly, though I think the professor got his feathers ruffled a bit. But he'll get over it. You have to develop a thick hide to play in the big leagues. As for Sue, she understands it's not personal. I was only doing my job."

"I'm not so sure—"

Jana turned to her team. "Wrap things up, boys. We have an exclusive in the president's office."

At that moment Sue Ling came toward us, her face expressionless.

"There she is now!" Jana said cheerily.

Sue didn't acknowledge Jana. She walked up to me. "Grant, the professor would like to talk to you."

"Should I wait here?" Jana asked.

"What?" Sue turned on Jana with fire in her eyes.

"The exclusive," Jana said, taken aback.

"You don't have the proper credentials," Sue replied. "The exclusive was offered to a friend."

Turning her back, Sue walked away.

"You can't be serious," Jana replied. "I was just doing my job."

Sue turned back. "Grant, are you coming?"

Jana touched my arm, holding me back. "Grant is having coffee with me."

All of a sudden the proverbial rock and a hard place looked like the setting for a vacation retreat.

"Please don't do this, ladies," I said.

"The professor's waiting," Sue replied.

Jana intertwined her arm with mine. "Bruno's? Or would you prefer a coffeehouse?"

"Sue, would it be possible for me to meet with the professor this afternoon?"

Her reply was an icy stare.

"Jana," I pleaded. "How about lunch? You can pick the restaurant."

She released me and stepped away. "I see—"

"It's just that this is really important. Future of the world important."

"Can I quote you on that, Mr. Austin?" Jana said.

Sue interceded for me. "You do and our friendship's over."

"What friendship?" Jana replied, pivoting on her heel. "Come on, boys. Let's get out of here."

"Sue, wait for me!"

I'd lingered to make a final—unsuccessful—appeal to Jana, then had to run to catch up with Sue, who was propelled by a full head of steam.

"Don't you think you're overreacting a bit?" I said. "Jana's been your friend for a long time."

Without slowing down, Sue said, "She always has to have her way, no matter who it hurts. Everything's always about her."

"All I'm saying is that under the circumstances you should cut each other a little slack."

"A little slack?" Sue exclaimed. "She was out of line at the press conference and you know it."

While I was no stranger to Sue Ling's verbal jabs, I'd never seen her this upset. We walked the remainder of the distance to the president's office in silence.

Jana stormed across the parking lot like a tornado in search of a trailer park. Ostermann and the cameraman had to step lively to keep up with her.

Why is Sue Ling acting like this? Of all people, she should understand.

Jana yanked open the passenger door of the news van. She paused, glancing back at the campus. Ostermann climbed behind the wheel on the driver's side. The cameraman slid the side door open and loaded his equipment.

Jana slammed her door shut. "We're not done here."

With determined strides she reversed course. Ostermann and the cameraman exchanged glances. The cameraman shrugged and pulled out his equipment again.

At the top of the steps linking the parking lot to the campus there was a sign.

ADMINISTRATION BUILDING

An arrow pointed left. Jana turned right toward the heart of the campus.

The hallways could have been any small college in America between classes. Students strolled purposefully, but not hurriedly, to their next class. Clusters of friends formed, talking, shifting, and reshifting their textbooks as they walked.

Outside a classroom two girls huddled close together, their foreheads nearly touching. Suddenly a head popped up as though she'd sniffed an approaching threat. She turned in Jana's direction. Her eyes lit with recognition. She said something to her friend.

The girls looked Jana over as she drew closer, starting with her shoes and working their way up to her makeup and hair.

They reminded Jana of herself and Sue a decade ago at San Diego State. On any other day Jana would have viewed a cluster of coeds as a prime source of information. Today, she stopped a boy who was going the opposite direction.

She blocked his path.

"Excuse me," she said, touching him on the arm, "I was wondering if you could help me."

The boy reacted to her touch as though it were electric.

He appeared small to be in college, with a mop of brown hair that didn't show evidence of having been in the same room as a brush for at least a couple of days. The backpack under which he labored was plastered with comic book stickers.

Jana hadn't chosen him at random. His stature. The figures of superheroes on his backpack. The boy fantasized about heroes. She was going to give him a chance to live out his fantasy by rescuing a damsel in distress.

"I'm looking for Tiffany Sproul," she said. "I was hoping you could tell me where I might find her."

The boy stared at Jana as though she were a goddess having descended from Mt. Olympus. His jaw worked, but all he made were guttural sounds. He looked as if he might swallow his tongue.

"Um—Tiff—Tiff—Tiffany?"

"Sproul. Do you know her?"

A few feet away the coeds observed the exchange. If they knew Tiffany, they weren't offering any information.

Ostermann and the cameraman weren't helping. They made no attempt to conceal their amusement at the kid's expense.

"I th—think," the boy stammered, "Tiff—Tiffany has class now. I think. But I can't say with 100 percent certainty. Not 100 percent."

"Do you know which class?"

The boy's shoulders slumped. Desperately he wanted to know, but he didn't.

With sudden inspiration, he said, "The office! They'll know! I can take you to the office! They'll know!"

Had he a cape, he would have flown her there. But for Jana going to the office was out of the question.

"Thank you, all the same," she said.

The boy's enthusiasm collapsed. He couldn't have been any more defeated if she'd exposed him to kryptonite.

The hallway was emptying. It appeared Jana was going to have to ask the girls.

Just then, the boy straightened up.

"There!" he exclaimed in triumph.

Jana turned to see two girls walking toward them. Neither of them was Tiffany Sproul.

"The tall one!" the boy said. "That's Tiffany's roommate!"

Jana rewarded her hero with a smile and squeeze of his arm. His face and neck blazed red against the blue collar of his shirt.

Her heels clicking, Jana closed in on the tall girl, a model-thin brunette.

"Can I have a moment? I'm looking for your roommate."

The brunette did a classic double-take, the kind Jana encountered frequently whenever people recognized her. An instant later an invisible alarm sounded in the girl's head. Her expression became guarded.

Jana repeated her request. "Can you tell me where I can find Tiffany?"

"I don't think Tiffany wants to talk to anyone right now."

Jana used her celebrity smile. "I want to interview her for the news."

The brunette glanced at Ostermann and the cameraman. "Yeah—but, that's just it. I don't think Tiffany wants to be interviewed."

"Don't you think Tiffany should make that decision for herself?" Jana said.

The brunette didn't have a good answer for that question.

Moments later Jana was hurrying down another hallway as the bell rang, signaling the start of classes. Tiffany Sproul was at the far end of the corridor, just about to enter a classroom.

Jana called out to her. When Tiffany saw who it was, her face clouded over.

"Can we talk?" Jana labored for breath.

"I have class," Tiffany replied, half in and half out of the classroom.

A male voice from inside said, "Miss Sproul, will you be joining us today?"

"It will only take a few minutes," Jana insisted. "I'm sure your professor will understand."

"Miss Sproul," the voice boomed. "Either join us or close the door."

Tiffany glanced longingly into the classroom. With a sigh, she closed the door.

"Is there some place we can go?" Jana said.

"Not them." Tiffany indicated Ostermann and the cameraman. "I don't want to be on camera."

Ostermann started to object.

Jana cut him off. "All right. Fine. It'll just be you and me."

"No, not fine," Ostermann objected. "We need a film clip."

"Wait for me in the van," Jana said to him.

Ostermann began to object again. Jana shut him down with a glance. Letting loose an exasperated huff, he stomped away. The cameraman didn't seem to care one way or the other. He shrugged and lugged his equipment down the hallway.

"Out here." Tiffany led Jana to an open courtyard with trees planted in six-foot-square wooden boxes. The perimeter of the planters were benches.

Tiffany set her books down, then sat beside them. Folding her hands in her lap, she stared straight ahead. Jana reached for a recorder in her purse, then thought better of it.

"What do you want to know?" the girl said. "You were at the press conference. I have nothing else to say."

Jana suppressed a grin. It wasn't unusual for people she interviewed to attempt to control the direction of the interview, especially if they were hiding something. Tiffany didn't know it, but she had just confirmed Jana's suspicions.

"The press conference gave me the facts about the discovery," Jana said. "I want to know what it was like for you—a student and a young woman—to make such an incredible find."

Tiffany shrugged. "I got lucky, that's all."

She folded her arms defensively. Jana noticed the girl's shoulders. Swimmer's shoulders, wide and strong. This close to her, her freckles were prominent.

"OK, so you got lucky," Jana said. "A bored shepherd boy threw rocks into a cave and found the Dead Sea Scrolls. Sometimes that's how discoveries are made."

Tiffany turned away. She fought her emotions. "I just wish I'd never gone on that trip. I wasn't even their first choice, did you know that? A guy in Ft. Lauderdale was supposed to go, but he crushed his leg in a motorcycle accident. When they called me I thought it was a lucky break."

She chuckled at her unintended pun. Her grin faded quickly.

"But now—I don't know."

She began to weep.

Jana handed her a tissue and waited patiently for her to compose herself. Softly, she said, "Tiffany, something is obviously troubling you. With all the attention these manuscripts are generating, you know it's going to come out. What are you afraid of?"

CHAPTER

4

Dark mahogany wood dominated the décor in Dr. Whitson's office, complemented by forest green carpeting and drapes. It was as dim as a cave.

Four chairs had been arranged in a semicircle facing a laptop computer on the conference table. The professor had wheeled himself between the two middle chairs. Dr. Whitson sat to one side of him. Sue Ling took the chair on his other side.

As I maneuvered into the remaining chair next to Sue, the professor said, "Your girlfriend betrayed us."

"Former girlfriend," I corrected him. "Jana and I haven't dated since high school. And she didn't betray anybody. She was doing her job."

"Her job?" Whitson roared. "Blindsiding us in front of the cameras is her job? I thought you were going to talk to her beforehand."

"Didn't have time. She arrived just as the press conference was getting started."

"Well she certainly came loaded for bear," Whitson complained. "Do you have any idea what I looked like up there? I call on her, thinking we have an ally in the media, and the next thing I know I'm being blasted out of the water."

"Let it go, Marvin," the professor said. "What's done is done. The question now is, Where do we go from here?"

The professor was himself again. I've seen him get angry before. He has a summer squall temper. It passes quickly.

Sue, however, is a sulker. She slouched in her chair, her eyes fixed on things only she could see.

"Did you really think you could keep the third manuscript a secret?" I asked no one in particular. "Between news services and the Internet, everyone has instant access to everything."

"We have an agreement with the Egyptians," the professor replied. "They agreed to keep the contents of the third manuscript under wraps to give us time to investigate its authenticity."

"To reveal it for the humbug that it is," Whitson asserted. He was still heated.

I said, "It seems the director of antiquities has forgotten your agreement."

"So it would seem," the professor replied. "Marvin, have you seen the releases Miss Torres was quoting from?"

Whitson shook his head. "She probably fabricated them."

"Jana wouldn't do that."

I was about to say the same thing. Sue beat me to it. She was still angry and sullen, but she knew Jana better than anyone.

"So then, what's the big deal?" I asked. "If the manuscript is obviously fraudulent, where's the threat? Whoever put it in the jar with the other two manuscripts made a mistake. Grabbed the wrong scroll. Maybe he was in a hurry. Maybe he loved spoofs and slipped it into the jar as a joke. You know, something to confound future scholars. A time-released joke. Why not just refute it? It's not like this is the first time this has happened. Just a few months ago . . . what was that manuscript that the media were fussing over?"

"The *Gospel According to Judas,*" Sue said.

"That's it. And weren't there others?"

"A number of others," the professor replied. "The *Acts of Thomas,* the *Epistle of Barnabas,* the *Epistle to the Laodiceans.*"

"And the one about Jesus' boyhood," Sue said.

"The *Infancy Gospel of Thomas,*" Whitson said, identifying it.

"Stories of Jesus' boyhood?" I prompted.

Whitson elaborated. "A young Jesus fashioning pigeons out of clay and bringing them to life; bringing a dried fish to life; cursing a boy who fell dead on the spot; resurrecting a man who fell off his roof; carrying water in a cloth; stretching a wooden beam so that his father could finish constructing a bed."

"So how is this third manuscript different?" I asked.

"Let me put it this way," the professor said. "If Hollywood were to write a blockbuster script so as to undermine and discredit Christianity, this would be it."

Whitson added, "We just can't take the chance of its getting out until we've accumulated the necessary evidence to refute it."

"How long will that take?"

Whitson and the professor exchanged glances.

"Show him the video clips," Sue said.

Looking to Whitson for a decision, the professor said, "We've brought him in this far, might as well go all the way."

"All right," Whitson conceded, though not without a moment of hesitation. He stood. "You show him the clips. I'll see if I can find out why Dr. Zahin has gone back on our agreement."

As Whitson left the room, Sue moved to the laptop. The arrangement of the chairs suggested they had been watching the video clips while waiting for me to arrive earlier. With a combination of mouse-clicks Sue summoned the video to the screen.

The professor provided an introduction. "This was taken a week ago in the Jewish Quarter of Jerusalem."

I leaned forward in my chair.

The video was raw footage of an archeological dig. The area was marked with stakes and string. Two heavily bearded men brushed dirt from what appeared to be the foundation of a very old building.

"The house of Caiaphas," the professor explained. "He was—"

"—the high priest when Jesus was crucified," I said.

Sue glanced at me, surprised that I knew that.

"All that Gospel reading in preparation for my showdown with Semyaza," I reminded her.

On the video, one of the men traced the edges of a brick with the point of his trowel. The brick became loose. The dirt of time, not mortar, had held it in place.

The trowel gave way to fingers that worked the brick side to side, then pulled it from its place. It came free with surprising ease.

I had no idea how many people were witnessing this event as it was being recorded, but I can tell you none of them were breathing. The only sound was the scraping of brick against brick as it was extracted.

The camera and light were lowered to get a look inside the cavity. Harsh shadows made it difficult to discern what was inside, if anything. A hand reached in.

There was an audible gasp and someone muttered in Hebrew. When the hand withdrew, it clutched something in its palm. Fingers unfurled to reveal tattered remnants of a pouch and a mound of coins, all of them identical. Several more extractions were necessary to retrieve all the coins. They were then counted as the camera recorded the tally. An unidentified voice provided the count in Hebrew.

At sixteen, my mind wandered for a moment and I lost count. So I was grateful when the professor picked up the count, interpreting the Hebrew.

"—twenty-seven, twenty-eight, twenty-nine . . . thirty." There was a pause, then a concluding sentence.

"Thirty pieces of silver," the professor interpreted.

The video clip ended.

"Are those the coins I think they are?" I asked.

"Given to Judas to betray the Christ," the professor said. "The text of the manuscript told us exactly where to find them."

"OK." I thought out loud, attempting to assess the damage. "So whoever penned the manuscript knew where the coins were hidden. He obviously knew someone, or overheard it. That doesn't mean that everything in the manuscript should be taken at face value."

Sue said, "In Ephesus, three jars have been unearthed. One contains gold. The other two contain remnants of frankincense and myrrh."

"The gifts of the Magi," I said. "In Ephesus?"

"On the cross Jesus entrusted his mother to John's care," the professor explained. "Tradition holds that he took her with him when he went to Ephesus."

"OK, so the author of the third manuscript was privy to two secrets," I said. "That still doesn't mean—"

"In Rome," the professor interrupted me, "Pontius Pilate's report to his superiors has been discovered. It details the trial and execution of a certain Nazarene. The collection of documents includes the report on the criminal violation of the tomb, the report of the watch, and the circulating rumors that the Nazarene had risen from the grave."

"All right," I said, a little less enthusiastically, "so whoever wrote the third manuscript was a keeper of secrets. That doesn't mean—"

"We have people scouring Jerusalem excavating sites. To date we have found a carpenter's shop in Nazareth, the four-drachma coin Peter found in a fish to pay his taxes, and the bones of John the Baptist."

"What? No Holy Grail?" I quipped.

The professor chuckled at my exasperation. He shared it. "You'd think that would be at the top of the list, wouldn't you?"

"That in itself could be used as evidence of the manuscript's authenticity," Sue said. "The items you'd expect to be on the list, aren't—the cup of Christ, remnants of the cross, the shroud. Many of the items are personal artifacts, indicating that the author of the manuscript wrote from firsthand knowledge, that he was obviously an insider, someone the inner circle trusted."

"I take it you've read the text," I said to Sue.

"Portions of it," she replied.

"The science. Was Jana correct about the science? Does the author demonstrate a true knowledge of modern discoveries, or are the statements like those of Nostradamus, generalizations that people can read into whatever they want?"

"The language is different," she said. "It doesn't use the same terms we use today, such as string theory or general relativity."

"So you're saying Jana's source has an agenda?"

Sue looked at the professor before answering. "No. That's not what I'm saying."

I sat back in the chair, unprepared for what she would say next.

"While the language is different," she said, "the concepts are advanced physics. Very detailed."

"I can't believe that!" I said.

"In fact, in some places it seems to go beyond our present understanding."

"Beyond?"

"We can't know for sure until we run some tests."

I ran a hand through my hair. It was worse than I could have imagined. No wonder everyone was on edge. Who was going to get excited over a couple of ancient songbooks when presented a treasure map of New Testament artifacts and the keys to the universe?

The professor and Sue Ling waited patiently for me as this whirlwind of information settled in my mind. It was a lot to take in all at once. But we weren't done. I could tell by their expressions.

"Don't tell me. The manuscript identifies the location of the bones of Jesus."

"Of course not," the professor said. "There are no bones to be found. Jesus rose from the grave."

"The manuscript is quite adamant about that fact," Sue added. "It confirms the resurrection in great detail."

"Well, that's good. Isn't it?"

The professor gazed at me soberly.

Before he could answer, the door flew open. Dr. Whitson charged over to a cabinet and opened it to reveal a television. He switched it on.

"That woman!" he seethed.

The face of Jana Torres filled the screen. A banner across the bottom of the screen read: LIVE FROM HERITAGE COLLEGE, EL CAJON, CALIFORNIA.

Sue went to the window and drew back the drapes. Jana and her crew could be seen standing in the parking lot broadcasting the news story.

> *This is Jana Torres, reporting live from Heritage College in El Cajon, where a short time ago a press conference concluded during which it was revealed that there has been a historic archeological discovery made in Alexandria, Egypt—one that may well eclipse the finding of the Dead Sea Scrolls.*
>
> *But while scholars and academics expressed excitement over two of the scrolls that were found in a clay jar at the bottom of the sea—scrolls with ties to the Old Testament—the real story seems to be a third scroll, which is proving to be highly controversial.*

"That's it?" Whitson barked at the television. "After centuries of being lost, that's all she's going to say about the Book of Jashar and the Book of Wars?"

> *A few moments ago, in an exclusive interview, this reporter spoke with the young woman who is credited with making this extraordinary discovery. She declined to be interviewed on camera.*

"Oh, my." Sue Ling covered her mouth. "I'd better check on Tiffany and see if she's all right. Does anyone know what room she's in?"

"Helen can help you locate her," Whitson said, referring to his secretary.

Sue Ling hurried from the room.

Of her discovery, Tiffany Sproul, a junior at Heritage College and an accomplished scuba diver, said she was just lucky—or unlucky, as the case may be. For a few moments later, she told me, quote: "I don't want to be known as the person who unmasked Jesus."

Whitson spun around. "Can this get any worse? Can this *possibly* get any worse?"

"Give the girl a break, Marvin. She's only a junior," the professor replied. "We shouldn't have left her alone."

"Well, who would have figured that woman would track her down during classes?"

He glared at me as though it were my fault.

"I thought she'd left campus!" I said, defending myself.

A tearful Sproul told me she fears the content of the third scroll will undermine the life work of her conservative pastor father and do irreparable harm to Christianity. She told me, quote: "The Jesus in that manuscript is not my Jesus."

"That much is true," the professor said.

At the press conference, all of our attempts to verify the content of the third scroll were met with patronizing statements dismissing the scroll as an amusement. When this reporter persisted, the tone of the press conference turned ugly.

A film clip of the professor yelling, "That's enough! This press conference is over!" was played. Whitson and the professor viewed it without comment, though I noticed the professor's hand gripping the arm of his wheelchair.

> *Here's what we know about the third scroll from an earlier press release from the Museum of Egyptian Antiquities in Cairo. It has been dated to around 100–125 C.E., about the same time as the New Testament. Its authorship is in dispute, though no one is stating publicly who the author is. And—this is the intriguing part—it apparently makes reference to scientific knowledge that was unknown in the second century, facts that our scientists are just discovering now.*

Whitson slumped into a chair. "She has single-handedly undone everything we attempted to accomplish today."

"It was going to come out eventually," the professor replied philosophically. "We'll survive this. It may be rough sailing for a while, but we'll survive."

> *Which begs the question, what is in the third scroll that so frightens church leaders that they have to hide it? As the truth of the third scroll is revealed, will Tiffany Sproul's fears be realized? Will we discover that Christianity has been misleading its followers for centuries?*
>
> *This is Jana Torres, reporting live from Heritage College.*

Jana coiled the cord of her microphone while Ostermann and the cameraman packed the equipment. She glanced up and saw Sue Ling, arms folded, looking down at her from the campus walkway.

Even at this distance Jana could feel Sue Ling's anger. The

two women exchanged a long, uncomfortable glance before Jana turned her attention to the microphone cord. When she looked up again, Sue Ling was gone.

"Don't let it bother you," Ostermann said, having witnessed the silent exchange.

"I would have to care for it to bother me." Jana coiled the cord.

"All I'm saying is that sometimes you have to choose between getting the story and having friends. You can't let your friends get in the way of the story. You were a professional today."

Carrying the cord, Jana plopped it down on the equipment waiting to be carried to the van. She took another glance at where she'd last seen Sue.

"And sometimes your friends make the choice for you."

The three of us in President Whitson's office stared at a blank television screen, each of us absorbed in his own thoughts.

The door to the outer office opened. Whitson's secretary didn't ask why the three men were watching a television screen with no picture. She dutifully approached Whitson and handed him a sheet of paper.

"This fax just came in. It's from Dr. Zahin."

As Whitson read the fax, his secretary excused herself.

"And the hits just keep on coming," he said, reaching for the television remote. He checked his watch, then hit the button that brought the television screen back to life.

A dirty hand filled the screen as it dropped one coin at a time into a pile. " . . . twenty-three . . . twenty-four . . . twenty-five . . ."

The same video clip they had shown me in private was being aired by a national network. By way of explanation, Whitson held up the fax.

"Dr. Zahin apologizes for breaking our agreement. He says unforeseen developments forced his hand and insists that if I were in his position I would take a similar course of action."

Following the counting of Judas's coins, a news analyst described for the television audience the significance of the find. A graphic of one of the coins was added to a list of graphics identifying the other artifacts identified in the third manuscript—the gifts of the Magi, Pilate's reports, Peter's taxes, the shop in Nazareth. The whole world knew about them now.

The professor stared at the graphics. "We need to move quickly. Grant, how soon can you leave for Jerusalem?"

Whitson and the professor both looked at me, awaiting my answer.

"Wait a minute." I took a step back. "No one said anything about Jerusalem."

"Things are happening too quickly," he replied. "I need someone in Jerusalem to be my eyes and ears."

"I agree," I said, "but why does it have to be me?"

"It isn't you," the professor said. "I'll send Sue as my representative. I want you to go with her, just in case she comes across some of our old friends."

An icy shudder shook my spine. By "old friends," he meant rebel angels and their demon horde. I had barely survived my last encounter with them and wasn't ready for a repeat showdown.

"No," I said. "When you said you needed my help, you didn't say anything about international travel or hand-to-hand combat with unfriendly angels. I'll pass."

The professor swung his wheelchair so he was facing me

directly. "What do you mean, you'll pass? That's not an option."

"Of course it's an option. Free will makes it an option. If there's one thing I learned from recent experience it's that we all have choices. And I choose to pass on this one."

"Your fear is unfounded," Whitson said, adding his voice to the professor's. "We don't know that angels have anything to do with this."

"It's not that," I lied. "I got a call from my publisher. They're offering me a new book deal, and they're throwing a lot of money in my direction. I can't pass this up. It's my chance to re-establish my reputation in the industry. Sorry, but playing Indiana Jones doesn't pay the bills."

The professor folded his hands in his lap. He stared at me long and hard. "Looks to me like you're digging a hole."

We both knew what he meant. I'd once accused him of hiding from danger.

"One man's hole is another man's vocation," I said.

Yeah, it sounded that stupid when I said it, too. But they knew what I meant. I left them to fight their own battles.

In the parking lot I called my publisher.

"Consider the contract signed," I told him. "I'll overnight it to my agent."

With that phone call my bank account had just gotten a lot fatter. So why didn't I feel like celebrating?

"Good work, kiddo. The networks are running with your exclusive," Matt Gabra said, coming up behind Jana. "They'll air it tonight on the evening news."

Jana was watching a tape of the broadcast that had aired

while she and Ostermann were returning to the station. She watched with fascination as the thirty pieces of silver were counted. The producer waited for the clip to finish before continuing.

"Once again, you impressed them," her producer said of the networks. "I wish I could say I passed on the chance to gloat that you signed with us. But I'm not that big a man."

Jana swung around. "I'm going to Jerusalem and Cairo."

"Whoa! Hold on there!" Gabra cried. "You did good today, but the public attention span for religious stories is a couple of sound bites long."

Jana wasn't listening. She strode toward her desk with Gabra hot on her heels.

"You said I could choose my stories," Jana reminded him as she transferred pens and writing pads from her desk to her purse. "You increased my budget. I'm going."

"Now wait just a nanosecond. Hear me out. I know what I told you, but I'm still the producer here, and as the producer I'm telling you that this story doesn't have legs. This whole thing will have blown over before you get halfway to Jerusalem. I'm telling you, it's a wasted trip."

"You know what I think?" Jana replied. "I think that this story not only has legs, it has wings."

Hoisting her purse over her shoulder, she called across the room. "Ostermann! Pack your bags. We're going to Jerusalem."

With Christina in D.C. lobbying for Senator Vogler and Jana angry with me, I had no one with whom to celebrate the signing of my new book deal. So I ordered a pizza with the works and pondered the fact that my only friends were a professor, former girlfriends, and a prospective girlfriend. I needed to get a life.

Three hours later I regretted that decision. Indigestion and the late-night news are a painful combination, even though Jana looked terrific on the screen. Very professional. Even the news anchors were impressed. What they didn't know was that she'd seriously wounded a friend to get the story.

For an hour I tossed in bed. Unable to sleep, I got up and read a World War II novel about an American nurse and a German soldier caught between lines in the Ardennes forest. An hour later I returned to bed, and another hour after that I managed to fall into a fitful sleep.

I dreamed I was in a forest being chased by German soldiers. Having no weapons as they closed in on me, I figured my only recourse was to fly to safety. I spread my arms like wings and lifted my chin heavenward. I never got off the ground. Bushes snagged my clothing. Roots clawed at my feet. I was held earthbound. Hands clutched at me. I turned to fight them off and saw—

—a dark figure standing at the foot of my bed.

I screamed like a little kid.

"Fear not," said the dark figure. "I am an angel."

Finding my voice, I replied, "Forgive me if I don't find comfort in those words."

The being provided his own light to reveal himself. His radiance filled the room.

"Abdiel! Why didn't you tell me it was you? Better yet, why didn't you knock, or choose a more suitable hour, like one in the daytime?"

"Angels do not heed time zones."

"Well, for humans they come in pretty handy."

He stared down at me. "You're not going to Jerusalem. Why?"

I reached for the bedside lamp.

"Nothing personal," I told him as I clicked it on, "but I tend to get distracted by intruders that glow in the dark."

"You haven't answered my question."

"The professor sent you, didn't he?"

Squaring his broad shoulders, Abdiel said, "I do not take orders from men. Why are you not going to Jerusalem?"

I looked at the clock on the nightstand. I'd been asleep a little less than an hour.

"It's three-seventeen in the morning," I told him. "I don't justify my decisions to anybody, angels included, at three-seventeen in the morning."

"Would you prefer we have this conversation later?"

"I'd prefer not to have this conversation at all!"

To make my point, I switched off the lamp, though with Abdiel glowing it made no difference. I flopped down onto my pillow. Abdiel remained at the foot of the bed.

"How do you expect me to sleep with you standing there?"

"Too bright?"

He dimmed himself.

"Better?" he asked.

"No, it's not better. I can't sleep if you're here."

"Do not humans pray for angels to watch over them while they sleep?"

Exasperated, I switched on the lamp again.

"All right. I'm not going to Jerusalem because I have a new book contract with a tight deadline. Now you know."

"This book. It must be written?"

"This book is my chance to redeem my reputation as a researcher and author. Plus, it pays well."

"Your reputation among men is important to you?"

"Of course it's important to me! This is my life we're talking about."

"Correct me if I'm wrong, but it is your reputation as a writer that has suffered. You are confusing your life with your profession."

"My profession is my life," I said. "Maybe you don't see it that way, you being an angel. But that's the way I see it and the last time I checked, it's my call to make."

He stared at me for several moments. His lack of response unnerved me.

"It is my call, isn't it? I still have free will, don't I?"

"You would have me instruct you about that which you already know so well? Free will cannot be taken from you by anyone save the Father."

"Naturally. That's the way it should be," I said, relieved the rules hadn't changed. "And so I choose not to go to Jerusalem."

"If that is your . . ."

"It is. And now I'm choosing to go back to sleep."

Before he could say anything more, I switched off the light, huddled beneath the covers, and closed my eyes. I resisted peeking for as long as I could. When I did, Abdiel was still there.

"And I choose to stay until this conversation is finished," he said.

If there is anything more exasperating than a stubborn angel, I don't want to know about it. I sat up. "You think I'm afraid to go, don't you?"

"Are you?"

"Of course I am!"

"As you should be," Abdiel replied. "What I find difficult to understand is why you would intentionally choose a life of mediocrity."

"Mediocrity? Do I need to remind you that I won a Pulitzer Prize for my writing? That may not carry a lot of weight in heaven, but here on earth it's downright impressive."

"Do I need to remind you that you bear the mark of God?"

My hand rose instinctively to my forehead. Why, I don't know. It had never been revealed to me where the mark was or what it looked like. All I knew was that every angel—good and bad—could see it.

"I have not forgotten," I said. "And believe me, I'm grateful for it. It's my ticket to normalcy. The way I see it, as long as I have the mark none of you can touch me."

"I have no desire to touch you."

"You know what I mean. No one can drag me into the middle of your angel war. Call it mediocre if you wish, but all I want is the chance to live a normal human life."

"You wish to be normal?"

"I wish to be the poster boy for normal. I want a normal job with normal working hours so that I can buy a normal house on a normal street where my normal wife and I can raise normal kids, free from the threat of warring angels and life-sucking demons who want to turn my body into a hotel for the damned."

Having spooked myself with the memory, I checked the dark recesses of the ceiling for hungry, sticky gargoylelike creatures.

"You wish to be normal," Abdiel repeated.

"That's the plan."

For a long moment he stared at me, unblinking. "But that is not who you are. You are part angel."

"Yes, but don't you see? That's the beauty of free will. I choose to ignore that fact."

Abdiel turned aside. For a moment I thought he was going to leave.

"I was there in the days when Nephilim inhabited the earth; like you, part human and part angel. I saw what they could do."

"Really?" That got my attention. "Tell me. What could they do?"

"Of all men, you alone have been given the chance to know the power of Nephilim."

"Power?"

"I can tell you this about the Nephilim of old," he said. "They did not choose to live mediocre lives. They were heroes and men of renown."

I tried to imagine an entire village of beings half human, half angel. Midreverie I caught myself.

"Sorry—I'm not falling for it," I said. "You're forgetting, I've already taken a ride on the wild side with your kind. I think I'll stick to the kiddy rides."

He nodded. "If it is your decision for the rest of your days to wonder what powers lie within you, I will honor that."

He disappeared.

The only light in the room was the sixty-watt bulb of my bedside lamp. I switched it off and tried to go back to sleep.

Thirty frustrating minutes later I threw back the sheets and went to the closet and pulled out my suitcase. I could sleep on the flight.

CHAPTER
5

The coastline of Tel Aviv stretched impressively into the hazy northern horizon, a captivating view from the air even though my knees were screaming to be stretched.

Twenty hours after departing San Diego we were approaching our destination after a four-hour layover in New York, during which time I was detained by security. An agent recognized me. She was insistent she'd seen my picture on a printout of suspected terrorists. Come to find out, she'd seen it on the back of my book in her supervisor's office.

Seated next to the window, Sue Ling seemed to be enjoying the view. I was lucky in that I had two views. The one out the window and the one seated next to me.

I don't know how Sue Ling did it, but she looked as fresh as she did when we boarded the plane in San Diego. And while she'd maintained a business demeanor throughout the flight, there is an intimacy to travel that made the long trip enjoyable. At least for me.

We talked. Of course we talked. I learned that she has seen every Alfred Hitchcock movie ever made, that she loves anything made with pasta and has been known to eat cold spaghetti for breakfast, and that she has a rabid fascination with roller coasters that I don't understand: the wilder, the better. I also learned that she is a dissertation away from earning her Ph.D., and that she's put off writing it for over a year. I didn't have to ask why. All of her time is spent with the professor.

As a researcher I've developed subtle interview skills that are designed to draw people out when they're reluctant to talk. I've made it my practice not to use these skills in casual conversation with the opposite sex. The way I see it, if a woman is hesitant to talk about something, that's her right. Call me old-fashioned, but I'd rather she reveal her heart to me in her own time and in her own way.

I broke my own rule with Sue Ling. I probed. I'm not proud of myself, but I had to know where I stood with her. I didn't want to make a fool of myself.

After a few questions she opened up. I think she wanted to. She's quick. I think she saw where I was headed and did us both a favor by dousing any romantic thoughts I might be kindling.

I learned that Sue Ling considers herself to be the professor's wife, if not legally and physically, at least emotionally. For better or worse, until death do them part. She told me that two years ago she invited him to propose to her. He declined.

It wasn't for lack of affection, nor did his disability figure into the decision. He told her he couldn't marry again for fear that what happened to his wife and daughters would happen again. He couldn't take the chance that rebel angels would hurt or kill her to get to him.

Sue loved him even more for turning her down and pledged herself to him for as long as they both shall live. When she told me of her pledge, she insisted a physical relationship and children didn't matter to her. But there was sadness in her eyes when she said it.

Our seats dropped from beneath us as we descended. The Israeli countryside was a blur. Ben Gurion airport lay directly ahead. There we would meet our contact, a twenty-two-year-old archeology student named Choni Serrafe. He would be our guide and drive us the remaining fifty kilometers to the Crowne Plaza Hotel.

"Looks like we're in for a storm." I pointed out the window.

An impressive thunderhead was building over the eastern mountains, similar to the way it does in east San Diego county as the cool ocean air collides with hot desert winds.

We landed without incident and began the tediously slow march through customs and security. It seemed like half the world was trying to get into Israel, which wasn't surprising considering all the attention the Alexandrian manuscripts were getting in the press. Naturally you'd expect biblical scholars from all over the world wanting to get into the country to see for themselves. It was the hordes of doomsayers and end-of-the-world fanatics standing in line that I found annoying.

I blamed the media. From the start they had been trumpeting every imaginable rumor that had to do with the third scroll, the crazier the better. One of the most repeated rumors was that the third manuscript had revealed the location of Jesus' tomb, where researchers had unearthed a complete skeleton. Variations of the story ran rampant.

One held that, by order of the president of the United States, secret military operatives had raided the site and massacred the scholars in the act of authenticating the bones of Jesus. The bones of Jesus were confiscated and crushed to dust and scattered over—take your pick: Texas, Wall Street, Las Vegas, or

Elvis's grave. One man in Houston claimed to have a NASA memo to the effect that Jesus' ashes would be launched into space aboard the next space shuttle.

Why would the president of the United States order the destruction of Jesus' bones? To keep the Christians in America from turning into godless hordes and endangering civil order and the world economy.

A different rumor claimed that the text of the third manuscript revealed that Jesus was a super-intelligent alien from the same race that built the pyramids in Egypt.

Still another report held that Dan Brown was an alien who discovered a copy of the manuscript text and plagiarized it, publishing it as *The Da Vinci Code*.

Then there was the *National Enquirer* story reporting that Jesus faked his own death in order to escape the Temple money-changers who had put out a contract on him.

While in the airport waiting to board I watched an *Entertainment Tonight* segment that reported the manuscript was being hushed up because it gave a detailed and disturbing physical description of Jesus. That instead of an attractive man with long hair Jesus was in reality fat and bald.

The consensus seemed to be that whatever the text of the third manuscript revealed when it was released, there would be a radical revision of the historical Jesus.

Reaction among churches was mixed. Liberal denominations welcomed a fresh interpretation of the historical Jesus, while conservatives insisted that no matter what the Alexandrian text revealed, they would not alter their teaching of Jesus since it was not part of the inspired canon of Scripture.

The next thing I knew I got an elbow in the ribs as a short, bony young man pushed me aside. He was wearing a T-shirt that said: THE ALEXANDRIA MANUSCRIPT—OPRAH'S BOOK OF THE

MONTH. He pulled his girlfriend with him to the front of the line.

My cell phone rang. "Hail to the Chief." I kept meaning to change the ring tone.

"It's Christina," I told Sue just as her cell phone rang.

"The professor," she said.

We turned away from each other and took the calls. My conversation ended before hers.

"Christina wants me to call her as soon as we have anything new, day or night," I told Sue when she was finished.

"Are you and Christina back together?"

"I'm a source, nothing more. Didn't I tell you? She's on Senator Vogler's staff."

"Rebecca Vogler? Impressive."

"Christina's her chief of staff."

"Now I'm really impressed."

"What about the professor? What time is it in San Diego?"

"Four A.M." She appeared troubled. "He said he just wanted to make sure we'd arrived safely." She mulled a moment, then added, "I shouldn't have left him alone."

I glanced at the long line ahead of us. "I don't think the Israelites had this much trouble getting into the land when Moses led them."

Behind me were two Orthodox Jews. They didn't think my joke was funny.

Choni Serrafe put the airport behind us as he swerved in and out of traffic like a New York cabbie on steroids.

"Is this your first trip to Israel?" he asked with a toothy grin.

We both replied that it was. Sue sat in the backseat with the luggage. She was actually enjoying the ride. Then I remembered her fascination with death and roller coasters.

Choni was the genial sort, thin and sinewy with short, black, curly hair and a five-o'clock shadow.

"Has your father made progress since speaking to the professor?" Sue asked from the backseat.

His father was a professor of antiquities at the university and one of the team of translators.

Choni looked at her in the rearview mirror. "He'll want to report to you himself. I'll take you to the university after you check into the hotel."

"He must be excited," Sue said.

"It wore off quickly. He's too exhausted to be excited."

Ahead of us dark clouds continued to build on the horizon. There was something about them that mesmerized me. I couldn't stop looking at them.

"Don't you have thunderstorms in California?" Choni asked.

The golden cupola of the Dome of the Rock glistened in the afternoon sun, catching my eye every time I looked up from unpacking. Abandoning the luggage, I finally gave in to the lure of the landscape. Pulling back the curtains, I slid open the door and stepped onto the balcony. The view of the old city was breathtaking. I couldn't believe I was here in the ancient city where every street, every stone was saturated with history. If nothing else happened during the course of our stay, this moment, this view alone, was worth the trip.

The air was warm and musky, heavy with the threat of rain. A massive thundercloud formed a backdrop to the scene with the lowering sun a singular stage light. The last time I'd seen clouds this dramatic—

My next word caught in my throat. I swallowed hard.

"San Diego," I murmured. "The day the president was assassinated. Only they weren't clouds then, but armies of angels."

Could it be? Was that the reason I was so captivated by these clouds? Was there something more to them? Something ordinary human beings couldn't see?

On the day of the assassination I had stood on the deck of the aircraft carrier *Midway*. Semyaza, Lucifer's lieutenant, stood beside me. He lifted the blinders from my eyes and I saw angels. He also expressed surprise that I needed his aid to see them.

Had the Nephilim of old been able to see angels in their natural state? It made sense that they could. What kind of sustained relationship can be had with invisible partners?

Maybe they could do it, but could I? And if I could, how?

Gripping the railing with both hands, I set my gaze on the clouds. *Somehow I need to tap the angel within me.* I lowered my head and concentrated hard on the clouds and . . . succeeded in giving myself a headache.

Glancing away, I rubbed my eyes. I tried again. Same result. Eyestrain. Headache. No angels.

But I could feel an attraction from the clouds. Call it psychic or whatever you wish, they were calling to me. No, it was stronger than that. There was force. They were pulling on me.

That was something, wasn't it? How many people are drawn to clouds by force? Maybe that was the extent of my angelic abilities.

Then something came to mind. Maybe I was going about it all wrong. While I hadn't thought of them in years, for some reason stereograms came to mind. They were a fad a few years ago. Optical illusions, they were three-dimensional objects embedded in two-dimensional prints that at first glance appeared to be nothing more than a splattering of random dots.

People bought books with page after page of stereogram pictures. They stood in galleries staring at framed prints. Some people, no matter how hard they tried, couldn't break past the surface dots to see the three-dimensional image within. They were encouraged to place their noses on the picture and slowly pull it away. All this to see airplanes and faces and teapots.

Was that the key to seeing angels, too? Sticking my nose in the clouds wasn't an option, but what if I stared past them with unfocused eyes?

What did I have to lose?

Turning to the clouds, I steadied myself against the railing and gazed at the eastern sky. I took a cleansing breath. Relaxed my muscles. And stood there. Not so much looking at the clouds, but through them, beyond them. I concentrated on not concentrating. I breathed deeply and tried simply to be.

Nothing happened.

The urge was to focus. I resisted it.

I saw clouds. Highlights. Shadows. Movement. Billows. Cavernous depths. Angels.

So startled was I when I saw them, they disappeared from view. Setting myself again, I forced myself to relax, fighting off my rising excitement.

There were thousands of them and they were massing. Robed. Shining with a heavenly glory that was mesmerizing and fearful. Moving with grace. Solemn. Silent. They filled the sky stretching north to south from horizon to horizon and upward in a column that reached to the heavens. Was this the ladder that Jacob saw?

But unlike Jacob's angels who ascended and descended the ladder, these angels traveled a singular direction, from heaven to earth. Their assembly had the appearance of a grand choir.

I laughed out loud. Wasn't it a mere five miles south of here that they had assembled in similar fashion to announce the birth of the Christ child? And now here they were again. To announce what?

There was a tap at my door.

"Grant? Are you ready?"

I bolted across the room and startled Sue Ling with the suddenness of the door opening. Grabbing her by the arm I pulled her across the room.

"You have to see this!"

"Ouch! Grant, you're hurting me—"

"Sorry, it's just that—" I pulled her onto the balcony. "— look!"

With the sweep of my hand I showed her the angels.

"I know," Sue replied, unimpressed. "I have the same view from my balcony. That's why I brought an umbrella. Oh, look, what good timing. Choni's in the parking lot waiting for us."

"Sue? Can't you see them?"

Of course she couldn't see them. But at times like this there is no reason, only excitement and desire. I so wanted her to see what I could see. Maybe if I wished hard enough. Maybe if I clapped my hands.

"Well, we're off!" she said cheerily.

I blocked her with my arm.

"Sue, I see angels."

Her genial expression faded.

Sue Ling didn't need to be convinced of the existence of angels. As the professor's assistant she'd seen Abdiel often enough, possibly even conversed with him. She also knew enough to know that seeing angels wasn't always a good thing.

"Angels," she repeated. "How many and where?"

She scanned the rooftops in anticipation of viewing the location, if not the angels.

"Thousands," I said. "Thousands upon thousands. And not down there. In the clouds."

With fervent gaze she scanned the clouds. With reverent voice she said, *"And they will see the Son of Man coming on the clouds of the sky, with power and great glory.* Matthew 24, verse 30."

"We have to get down there," I said.

It took a moment for my words to penetrate. When they did, she grabbed me by the arm and pulled me out of the room.

"Ouch! Sue, you're hurting me—"

She let go of my arm in the elevator. I rubbed it.

Her eyes were fixed on the floor indicator, urging the elevator downward. As soon as the doors started to open, she was pressing to get through and ran into a woman and two men who were getting in.

"Jana!" she exclaimed.

The collision knocked Jana back a step into her bow-tied co-worker and cameraman, whom I recognized from the press conference, though he wasn't carrying a camera at the moment.

When Jana recovered, she looked at Sue, then at me. "What are you doing here?"

Sue stepped around her and waved for me to do the same. "Grant, we're late," she said, hurrying on.

"Hi, Jana." I stepped to one side to let her into the elevator. "You're a long way from home."

"Grant!" Sue called to me.

"Sorry, Jana, I have to go."

I was halfway across the lobby when—"Grant!" It was Jana. I turned back.

"Grant?" Sue held the lobby door open.

Once again I found myself forced to choose between my former girlfriend and the woman I was attracted to but couldn't have.

But from the expression on Jana's face, she wasn't expecting me to make a choice. She was sizing me up.

She turned to the cameraman. "Get your camera. Move!" To the bow tie, "Get the car." Then she fixed her sights on me. "Grant, what exactly are you doing here?"

A vise grip clamped onto my arm. It was Sue. She pulled me across the lobby. At the door, I said to Jana, "Sorry—"

Jana followed us into the parking lot where Choni stood beside his car and waved at us.

"Take us to Mt. Olivet," Sue ordered.

The sharpness of the command wiped the smile off Choni's face. As Sue bundled into the backseat and I climbed in front, Choni slipped behind the driver's wheel.

Putting the car in gear, he said, "It would be better to sight-see another day. My father is expecting—"

"Mt. Olivet," Sue repeated without explaining herself.

She looked out the back window. Jana was standing in the middle of the parking lot watching us.

Had it been me giving the orders, Choni would have argued with me. But women have a certain tone men and children have learned not to argue with. Sue used that tone. She used it well. I doubted it was the first time she'd used it.

"It is important you get to Olivet?" Choni asked.

Sue and I exchanged glances. "Has anything changed?" she asked me.

I looked eastward at the clouds. "Unchanged," I replied.

"End-of-the-world important," Sue said to Choni.

"And that woman?" he asked, motioning to Jana.

A small car screeched to a halt beside her. The cameraman, carrying his camera, emerged from the hotel at a dead run.

"She's of no consequence," Sue said, "but if you lose her, it wouldn't break my heart."

Choni smiled. "A chase scene. I've always wanted to do an American chase scene."

Exiting the hotel parking lot he sped down the access road and onto the main thoroughfare. Then he turned hard left into a housing district.

"A shortcut," he explained. "I used to date a girl who lived here. I thought it was serious, like she was the one, you know? She broke it off because her dog didn't like me. It's not like I wanted to marry her poodle."

Jana's car followed us in.

The housing district was a maze, every few hundred feet a turn. The cloud of angels swung from my side of the car to the front, to the driver's side, to the back, to my side again, and finally to the front as we exited onto the main road.

I stuck my head out the window to get a better view. Sue rolled down her window and did the same.

"I've never seen anyone so fascinated with a thunderstorm," Choni said. "I must visit San Diego and see this city that has no weather."

We exited the maze. Sue watched the exit for Jana for as long as she could see it. Jana's car never came out. Sue faced forward with a satisfied grin.

The road we were on skirted the southern edge of the Temple Mount running parallel to ancient walls. At the southeast corner the road turned north.

"We're entering the Kidron Valley," Choni said. "Mt. Olivet is on the right."

At the base of the slope was a huge graveyard that stretched farther than we could see.

The car slowed.

"Why are we stopping?" Sue asked.

Choni motioned to the road ahead. A tour bus had stopped and was blocking the road. The panel to its engine was raised.

Tourists buzzed around the bus doing what tourists do. They wandered mindlessly in search of suitable backgrounds to take pictures of their spouses and friends. Several of them were standing shoulder-to-shoulder in the middle of the road, smiling and saying, "Cheese," with the ancient city at their backs.

Sue climbed out of the car.

Choni and I exchanged puzzled looks. "I can get around them," he said of the tourists.

"Sue?" I climbed out of the car.

She was standing on the shoulder of the road, taking in the surrounding area.

"The Golden Gate." She pointed to a double-tiered archway that was embedded in the wall. "Also called the Gate of Mercy and the Beautiful Gate."

Maybe at one time it had been a gate, but the archway had been filled in. Now it was just part of the wall with graves scattered in front of it.

"Jesus and his disciples walked through that gate to go to the Temple," Sue said. "It was through that gate that Jesus rode a donkey while the crowd waved palm branches."

I nodded. I could see it. The gate was situated in line with the Temple Mount.

"On this side," she said, indicating our side of the road, "is the Garden of Gethsemane where Jesus was arrested." Her gaze moved up the hill. "And Mt. Olivet, where he ascended into heaven in a cloud of angels. I can see it."

"I can, too," I said. "It's just as the Bible describes it."

"No," she said. "I mean, I can see them. The angels. I can see them."

If she was pulling my leg, she was doing a masterful job of it. The expression on her face was one of awe and wonder.

"You saw this at the hotel?" Choni asked.

His face was just like Sue's. He could see them, too. He stood inside the open door of his car, his arms resting on the top, his mouth open, his eyes wide and fixed on the clouds.

"Well, will you look at that?" one of the tourists said with a southern drawl. "Jubal, lookie up there at them special effects. Looks like angels in the clouds, don't it? How do they do that?"

Jubal glanced upward and squinted his eyes. "Thas nothin'." He spat. "I seen better special effects at Disney World."

A line of cars had queued up behind us. About a dozen or so cars back was Jana. Like everyone else, she was gazing up at the sky in wonder. As she gazed, she directed her cameraman to record the event. She needn't have bothered. His camera was pointed at the clouds.

"We need to get up there," Sue said.

Choni assessed the situation. In both directions now the road was jammed with people. Everyone was getting out of their cars and staring at the angel-filled clouds over Mt. Olivet.

"Only one way I know of to get to the top of the mountain," he said.

Vaulting over the edge of the road he slipped and ran down the bank. Sue and I were right behind him.

As I made the leap I glanced in Jana's direction. She was recording a report. Her cameraman was lying on his back in order to get the angels in the background. Our movement caught Jana's attention. She said something to the cameraman, and seconds later they were running down the slope after us with Jana in the lead, the cameraman on her heels, and the bow-tied reporter trailing. He was carrying a small monitor.

We crossed the Kidron and began climbing, weaving through olive trees that were part of the Garden of Gethsemane. Choni led us to a path that crested onto a road.

"Come, come!" he urged us, with a huge kid's smile.

He reached for Sue Ling's hand and pulled her up, though she didn't appear to need help. I, on the other hand, was wheezing like an old man.

"Don't tell me," I said to Sue Ling. "You're a jogger."

"Five miles every morning."

"I plan to start Monday."

We crossed in front of the Church of All Nations with its colorful mosaic façade. It was easier going here. Level ground.

Cars had caught up with us. A steady stream snaked up the side of the mountain. Behind us Jana and her crew were climbing onto the road.

The church's retaining wall came to an end and we began to ascend. We came to a fork in the road.

Choni went left. The steeper road.

A crazy thought born no doubt of oxygen deprivation popped into my head. It would be just my luck to drop dead of a heart attack minutes before the greatest spiritual event in the history of the world since the Resurrection.

I was falling behind. Sue slowed for me to catch up.

"Do you need help?" she asked.

"Thanks. No. I'll make it."

Apparently I wasn't convincing.

"We can walk. Or hitch a ride."

The idea of slowing to a walk was tempting. The possibility of catching a ride was not likely. While the cars were bumper to bumper, they were moving at a quick clip and the roads were narrow. Stopping would back up everything. Besides, most of the cars were packed with passengers. Some even had young men riding on the hoods and tops and trunks.

"Lets. Just. Keep. Going," I said.

While she could have run ahead, Sue stayed with me.

With my lungs bursting with pain, my knees threatening to collapse, and white spots floating in my vision, we crested the round summit. From here everything flattened out.

There were people everywhere, heads tilted heavenward, mouths gaping at the angelic assembly overhead. For their part, the angels were oblivious to our presence. They moved into place and stood with solemn reverence, eyes forward, not looking down.

"Have you ever seen anything like this?" Tears moistened the wrinkles of Choni's eyes.

Actually, I had, but I didn't tell him that. The last time I saw an assembly of angels of this magnitude I was standing atop a skyscraper in San Diego in the center of it all. I liked this time better. No one was paying attention to me.

Hunched over, my hands were on knees as I tried to catch my breath.

Choni came up to me. "You knew before they appeared. How did you know? Are you a prophet?"

"I have a better question," I said. "Where from here?"

"Yes, yes—" Sue exclaimed, looking around. "Choni, there are three locations that claim to be the place where Jesus ascended."

Choni nodded. "Traditions, at best. All we have from Scripture is that Jesus ascended in the vicinity of Bethany."

"Where's that?"

"Here. Somewhere."

"So you're saying—"

"We're close enough. From here it's anybody's guess."

My breathing was such I could straighten up again. I looked up, wondering if I could see something the others couldn't see. But all I saw were angels.

A young man ran from group to group, showing everyone a picture on his cell phone. People were nodding and grinning when they saw it.

He approached us and held up his cell phone. It was a picture from space of the phenomenon localized over Jerusalem. There was enough detail to see that the clouds were inhabited with figures. The central passageway, Jacob's ladder, appeared as a laser beam shooting into space.

"Where did you get this?" an excited Choni asked.

"Internet," the boy replied proudly. "This one—" he said, changing the picture, "—is from the Israeli air force."

It, too, was from an elevated perspective with greater clarity and detail.

A short distance away three men with open Bibles began reading aloud, one at a time.

> *And while they looked steadfastly toward heaven as he went up, behold, two men stood by them in white apparel; Which also said, Ye men of Galilee, why stand ye gazing up into heaven? This same Jesus, which is taken up from you into heaven, shall so come in like manner as ye have seen him go into heaven.*

> *. . . and they shall see the Son of man coming in the clouds of heaven with power and great glory. And he shall send his angels with a great sound of a trumpet, and they shall gather together his elect from the four winds, from one end of heaven to the other.*

People around us hushed as they recognized the familiar verses that were being revealed over our heads. The third man read:

> For the Lord himself shall descend from heaven with a shout, with the voice of the archangel, and with the trump of God: and the dead in Christ shall rise first: Then we which are alive and remain shall be caught up together with them in the clouds, to meet the Lord in the air: and so shall we ever be with the Lord.

At the reading of this verse a cheer resounded atop Mt. Olivet.

"Grant Austin!"

A hand grabbed my shoulder and swung me around to face the fury of Jana Torres.

"Why didn't you tell me at the hotel? You saw this, didn't you? You saw it before anyone else did. And you didn't tell me? You ran away and didn't tell me?"

I went from feeling elation to scum in a nanosecond. "Jana, I'm sorry. At the time, I didn't know exactly what I was seeing."

I hoped the excuse wasn't as lame as it sounded.

From Jana's expression, it was worse than it sounded. "After all we've meant to each other . . ."

Sue Ling watched our exchange from a distance.

"Something's happening!" Jana's cameraman yelled.

With a smooth motion he swung his camera onto his shoulder, pointing it heavenward. All around us people did the same with video recorders, cameras, and cell phones.

An unseen trumpet sounded. Clear. Unwavering. Its sound came from above us and resounded all around us.

People fell to their knees. Young and old, male and female. They lifted clasped hands to heaven. Tears streaked their cheeks.

Above us the angels appeared agitated. They gave a mighty shout.

It was a shout such as I had never heard. It passed through me like a wave, knocking me to my knees.

Choni was beside me, weeping with both hands raised. Sue Ling appeared positively beatific, as did Jana on my other side. What kind of friend was I to deny her this experience?

A collective gasp rose upward as the heavens parted, and there shone a great light. The light took the form of a man, descending from the clouds. His radiance outshone the angels and illuminated the thousands of faces looking up at him.

His garments were translucent and white as snow, rippling as though in a breeze. His arms were outstretched all at once to embrace us, and to show us the nail scars in his hands. His face was unblemished. His eyes . . . his eyes . . . his eyes . . . took you in and warmed you and loved you.

A few feet above us he slowed his descent. The crowd shrank back. He was no more than ten feet from us as he completed his descent.

His expression serene, a portrait of peace, the earth still. It was as though all of nature held its breath.

Jesus gazed lovingly upon us and we upon him. His arms swept slowly side to side in blessing.

As he glanced in my direction, he broke into a smile, then a chuckle. He held it back. Then he couldn't. He laughed, caught himself, tried to hold it back, then laughed again.

The dam burst. Despite his every effort, Jesus let loose with laughter until tears filled his eyes. He doubled over he laughed so hard.

"It was a joke, people!" he whooped.

CHAPTER
6

After having his laugh, Jesus disappeared and all the angels with him, leaving us to the thunderclouds. The downpour was torrential. Having been raised on Hollywood humor, I kept thinking of Jesus balancing a bucket of water over heaven's doorway and instructing the last angel to slam the door shut on his way out.

Like fools we stood there, staring up at the clouds, with the rain pelting us in the face until we were drenched. When it was obvious there would be no encore, we trudged down the hill.

The exodus off the Mount of Olives was a somber trek. There were some, like Choni, who remained upbeat despite the bizarre ending to what had been a dramatic buildup. Most, however, were somber. Gone was the thrill of expectation that had marked our ascent. For people who had expected to be taken up into the clouds where they would reunite with their loved ones as they had been taught in church, trudging down a slippery, muddy slope was disappointing.

The car was where we'd left it. A flow of vehicles meandered around it like a stream around a rock. With Choni driving, we waded into the flow of traffic and continued northward to Mt. Scopus and the Hebrew University of Jerusalem, our original destination.

When we arrived, it was dark and the campus was deserted. Sue and I followed Choni to the Institute of Archeology. The institute had been pressed into service because of its advanced technical facilities and close proximity to the artifacts identified in the Alexandrian manuscript.

Choni identified himself to a security guard, who checked a log sheet. He commented on the tardiness of our arrival, then radioed a buddy announcing our arrival.

Moments later Choni's father emerged through a set of double doors. He embraced his son with a weary smile and made a comment about him not having the good sense to come in from the rain. He then shook Sue Ling's hand and my hand in Western fashion.

Dr. Gershom Serrafe was a kindly man, small, with broad shoulders and a bad combover. Both his hair and his bristly mustache were more white than gray.

"How is John these days?" he asked Sue, his eyes twinkling.

It took an awkward moment for me to realize he was inquiring after the professor.

"Professor Forsythe sends you his best," Sue Ling offered. "He wishes he could have come himself."

"He wishes he could climb up out of that straitjacket on wheels and get back into the field, that's what he wishes," Serrafe said ruefully. "But archeological digs are for the young, and John and I must content ourselves with more cerebral endeavors. Speaking of which, the manuscript in question would have been a waste of his time."

"How can you say that, Papa, after what has happened?" Choni said.

Serrafe eyed his son without comment.

Choni was aghast. "Have you really been stuck so deep in this cave that you do not know what has happened?"

"Mt. Olivet," Serrafe replied.

"Of course, Mt. Olivet! We were there! We saw! Angels, Papa! Thousands of them!"

"And you saw them, too?" Serrafe asked.

He looked directly at me. I wondered if he knew about me.

"We all saw," Sue Ling said, answering for both of us.

"It was awesome, Papa!" Choni said. "Absolutely astounding! When he spoke, we all heard him in our own languages. I heard him in Hebrew. They heard him in English."

"Awesome . . . astounding—" his father repeated. "It would take awesome and astounding to rid the parking area of those jackals with their microphones and cameras and satellite dishes. May their vans get mired in the mud."

With a flick of his finger he indicated we were to follow him. He turned and led us through the double doors.

A wide corridor led to another pair of doors, which opened to a huge library study area. The tables and chairs had been re-arranged to form seven groups of language scholars—each working on a separate translation of the Alexandrian manu-script. This must have been what Babel sounded like when God confused the tongues of man.

A half-dozen televisions were hung on ceiling mounts around the room. Following Serrafe's lead, we gravitated around one just inside the door.

On the screen a distinguished-looking male commentator was delivering the news in Hebrew. I didn't understand a word he was saying. I didn't have to. The footage accompanying the story was from Mt. Olivet.

"They are calling him the Laughing Jesus," Serrafe translated for us.

The most dramatic footage was accompanied by a banner at the bottom of the screen identifying the source as courtesy of KTSD, San Diego. Jana and her team had scored an international journalistic coup.

"We were right next to that cameraman, Papa," Choni exclaimed, pointing at the television. "That's exactly what we saw."

Unimpressed, his father walked to a table, picked up a book, and slapped it against his son's chest. "Matthew 24:3–5. Look it up."

Choni's expression soured, the way it does when someone resists reality, preferring that his excitement go unchallenged.

"Read it aloud," Serrafe said.

Choni read:

> As Jesus was sitting on the Mount of Olives, the disciples came to him privately. "Tell us," they said, "when will this happen, and what will be the sign of your coming and of the end of the age?" Jesus answered: "Watch out that no one deceives you. For many will come in my name, claiming, 'I am the Christ,' and will deceive many."

Choni looked up. "But, Papa—"

Serrafe cut him off. "You're not done reading. Read verse 23."

Choni lowered his head, found the verse, and read:

At that time if anyone says to you, "Look, here is the Christ!" or, "There he is!" do not believe it. For false Christs and false prophets will appear and perform great signs and miracles to deceive even the elect —if that were possible. See, I have told you ahead of time.

Serrafe took the Bible from his son and shook it at him. "This is why we study Scripture! So that we are not tossed here and there by every drama, no matter how awesome. Do you think what happened on Mt. Olivet today is a coincidence? Come, I will show you."

We snaked through the room to the opposite end, where several rows of long tables had been placed end to end. Brightly lit with portable lights was the Alexandrian manuscript itself. While the translators worked mostly from photo and computer images, occasionally they rose from their workplaces to consult the manuscript itself.

Despite Professor Serrafe's overt disdain for it, the manuscript itself was impressive—hand-printed black Greek letters on ancient papyrus, brown and brittle with age.

He turned to Sue and me. "You have read the text?"

"I have," Sue replied.

"And your field of study?"

"Physics."

"Ah, then you know our dilemma," the professor said. "And you, what is your field of study?" Tired eyes focused on me, awaiting an answer.

"I'm a writer. A journalist. Well, actually, a biographer." I paused and looked to Sue Ling. When she didn't offer the information for me, I added, "My biography of President Douglas won a Pulitzer Prize."

"A journalist." Serrafe sniffed. "So you are here as—how do you say it—Miss Ling's protection, her um . . . her body-guard."

Sue Ling laughed. I didn't think the professor dismissing my credentials was all that amusing.

Choni stood with his hands behind his back, leaning over the manuscript reading. He didn't appear to be having any trouble reading the text even though there were no spaces between the words. As he read, his brow wrinkled.

"The Alexandrian text reveals a darker side to the Laughing Jesus," Serrafe said. "To label him the Joker Jesus would be more accurate."

Sue nodded her agreement.

"Jesus as portrayed in this manuscript," Serrafe continued, "is a being not of this world who visited this planet in the first century and fashioned himself as the Jewish Messiah as a practical joke. The evidence offered in support of his claim is three-fold. First, the date of the manuscript itself."

Serrafe placed his hand over the manuscript without touching it. "The papyrus, ink, style of writing, and vocabulary are without doubt from the first century. Second, the precise locations of the artifacts—the thirty pieces of silver, Pilate's documents, the coin the Apostle Peter pulled from the mouth of the fish—all prove an intimate knowledge of the people and events to which they're attached."

I was beginning to understand why Tiffany Sproul was a reluctant celebrity, and why the college was buying time to formulate a public statement regarding the manuscript.

"Third," Serrafe said, "and most difficult to explain, are the modern scientific references."

"All the things Jana mentioned at the press conference?" I asked Sue.

"Dark matter, DNA, black holes, entanglement, and more," she replied. "Much more."

Choni looked up from his reading. His eyes were dark. Disturbed. Without his smile he looked like a different person. "And now we have a face to put with the manuscript."

"Of one thing I'm certain," his father added. "We haven't seen the last of him."

"Grant? Higgins. Did I wake you? You sound tired."

With a six-hour difference separating us, it was five o'clock in the afternoon in New York, eleven o'clock at night in Jerusalem. Choni was driving us back to our hotel. At his request Sue was sitting in the front seat. He was quizzing her about the physics in the manuscript when my cell phone rang. I'd been nodding off in the backseat for the past twenty minutes.

"It's been a long day," I said, stretching.

"A long day? It's only two o'clock in California. Please tell me you're getting up early to write."

I was slow in coming up with an excuse.

"You are working on the book, aren't you?"

"Um—not at the moment."

"Watching television? Can't say that I blame you. That's some video from Israel, isn't it? You've seen it, haven't you?"

"Yeah, I saw it."

"What's your take on it?"

"Um—I'm not quite sure what to make of it yet."

"It's so obviously a hoax. You know, like that Blair Witch movie those kids made. They had everyone believing something spooky was chasing them in the woods. This is no different. You watch: In a day or two a couple of pimply faced nerds will come forward, explaining how they did it. So, when can I see some chapters?"

The question took me by surprise. It shouldn't have, but it did. Problem was, I hadn't written any chapters. I had flown to Jerusalem instead. All I had were some outline notes.

"When do you need them?"

"Yesterday. Marketing wants to get a feel for the book. So do the cover design people."

Great. "Let me . . . um—let me whip them into shape and I'll get them to you tomorrow."

"They don't have to be in your usual Pulitzer Prize–winning form, Grant. Rough draft is fine. Email them to me."

"Yeah, well . . ." I stammered. "It's what time in New York? Five, right? Nobody's going to get anything done today. Let me work on them, and I'll have them on your desk first thing tomorrow."

There was a long pause.

"Eight o'clock New York time, Grant. No later."

He sounded suspicious. Probably from years of dealing with authors like me.

"You got it," I said, trying to sound cheerful, optimistic, even carefree.

We chatted about restaurants and baseball for a few minutes. He said good-bye by telling me he looked forward to reading my chapters.

After I hung up, I did some quick mental calculations. Eight o'clock in the morning in New York was two o'clock in the afternoon in Jerusalem.

"I can do this," I told myself, as if putting it into words would somehow make it true.

CHAPTER 7

Before climbing into bed I set out my notes, the journal of my White House experience, and my laptop, and set the clock alarm for 5:00 A.M. I figured if I hit the ground running I could have a couple of chapters written by my publisher's New York deadline.

Sleep was fitful, fueled by the day's events. Seeing the assemblage of angels sparked flashbacks of my showdown with Semyaza on top of the Emerald Plaza tower. The nightmares of that night always left me writhing, with entangling bedsheets playing the role of demons. When the alarm went off I was exhausted. But getting up and working was more attractive than staying in bed and dreaming.

With a pot of room-service coffee fueling me, I fashioned a rough outline of chapter one and by 6:00 A.M. I had a suitable first paragraph. By 6:30 A.M. I was hitting my stride. At this pace I would meet my deadline with ease.

A soft tapping at the door interrupted me.

"Grant?"

My fingers froze over the keyboard. With writing, momentum is everything, difficult to generate and difficult to regain once it's lost. It's not something a writer surrenders willingly.

"Grant? Are you awake?"

The voice was feminine.

If I remained silent, would she conclude I was sleeping and go away?

But then paranoia kicked into gear. What if she was ill? A change of time zones, diet, the excitement of yesterday. It was enough to throw anyone's system off. What if something was wrong with the professor? What time was it in San Diego?

"Grant?"

"Coming," I said.

Abandoning chapter one, I crossed the room and opened the door.

"Jana!" I said, surprised.

"I need to talk to you." She stared past me into the room. "Is this a good time?"

I looked at my watch.

"I know it's early," she said. "I wanted to catch you before you got away. Good, you're dressed. Do you want to talk here or go down to the coffee shop?"

Glancing over my shoulder at my open laptop, I felt my writing momentum slipping away.

"I have a pot of coffee," I said. "I know you prefer tea."

She stepped past me and crossed to the curtains I hadn't yet opened. I'd kept them closed to shut out the distraction of Jerusalem. I half-feared I'd see angels. If that were the case, I'd never get any chapters written.

"Do you mind?" Jana said, pulling the curtains back, letting the sun in.

A glance out the window revealed a sky clear of angels.

With an inward sigh over lost momentum I tidied up the table, shuffling my notes to one side and closing the laptop. To hope that this would be a short conversation was a fool's wish. This was Jana.

I righted the second cup on the serving tray and poured Jana some coffee, setting it in front of the chair opposite mine along with the sugar packets and miniature crème pitcher. Jana had always doctored her coffee heavily.

She pulled out the chair and pushed the crème and sugar aside, sipping her coffee black. "I want to know where I stand with you." Holding her cup in both hands, she peered at me with serious brown eyes.

I sat and topped off my own cup. "I saw your video clip on the news. Your producer must be ecstatic."

"You tried to ditch me yesterday. Why?"

I didn't have a good answer for her, so I offered the only answer I had. A lame one.

"You caught us by surprise. We had no idea you were in Jerusalem."

Her eyes narrowed. "We—is this about Sue Ling?"

I set my coffee cup down with a purposeful clink. "Why don't you tell me, Jana? If you and Sue Ling have something to work out, do it on your own. I don't appreciate the two of you putting me in the middle." I matched her gaze with my own.

"You saw the angels before anyone else yesterday, didn't you?"

"Yes."

"You were going to the Mount of Olives when you ran out of the hotel."

"Yes."

"Why didn't you tell me? After all we've been through, certainly you must have known I'd want to know."

"Like I said, we were in a hurry, you caught me by surprise. I wish I had a better explanation than that, but I don't."

"You tried to ditch us."

"That wasn't my call. I admit I do a lot of dumb things, but this wasn't one of them. I wasn't driving, and it wasn't my call. If I had something to apologize for, I would."

She thought about that a moment. Sipped her coffee. Then said, "True, you have been known to do a lot of dumb things."

She offered a half-smile. A good sign.

"So where does that leave us?" she asked again.

"You tell me. If I continue working with the professor and Sue Ling, can we still be friends?"

Her smile faded. She became Jana the reporter. "I have to ask the hard questions. It's my job."

"I would expect nothing less."

"But can you live with it? I won't be anyone's press secretary. Not yours, not the professor's."

"The professor was wrong to try to use you like that," I said.

My answer surprised her. "Sue Ling wouldn't agree with you."

"At times Sue Ling's feelings for the professor cloud her judgment." I paused. "You want to know where you stand. I'll tell you. I am your flawed but devoted friend. Nothing between us has changed."

Her smile was full. The reporter was gone. My friend Jana was back.

She reached across the table and squeezed my hand. "Thank you."

She sat back.

"Now," she said, pulling a pad from her purse, "where did you go after you left Mt. Olivet yesterday?"

The reporter didn't stay away for long.

I told her of our trip to Hebrew University and how, based on the text, Professor Serrafe had dubbed the Jesus of the manuscript Joker Jesus. Jana chuckled and nodded. She wrote that down.

"And what were your impressions of the Jesus on the mountain?" she asked.

"Same as everyone else, I guess. Dumbfounded."

"Did you recognize any of them?"

I sat back in my chair. "I hadn't thought about that."

So now I did. I replayed what I saw in my mind, scanning the faces of the angels. "No." I shook my head. "I didn't recognize any of them, which is really odd."

"So how did you know to be here?"

I told her that both Sue and I were here as the professor's eyes and ears, and how I felt the clouds calling to me, and how I tested my abilities.

"So nobody forewarned you," she asked, "no angel, that is?"

I shook my head.

"What's next?"

"I'm writing another book." I motioned to the laptop. "It will be about the deception at the White House while I was—"

"I mean, what's next on the angel's agenda?"

"Your guess is as good as mine. I'm not exactly on their newsletter mailing list."

There was a knock at the door.

"Grant? Are you awake?"

I looked at Jana but saw only the top of her head. Both hands were in her purse. She was packing up.

I opened the door.

"Good, you're dressed," Sue Ling said. "I just got a call—"

She saw Jana standing at the foot of my unmade bed.

"Oh—" Sue said.

Jana caressed my arm in passing. "Call me if you get wind of anything," she said, exiting the room without a word to Sue.

"Jana was just—"

Sue cut me off. "I'm establishing a video link to the professor," she said without looking at me. "He wants to talk to you."

She turned to go.

"Sue—Jana just stopped by to—"

"Five minutes," she said over her shoulder.

The laptop sat idle on the desk. I hoped the call to the professor wouldn't take long. Meanwhile, I had five minutes to knock out a paragraph.

My cell phone rang. It was Christina. She said she would be briefing Senator Vogler in ten minutes on the situation in Israel and wanted to know if I'd seen the Mt. Olivet video.

"Doesn't anybody sleep in the States?" I grumbled. After finishing my call to Christina, I had just enough time to get to Sue's room for the video call to the professor. "What time is it in San Diego?"

"Ten-thirty P.M.," Sue said, adjusting the camera on her laptop computer. "We're a day ahead of them."

She had propped the door open so I wouldn't have to knock. Her room was a mirror image of mine. She'd set her computer on my working table's twin and was busy opening the communications software program. She avoided eye contact with me. All we needed now was the professor. He had yet to log in.

Sue drummed her fingers impatiently on the table. She waited a minute longer, then picked up her cell phone and talked the professor through the procedure to get online. Soon afterward we had picture and sound.

"Pull up that chair," she told me, scooting over so that both of us would fit into the camera's field of vision.

"Quite a display on Mt. Olivet," the professor began.

His backdrop was a living room in disarray, a testimony to Sue Ling's absence. She always kept it clean and orderly for him.

Turning his head, the professor spoke to someone off camera. "Good, you're here."

Though we couldn't see him, we recognized Abdiel's voice.

The professor faced the camera again. "Grant, Sue tells me you saw the angels massing even before they revealed themselves. How did you do that?"

I explained how the cloud called to me and described my attempts to see them. I don't know what pleased the professor more—my initiative or my newfound ability.

"Now that you've done it once," he said, "it should be easier to do again. Have you seen any more angels?"

I told him I hadn't.

He inquired about our meeting with Professor Serrafe. Sue gave him a concise report.

"The translations. When do they expect to release them?"

"Within the week."

"That soon?"

"Since the appearance on Mt. Olivet, the Egyptians have been pressing to release the original text immediately."

"That's exactly what they want," the professor said. "They want to keep us off balance."

"The Egyptians?" I asked.

"The rebel angels," the professor replied. "Olivet tipped their hand. Until then we only suspected they were behind the manuscript. Now it's obvious they planted it."

"So the Jesus we saw yesterday—"

"An angel," the professor said. "You have to hand it to them.

The detail was incredible. They staged everything according to Bible prophecy."

"If everything was according to prophecy," I said, "how can we know that it was an impostor?"

Sue looked at me as if I were crazy for asking the question.

A voice came from off camera. "Had it been the Divine Warrior himself, I would have been there with him," Abdiel said.

"The Divine Warrior is the Christ," the professor explained, in case I missed it.

It made sense that had the event been genuine Abdiel would have known about it.

"Abdiel recognized some of the host," the professor added. "They're all on the rebel side."

"Did he recognize the impostor angel?" Sue asked.

"Abdiel's inquiring into the angel's identity," the professor replied. "You know, there's another way to verify that it wasn't Jesus who appeared on Mt. Olivet."

"He never touched down."

The voice came from behind us. Nearly jumping out of our seats, both Sue and I turned to see Abdiel standing in the hotel room.

Did I say standing? I meant floating. His feet weren't touching the carpet. It was the first time I'd seen him barefoot.

A revelation hit me like a thunderbolt. "Doc!" I exclaimed. "Doc Palmer! When I went to see him in Montana, he held a shotgun on me and made me take off my shoes and wiggle my toes in the dirt. He wanted to make sure I wasn't a rebel angel!"

"That makes no sense," Abdiel said. "Projectile weapons cannot harm us."

I pointed at his feet. "This thing about not touching the ground. Is it true of all angels?"

"It is true," Abdiel said.

"The incarnate Christ touched the ground," Sue said.

"When he walked, he left footprints," Abdiel said, with a surprising touch of emotion.

The professor's voice came over the computer speakers.

Who, being in the very nature of God, did not consider equality with God something to be grasped, but made himself nothing, taking the very nature of a servant, being made in human likeness.

"Philippians, second chapter," Sue said, stamping the quotation with its biblical reference.

The hotel room door flew open and banged against the wall.

"I thought we had an agreement," Jana screamed.

I was on my feet. Abdiel was gone. Sue was glowering. On the computer screen the professor was demanding to know what was going on.

"You didn't lock the door?" Sue yelled at me.

"You had it propped open, I thought you—"

"I propped it open to let you in, not her!"

Jana stormed to the window and threw back the sheer curtains. "What's this?"

In the distance, beyond the city, an unwavering beam of light blazed down from the heavens against a cloudless sky, hitting the top of Mt. Olivet. When I turned to say something to Jana, it wasn't Jana who was standing beside me, but Sue Ling, as amazed as I.

Jana had the television remote control in her hand. She opened the media center's cabinet doors and pointed it at the set.

A local station was broadcasting live from atop the mountain. The banner across the bottom of the screen said, JESUS RETURNS.

In better control of himself than he was yesterday, a genial Jesus was answering questions from reporters.

> *—was sudden, but how does a person return after a two-thousand-year absence if not suddenly? I know you have a lot of questions. That's why I'm here. I want to answer them—*

"Tell me you didn't know about this!" Jana said.

"I didn't," I insisted.

"What's going on?" the professor was shouting.

Sue told him to turn on his television set. He disappeared from view.

"Jana, I didn't know!" I said again. "If I knew, do you think we'd be standing here?"

My point was sharp enough to deflate her.

We stood three abreast watching the interview.

> *—best way is to show you. Tomorrow I will appear again, this time in Galilee, Cana. Be prepared to see something that hasn't been seen in two thousand years.*

He disappeared. The suddenness of his departure left the reporters scrambling for places to do their wrap-ups.

Jana's phone rang. Grimacing at the display, she turned away from us and answered it. "He says he didn't know," she said into the phone. "Yes, I believe him."

The professor was back on the computer screen.

"Are they airing it there?" Sue asked him.

Apparently the professor had angled his television so that he could see it while sitting in front of the computer.

"Give me a second," he said, watching the television. "They're replaying the video."

The Jerusalem station was replaying their footage of a descending Jesus. Because I didn't understand Hebrew, the professor thoughtfully provided commentary from what he was watching.

"Apparently, this Jesus gave the Jerusalem stations thirty minutes' notice before his return," the professor said. "One reporter described the notification as hearing a voice in his head during a staff meeting. Nobody else at the meeting heard it."

The professor became agitated. "There! Look there!"

He was pointing at a screen we couldn't see.

"He's descending—"

A video of the event was playing on our station as well, a few seconds ahead of his.

"There! There! Do you see it?" the professor said. "His feet don't touch the ground!"

They didn't. The feet of the self-styled Jesus clearly did not touch the ground.

"Is that something important?" Jana asked, slipping her phone back into her purse.

I explained the significance of the feet to her.

As I did, the professor mulled over the spoken instructions. "He didn't indicate a time; neither did he specify which Cana location. He assumed we knew."

"Do we?" Sue asked.

"Scholars don't agree on the location," the professor replied. Then his tone changed. He took control. "Call Choni. I want you to leave immediately. Tell him to take you to Khirbet Kana. It's in the Bet Netofa Valley."

Sue wrote as he talked.

"If he tries to talk you into going to Kefr Kana, don't listen to him. I imagine that's where most people will go."

Sue didn't ask the professor to defend his choice. After a quick good-bye, she closed the computer and was already packing her things.

"Did you get that?" I asked Jana.

"Khirbet Kana. Bet Netofa Valley."

Sue scowled at me—for fraternizing with the enemy, I guess.

"We'll meet you up there," I said to Jana anyway. "Wait. Better yet, why don't you follow us? Choni may know a shortcut or two."

Sue's scowl deepened. The ride to Galilee was going to be a long, silent one.

Returning to my hotel room, I threw a few things into a travel bag. My laptop lay open on the desk, the upright screen resembling a headstone. My unfinished first chapter was the epitaph.

It might as well have read: "Here lies Grant Austin's publishing career."

CHAPTER
8

M y fears of a long, silent ride to Galilee went unrealized. Looking back on it, I would have preferred the silence.

Choni argued the entire way that we were going to the wrong Cana. He insisted the professor was wrong about the location of the biblical Cana.

"It is not in the Bet Netofa Valley. It is too far north. Too far distant from Nazareth. The valley is marshy and difficult to cross. No, all reputable scholars agree that Kefr Kana, not Khirbet Kana, is the true location."

By all reputable scholars he meant his father and his father's colleagues. Sue was a rock. If the professor told her to go to Khirbet Kana, go to Khirbet Kana she would. To hear her argue you would have thought the location had been printed inside the King James Version of the Bible.

I learned later that a similar discussion was taking place in the news van behind us. In the van it wasn't so much an argument for the Kefr Kana location as it was the unquestioning acceptance of the professor's point of view. Jana's bow-tie colleague, a scientist by nature, wanted to know why other theories were being summarily dismissed without so much as a hearing.

As we neared Galilee, traffic thickened and soon we were slogging our way slowly north. All manner of vehicles clogged the road, not all of them motor-driven. Donkey-drawn carts, bicycles, and hundreds of walkers wanted to see what we'd come to see.

The argument came to a head when we reached the turnoff to Kefr Kana. Seeing the majority of travelers turn west, Choni became even more animated.

Sue was done arguing. She pointed north.

The road cleared, and we were able to make better time. But the heavy line of traffic going the opposite direction grated Choni's nerves and the longer we traveled, the more surly he became.

Craning my neck, I looked through the rear window and checked the van behind us. The cameraman was driving. Jana sat in the front passenger seat. An animated Bow-tie had wedged himself between them from the back. He was pointing at the line of traffic going the opposite direction, his head bobbing and his mouth running.

I made eye contact with Jana. She motioned with her hands, palms up. What should we do? I gave her a weak smile. Not the assurance she was wanting, but it was all I had.

It was early evening when we reached Khirbet Kana. There was some comfort that we weren't the only ones who thought this to be the biblical Cana. Vehicles meandered up and down the rustic streets of a village that was more ruins than village.

Choni pulled to the side of the road and we climbed out.

Bow-tie marched up to Choni and the Kefr Kana versus Khirbet Kana argument took on new life. Sue walked off by herself, taking in the village. The cameraman opened the side door of the van and checked his equipment. That left Jana and me. I did my best to assure her that we were in the right place.

"I hope you're right, Grant. My professional life is on the line."

She could have gone all day without saying that. I hated the thought that I could be responsible for killing two professional lives in one day.

There were only a few habitable structures in Khirbet Kana and they were occupied. There were no gas stations. No stores. We had to make the most of two vehicles and whatever we brought with us. It was going to be a long night, but at least we were in position for the appearing.

That is, if we had the right Cana.

I checked my cell phone. There was no cell phone service either. A blessing. I wondered how many messages my publisher had left for me on the answering service.

Morning dawned clear and fresh. I wish I could say the same thing for my fellow travelers.

Choni had slept fitfully in the driver's seat, unable to stretch out all night. He kept muttering that we had come all this way for nothing. Bow-tie kept blowing into his hand to check his breath. The cameraman squatted beside the van and faced the sun and ate a bag of peanuts. Jana fussed with her hair and makeup. Sue was awake when I woke up. Leaning against the car, she stared at the village, a motionless and silent sentinel.

I had given her the backseat for the night while I slept in the passenger front seat. Feeling the same leg cramping as Choni, halfway through the night I'd opened the door and stretched my legs outside, sleeping half-in and half-out of the car.

The village began to stir. Overnight the population of travelers had tripled. Everywhere we looked people had brought their ill and elderly, hoping for a miracle.

Still, the number of people was small compared to what we had seen going to Kefr Kana, but we were an upbeat gathering. The morning showed promise. Then, before we knew it, morning was gone.

Spirits were still high through early afternoon. By late afternoon a pall began to settle over the gathering. No one said it, but we were all thinking the same thing. We were at the wrong Cana. In our minds we could see the smiles of all the other travelers who had guessed right.

There were several false sightings. All it took to stir the troops was for someone to point to the sky and say, "Look!" or "There!" After a while, a small group thought it was funny to point and shout every two or three minutes. That got old fast.

"There!" Choni said.

I thought he was mocking us because instead of pointing to the sky, he was pointing down the road.

"No, really! There! He's coming!" Choni insisted.

To humor him, we looked.

Jesus walked toward us down the middle of the road, his flowing white apparel rustling with each step. The heat waves rising off the road provided a nice dramatic touch. I noticed he was wearing sandals. He approached Cana in Galilee as casually as if he was doing so in the first century.

People thronged to him. Surrounded him, keeping at a cautious distance. He smiled at them. Nodded greetings. And walked into the heart of the village.

I couldn't help but note Sue's reaction to his appearing now that her faith in the professor had been vindicated. She pushed off from the car and, unsmiling, followed the crowd.

At first Jesus appeared to be lost. He glanced this way and that, taking his bearings and muttering about how things have changed. Finally, when he was satisfied he had the correct location, he turned to face us.

He started to say something, stopped himself, then said, "Where is everybody?"

"Kefr Kana," a man offered.

"Kefr Kana?" Jesus repeated. "What are they doing in Kefr Kana? Don't they know their own land?"

I glanced at Choni, who shrugged sheepishly.

Jesus said, "Let's hope you know your Scriptures better than you know your geography. The wedding at Cana of Galilee was where I performed my first miracle. You've heard of it?"

Everyone claimed to know it.

"This is where it took place. You are standing at the bridegroom's house." When he noticed everyone trying to imagine what the house looked like from the visible foundation, he added, "Actually, you'd have to dig down five feet to find the ruins of the house, but trust me, this is the place. Let that be a lesson to all you housewives. Dust regularly. If you don't, before you know it, you're five feet underground."

Disturbed glances were exchanged. This wasn't the Jesus many had expected. Most had come hoping to hear Jesus bless the multitude and maybe see a miracle healing or two.

Jesus was unfazed by the crowd's muted response. "As you know, the groom's name was John. He was my cousin."

"John the Baptist?" someone asked.

"Bingo. My water-baptizing, desert-preaching kinsman. Do you know why he lived in the desert?"

"God sent him there to preach," an elderly, bearded man replied.

Jesus laughed. "That's the official story. Do you want to know the truth? His betrothed drove him into the desert. Puah. We called her Poo. She had to be the ugliest bride in the history of Judaism. I kid you not.

"Let me see if I can describe her. You know what John looked like, right? Big. Barrel-chested. Hairy. Put a wedding dress on him and you would have Puah on a good day. And her cooking? Compared to her dishes, dried locusts was a treat. It took me and the disciples five days to track John down and drag him out of the desert to his wedding.

"Now you can understand why the wedding party ran out of wine. We used most of it to get John drunk. It was the only way we could get him to lead the procession to fetch his bride. That took most of the night, and when we finally got to the bride's house, the bridesmaids had fallen asleep and their lamps had run out of oil."

Jesus cocked his head. "That would make a good parable, wouldn't it? Or have I already told that one?"

Jana stood next to me. She was holding a microphone out to record the audio while her cameraman shot the video.

She whispered to me, "He is quite a joker, isn't he? And look at his feet. They're touching the ground."

"He's wearing sandals," I said.

"That makes a difference?"

Jesus went on. "As we transported John and his bride back to his parents' house, there was music and gaiety, nuts were tossed to the children, we in the bridal party carried torches and myrtle branches, and the bridegroom wept.

"He wept during the signing of the kethubah. But you have to give John credit. As is the custom of all honorable Hebrew males, no matter how much he objected to this arranged marriage, he vowed to keep and care for his bride all the days of his life, which in John's case, were mercifully short.

"But I digress. It was during the feast that followed that we ran out of wine and my mother took it upon herself to make it our problem. So there you have it. There were six stone jars. I had them filled with water and zap! The next thing you know we got plenty of wine."

"How did your mother know you could do it?" Jana asked.

Jesus looked in the direction of the question and when he saw Jana, his grin spread into a warm smile. He stepped close, unaffected by the microphone. Looking past it to the person holding it, he said, "And who is asking this question?"

"Jana Torres, KTSD."

"You speak English. Your station affiliation is not local?"

"San Diego, California."

"The United States? You have traveled all this way and, unlike thousands of local residents, have managed to locate the biblical Cana. Tell me, daughter of beauty, how did you come to be so wise?"

Jana glanced toward me. Jesus followed her glance and did a double take. His grin widened even more. It was positively wicked.

"To answer your question," he said, turning his attention back to Jana, "when I was young, on occasion I would provide refills of the oil jar for my mother. She didn't ask. After hearing the story of Elijah and the widow, I thought it would be fun to see how long it took my mother to notice that the oil never ran out. She caught on quickly, and when she did I was punished, which I thought was amusing when at the wedding she expected me to produce the wine. She didn't object to my powers when it suited her purposes."

He swung around suddenly.

"Who wants to see a miracle?" he asked.

The crowd became agitated. This was what they had come for. Babies were held out to him. The weak and infirm were deposited as an invitation to him.

"No, no, no. Weren't you listening to the story?" he exclaimed. "Get me six stone water jars."

Everyone exchanged helpless glances.

"If you can't get me six stone water jars, get me the equivalent for today," he said, sounding miffed.

In short order an array of containers were lined up in front of him—four five-gallon military vehicle water containers and two ice chests.

"You know the drill," Jesus said. "Fill them with water."

The containers were filled with water.

"I need three tasters. You, you, and"—he swung around and pointed at me—"you."

I tried to beg off. He wouldn't let me. Jana was motioning me to do it. Sue Ling appeared skeptical. I approached the containers.

A woman offered each of us a Dixie Cup.

The first to try the miracle wine was a heavily bearded man, middle-aged, his skin bronze and leathery. He held out his waxy cup while the second man poured from one of the water containers. He sipped, made a face, and spewed the drink onto the ground.

His face scrunched with disgust, he said something in Arabic that I didn't understand.

Jesus said, "After two thousand years, I may be a little rusty, but that was uncalled for. That's quality stuff."

Taking a cue from the second man, a clean-shaven younger man, I took my turn pouring. The liquid that came out of the water container was brown. He sipped it and did the same thing as the first man. I couldn't tell what language he spoke, but he obviously didn't like the wine.

Jesus shrugged and looked to me.

I chose to dip my cup into one of the coolers. It was the same brown liquid that had come out of the water containers. I lifted it to drink, then hesitated.

Jana was thrusting the microphone my direction. The cameraman was zooming in. Sue Ling was a portrait of concentration. Jesus looked on, amused.

With everyone watching me, I touched the rim of the cup to my lips and took a sip.

I nearly laughed out loud.

Jesus did. "Have you tasted any better?"

"What is it?" Jana asked.

"Dr Pepper."

Jesus howled. "Correction. Diet Dr Pepper. It has no calories!"

The crowd was inching toward the containers. Looking. Sniffing. They didn't understand.

"I thought we might have some Baptists in the crowd," Jesus explained. "I didn't want to be a stumbling block."

He stepped close to me and took me by the arm. His grip was so tight it nearly brought tears to my eyes.

"I've heard of you, Grant Austin," he whispered close to my ear. "Why are you here, you foolish man? To flaunt the mark of the Father?"

I pulled away so I could look at him directly. "I know who you are."

It was an overstatement, but I enjoyed the flash of uncertainty in his eyes when I said it.

He grinned mischievously. "I wonder how the Israelis would

react if they knew an American Nephilim had infiltrated their borders?"

A chill swept through me. I had never given a thought to crossing into Israel, or any other country for that matter, as a Nephilim. I didn't want to find out what the Israelis would think of it.

He knew he had me at a disadvantage.

"Tomorrow. Capernaum. Three P.M.," he whispered. "And bring your gorgeous reporter friend with you." Raising his arms, he yelled to the crowd, "Tomorrow on the Sea of Galilee!"

Having walked into Khirbet Kana like a man, he departed in heavenly fashion. He rose upward into the sky and was soon gone.

"What did he say to you?" Jana asked, shoving the microphone into my face.

I placed my hand over it and lowered it.

She signaled her cameraman to stop recording.

Sue Ling was right there with her.

"He knows who I am," I said. "He threatened me."

"But the mark," Sue Ling said.

"The longer I have it, the more the mark seems like a target." Turning to Jana, I said, "He gave me the location and time for tomorrow. We're heading north."

The Sea of Galilee is a big place, but despite the lack of public directions the shoreline close to Capernaum was packed. I guess it just made sense. The historical Jesus was linked to Capernaum.

Ostermann, whom I've been calling Bow-tie because I'd forgotten his name, was no longer with us. Jana had sent him back to Jerusalem with the video of Khirbet Kana.

I'd watched her record the wrap-up. It was the first time she'd called him Joker Jesus on the air. Now that's what everyone was calling him.

Once again we had front row seats when he appeared, this time walking along the shore. He positioned himself in front of us and frequently spoke directly into the camera.

"The disciples and I spent many hours on this sea. You probably recall reading about our fishing excursions, rough weather experiences, and—who could forget—the walking-on-water incident. Since I haven't taken a stroll on water for a couple of thousand years, I thought I'd re-create that particular incident for you today."

The gasps from the crowd were audible. Applause rippled through it. People held up personal video recorders, cameras of every description, and cell phones to record the event.

He requested a fisherman sitting in a small boat take him a good distance offshore. It was unclear whether he'd arranged for the boat or if the fisherman just happened to be there. Once again the figure of Jesus wearing white garments, his long brown hair blowing in the wind, his bearded chin pointing out to sea could be seen on the Sea of Galilee.

When they were roughly a hundred yards from shore, the rowing stopped. Bending down and gripping the side, he swung one leg over the water.

The crowd stilled. The only sound was the lapping of the sea against the shore and the clicking of a thousand cameras.

His toe touched the water. He jerked it back. Embraced himself and shivered. "It's cold!" the Joker Jesus shrieked.

The crowd laughed. It was a different crowd from the one at Khirbet Kana. The humor didn't seem to offend them; in fact, they seemed to expect it.

A second time the Joker Jesus swung his leg over the side of the boat. This time he didn't recoil. He gained a footing. Transferring his weight to the foot on the water, he swung his other leg over, released the side of the boat, and stood as though on solid ground.

To one side of me Sue Ling was as entranced as any of us, but without the wonder. Jana's eyes were riveted on the spectacle as she spoke into her microphone, narrating the event with a golf sports announcer's whisper.

Then the comedy act began.

His arms swinging like windmills, the Joker Jesus looked like a tightrope walker who was losing his balance. Forward, his arms flailing, catching his balance, then, backward, arms flailing again.

After he'd milked this routine for all it was worth, he assumed a casual stance, his legs crossed at the ankles, his arms folded, as if to say there was nothing to it.

He broke into a soft-shoe dance, water splashing with each tap, with a big foot stomp finish and jazz hands.

The crowd laughed. Applauded.

Bowing, the Joker Jesus strolled toward us, then broke into a run. The next thing we knew, he'd tripped and was sailing through the air. He hit the top of the water and skid like a kid in his backyard on a Slip 'n Slide.

Coming to a stop, he picked himself up, dusted the water off his garments, shrugged, and said sheepishly, "Tripped on a fish."

The crowd went wild.

To enthusiastic applause, he completed the stroll to shore, halting a few feet from solid ground. For all the water tricks, he was completely dry . . . his face and beard, his garments.

A woman charged into the water toward him, shouting and screaming in Hebrew. Choni slipped close to Jana to translate. Sue and I listened in.

"She's angry," Choni said.

"I can see that!" Jana replied.

Overcome by emotion, the woman was shaking her fist at the Joker Jesus. In her fury she spat at him and splashed water. In her other hand she clutched a boy who looked to be about eight or nine years old, so skinny you could count his ribs from a distance. He had what appeared to be a pair of gray clouds in both eyes.

"She's calling Jesus a fraud and an impostor," Choni translated. "She says if he was truly the Savior, he would perform real miracles, not silly tricks."

The smile disappeared from the Joker Jesus's face. "Your son?"

The woman pulled the boy in front of her. Her story tumbled out. "He has been blind and deaf since birth. We walked all night to get here. My son has burns on his legs from walking into fires. He has been hit twice by cars running into the street. The doctors tell us there is no hope."

For all of his troubles, the boy appeared to be happy. Even while his mother was pouring out her heart, he was grinning and slapping the water with the flat of his hand.

The Joker Jesus waded to her and stretched out his hand. The mother pulled the boy forward. During the exchange, the boy became frightened. All he knew was that his mother was handing him off to another, and he didn't like it. He thrashed and fought to stay close to her.

Until his hand touched the hand of the Joker Jesus. The instant it did, the boy stopped thrashing. A calmness came over him. He willingly went to the Joker Jesus.

The crowd had stilled. Everyone watched to see what would happen next. We didn't know what to expect. Would the Joker Jesus heal him, or pull silk scarves out of the boy's ear?

Jana shot a glance at the cameraman. She knew him well enough to know he'd be getting this, but something inside her had to check to make sure.

The Joker Jesus dipped his hands in the water and then placed an index finger in each ear. I confess, my first thought was that he was giving the boy a Wet Willy.

But when the fingers came out, the boy gasped. He raised his hands to his ears and cupped them, then pulled his hands away, then cupped them again. He squealed and scared himself with his own voice.

His mother called to him.

He cocked his head. He'd never heard her voice before. He splashed to get to her and she to him.

"No!" the Joker Jesus said.

He held them apart. That in itself was miraculous. How could anyone keep mother and son apart at a moment like this?

Jesus stood the boy in front of him. He placed the fingers of both hands on the boy's eyes. Jesus didn't say anything. He didn't wet his hands first as he did with the ears. He just touched them. And when he removed his hands, the boy's eyes were clear.

He blinked. Then blinked again. Wider eyes I have never seen. He took in the Joker Jesus, the water, the sky, but when he saw his mother, I don't think the Joker Jesus could have kept them apart this time.

The crowd watched in silence at first, then there was the sound of weeping, followed by cheers and laughter and praises.

After several moments of having the stuffing hugged out of him, the boy turned to the Joker Jesus for a hug and was swept up out of the water by his healer's strong arms.

The Joker Jesus set the boy on his shoulder, both he and the boy grinning ear to ear. It was one of those moments that was captured by cameras and appeared on the cover of every major newspaper and news magazine in the world.

Even though I knew the Joker Jesus wasn't who he pretended to be, a shiver of excitement swept up my spine at what can only be described as a miracle.

CHAPTER
9

A
s he did at Khirbet Kana, the Joker Jesus told me where he would appear next.

"The Mount of Olives. Meet me at the top. We'll take a nostalgic stroll down the Via Dolorosa." Then he added, "Two girlfriends, Grant? You dog! Bring them both with you tomorrow."

He was wrong about the girlfriends, of course. But clearly he was being fed information, and I feared it was Semyaza.

When I told Jana his agenda, she hugged me and kissed me on the cheek. It was gratitude, nothing more. No other reporter in the world was getting inside information.

Sue saw the kiss. She turned away and acted as if it didn't bother her, but it did. This feud had gone on long enough. I determined to use the ride back to Jerusalem to talk to Sue and try to smooth things over between her and Jana.

That didn't happen. The entire journey Sue Ling was a stone

statue. She spoke to Choni only when necessary and to me not at all.

Choni on the other hand was a verbal fountain. He was like a kid on vacation. If he wasn't reliving Cana and the Sea of Galilee, he was speculating about what the Joker Jesus had in store for tomorrow. Mostly, though, he plied me with questions.

Why had the Joker Jesus singled me out? Why did he whisper in my ear? When he did, did he speak of anything other than his agenda? Why was I able to see angels before everyone else? Was it really the professor who knew about Khirbet Kana, or had I seen angels headed that direction?

Sue Ling broke her stony silence quickly enough to answer the question about the professor. She assured Choni that it was indeed the professor and not me who knew about Khirbet Kana.

Choni was taken aback by the heat with which she answered. "Are you and Grant having a lovers' quarrel?"

After sputtering a protest that she and I were not, had never been, and would never be lovers, she clammed up and said nothing to either of us the remainder of the journey.

On what would be referred to as "The Third Day of Miracles," the Joker Jesus descended upon Mt. Olivet in the cool of the morning. There was something different about him. He appeared somber and didn't look at anyone directly.

Levitating a foot off the ground, his eyes closed, his head lifted heavenward, his arms at his side, he hung in space for nearly an hour.

The gathering crowd arrived boisterous, but upon seeing him hanging there, matched his mood. Hushed and reverent.

He gasped as though he was coming up for air, raised his arms horizontal to the ground, and completed his descent, his sandals touching the ground. Turning west, he set his eyes upon Jerusalem.

Jana's cameraman backpedaled, recording every step as the Joker Jesus led us down the hillside, through the Garden of Gethsemane, across the Kidron Valley, up a steep embankment, and through a cemetery to the double-tiered Golden Gate.

He paused at the black iron fence that blocked us from the walled-up gate. No one had passed beneath the arches since the Ottoman Sultan Suleiman I sealed the gate, allegedly to prevent the Messiah's entrance.

The Joker Jesus stood there. He appeared to be looking for a doorbell.

A sizable crowd began running northward to the Lion's Gate, the modern entrance to the Via Dolorosa. They missed what happened next.

Four angels appeared, the kind you read about in the Bible with the flowing gold hair, white robes, and wings. Two at the iron fence, and two above, framed by the gate's arches.

The two angels at the fence lifted it effortlessly out of the way. The Joker Jesus approached the wall. As he did, the bricks crumbled and fell at his feet. The gate that had been shut for centuries was open once again.

We walked beneath the arches onto the Temple Mount.

Sue looked up in awe at the arches and the hovering angels. "No one has passed through this gate since 1541!"

"Since when?" Jana asked, hearing only part of the comment.

The icy anger that lay between them melted.

"Since 1541," Sue said. "The Muslims closed the gate and built the cemetery in the mistaken belief that Elijah, the forerunner to the Messiah, would not be able to approach it because he was a priest."

"Mistaken belief?"

"While a Jewish priest cannot enter a Jewish cemetery, there is nothing forbidding him from entering the cemetery of Gentiles."

Jana's eyes were sparkling. I could tell she was thankful for the information, but mostly because Sue was talking to her again. Beneath the double tiers of the Golden Gate, the two friends hugged.

I was smiling, too. My life had just gotten a little less complicated.

As the procession made its way toward the Via Dolorosa, the Israeli police made their presence known in force with a hastily erected barricade.

The Joker Jesus' pace never faltered. A vanguard of angels appeared with swords that burst into flame. The police fell back, their weapons rendered inoperative.

A growing parade of followers found palm branches and began waving them back and forth, shouting hosannas.

Upon reaching the Monastery of Flagellation, the Joker Jesus stopped and knelt in the roadway. Two Roman guards appeared from nowhere, dressed in first-century military uniform. They stripped his clothing from his back and whipped him and placed a crown of thorns upon his head.

It was a scene pulled from the pages of the Bible, if not for the crowd. Orthodox Jews dressed in black stood next to midwestern couples with cameras slung around their necks, who stood next to modern Israelis and Palestinians wearing burqas and backpacks and baseball caps and riding motorized scooters.

A wooden cross was laid on the Joker Jesus' back and the

drama continued to the top of Golgotha, where the Roman soldiers nailed him to the cross. Once it was erect, two other crosses appeared. The scene appeared just as it had been described in the first century.

It was noon. A black cloud blotted out the sun. The crucified Joker Jesus cried out and died. A soldier pierced his side.

This is where the script deviated from the record. Time was telescoped.

One of the Roman soldiers addressed the crowd. "Is there a doctor among you to certify this death?"

Several doctors came forward. Four were chosen without explanation. An Israeli, an Arab, an American, and a German.

The crucified man was taken down from the cross and each of the doctors was permitted to examine him. Each man reported to the crowd. Their diagnosis was unanimous.

He was dead.

I scanned the faces of the crowd. Some were crying. Some had smirks on their faces, expecting the Joker Jesus to pop up and say something funny.

No one appeared to claim the body. The Roman guards themselves carried Jesus to the garden tomb. They placed the body inside, rolled a large stone in front of it, sealed it, and posted a guard.

"Are we going to have to wait here three days?" Jana asked me.

I shrugged.

Anticipating the question, the Roman spokesman said in a loud voice, "In the end times, days will seem like hours."

I noted the time. We had three hours to kill.

For the first hour Jana and several members of the crowd questioned the two Roman soldiers who stood guard over the tomb. The soldiers must have been trained at the Buckingham Palace school for guards. They didn't speak. They didn't blink.

The second hour passed with most everyone having found a comfortable place to sit and wait. Conversations of every kind and in every language could be heard around us, but nobody's attention wandered far from the tomb.

With fifteen minutes remaining, people began getting to their feet. At ten minutes, several groups took it upon themselves to provide verbal announcements every minute. The announcements were not synchronized.

A minute to go. Thirty seconds. At ten seconds the countdowns began. The only thing missing was the Times Square descending ball.

". . . three, two, one!"

Nothing happened.

A few seconds later a different group began their countdown. ". . . three, two, one!"

After that, it became something of a competition to see which group would be closest to the actual time of the resurrection.

Then the Roman guards disappeared into nothingness. Two angels appeared. They broke the seal and moved the rock aside as though it were made of papier-mâché.

As the angels entered the tomb, the glory of their presence illuminated the inside walls. A moment later, one of them returned.

In a voice that carried effortlessly over the crowd, the angel said, "He is not here. He is risen!"

A cheer went up.

The angel selected a large, bearded man, a woman wearing a burqa, and Jana. "Come see. He is not here."

Jana pointed to her cameraman. "May I?"

The angel nodded.

Jana and the cameraman ducked their heads and followed the others into the tomb.

The bearded man came out grinning. "He is not there!"

The woman in the burqa came out weeping. "He is not there!"

The cameraman backed out, recording Jana as she appeared. In one hand she held a microphone, in the other the folded grave clothes. "The tomb is empty. This is Jana Torres, KTSD, reporting live from Jerusalem."

"Why seek you the living among the dead?"

The voice came from above us. Looking up we saw a circle of angels. In the center was a radiating Jesus.

He said, "And that's how, on the third day, I rose from the grave. No joke."

After four days with no more appearances, the professor suggested we return home.

I used those four days to pound out a few chapters of my book. On the day we returned to Jerusalem and cell phone service, I retrieved my messages. After the third one from my publisher, each one more ominous than the last, I called him.

He did give me credit for having the most original excuse for missing my deadline he'd ever heard. And while I expected him to demand I return the advance money because he was canceling the contract, instead he asked me to narrate the things I'd seen. As it turned out, he offered me a reprieve on my deadline if I agreed to be interviewed by Bart Dover, a professor of religion at Yale University who was writing a book on the Joker Jesus. His working title: *Is the*

World Ready for a Laughing Christ? It was one of those rush-to-publish projects.

We left Jana behind. Her producer wanted her to stay a few more days just in case the Joker Jesus made another appearance. She made me promise to call her if I got wind of anything.

Choni insisted on driving us to the airport. He had become something of a celebrity on the Hebrew University campus. He hugged us repeatedly and insisted he was going to visit us in California during summer break.

The twenty-two-hour flight home was unmercifully long. The only diversion was hearing firsthand the world's reaction to the Joker Jesus. Every station including the in-flight news led with footage of the miracles and speculation about what would come next. I must have seen Jana emerge from the tomb at least fifty times in a half-dozen different languages. Overnight she had become an international news celebrity.

Airport magazine racks and newsstands were plastered with stories of the Joker Jesus.

> *Time:* God Is Dead—Not!
> *Paris Match:* Miracles Make a Comeback!
> *London Times:* Resurrection Real!
> *Star:* Jesus to Bring Elvis on Next Visit

In Rome I made the mistake of telling someone I had just come from Israel and had seen the Joker Jesus. I was mobbed and, if security hadn't intervened, I would have missed my connection. From then on, I only listened and nodded.

We were in Atlanta when the published version of the Alexandrian manuscript hit the stands. I purchased a copy and read it on the flight to San Diego. It had teeth.

Home. My own shower. My own bed. No matter how anticipated the trip or how hospitable the host, a man is never as relaxed as he is in his own house.

I was eager to get on with my life. All that remained of my
obligation to the professor was a debriefing, after which I
planned to hole up in my condo and focus all of my energies on
writing the book.

Already the ideas were flowing. I loved this part of the cre-
ative process. If I could pull it off—and my confidence was
growing every day—this book would be better than the autobi-
ography that won the Pulitzer.

I arrived at the professor's house. Built in the forties with a
spacious front porch, it had an old-fashioned feeling of Mom
and apple pie. I felt like I was visiting family.

"Grant! Come in!" the professor said through the screen
door.

He looked tired. Not the lost-sleep tired, but the world-
weariness that ages a man.

"Sue is getting us coffee," he said.

The living room was back to its usual neat and orderly condition—not like it was when we spoke to him on the webcam. Sue
Ling had been busy since her return.

She emerged from the kitchen, carrying a tray with a white
carafe, three coffee mugs, sugar, and cream. The sugar was
cubed. I couldn't remember the last time I had seen sugar
cubes.

"I just spoke with Jana," Sue said to me as she set the tray
down. "She and her crew are at Ben Gurion airport and will be
flying out within the hour."

"Jana Torres has put herself and KTSD on the map," the professor boasted. There was no residual bitterness over the press conference. He set to work sweetening and creaming his coffee.

Sue appeared relaxed, happy to be home, happy to be with him.

"Abdiel will be joining us," the professor said, sitting back and sipping his coffee. "Sue tells me you read the Alexandrian text. What do you make of it?"

"Obviously it's overshadowed by his appearances. In some ways it's more threatening. The appearances combined with the archeological findings appear to validate it."

"Agreed. How do you feel about his recognizing you?"

"Like a marked man."

"For good or ill. It's the price you pay for the protection."

"I think I made him nervous. He threatened me."

The professor nodded. "Sue told me."

"Obviously he's not who he claims to be," I said. "He admitted as much to me in Khirbet Kana. And he's definitely taken everyone by surprise. But for all the slapstick humor, the thing that I'll remember is the little boy sitting on his shoulder, smiling and laughing, able to see and hear for the first time. Whatever we think about the Joker Jesus, that was impressive."

"What?"

The coffee tray rattled at the sound. Abdiel had appeared as I was speaking.

"What did you just say?" he bellowed.

"Calm down, Abdiel," the professor said.

"Not in the face of heresy. No, I will not calm down."

"I didn't say I believed in him," I said, defending myself, "all I meant was—"

"All you did was confess to being deceived by an agent of Lucifer," Abdiel said.

"I have not been deceived! I know who he is. All I'm saying—"

The professor came to my aid. "How can healing a blind and deaf boy be a bad thing?"

"Yeah. That's it exactly," I said. "Regardless of what else he's done, this was a good thing. If you'd seen the expression on his mother's face, you'd agree with me."

"The woman's prayers had been answered," the professor said.

"Yeah, her prayers—"

The comment brought me up short. The woman had prayed to God for her son's healing, and her prayer had been answered by an agent of Satan. I was beginning to see Abdiel's point.

"He is entertaining, this Joker Jesus," the professor continued. "He plays to the crowd. Gets them laughing. Then he dazzles them with a few signs and wonders."

"And, like me, people begin to think he's a good guy," I said, following his train of thought.

"The greatest evil comes with a smile, Grant," the professor said. "The grin of a drug pusher, the caress of a pedophile, the promise of a crooked politician, and the laughter of an impostor savior."

I had a sinking feeling, the kind of feeling you get the moment you realize you've been duped by a smooth-talking salesman wearing sandals.

"So why don't you make an appearance of your own?" I said to Abdiel. "Confront him. Reveal to the world that he's a fraud and a charlatan."

"We are pleased to serve the Father," Abdiel replied.

"What does that mean?"

"Each generation must find its own way," the professor said. "God doesn't swoop down every time evil presents itself. We must learn to recognize it, no matter what form it takes, and confront it in faith."

"But this is different! Nothing like this has ever happened before!"

"It is an ancient strategy," Abdiel said.

"He's right," the professor said. "He's correct. As far back as Jannes and Jambres in Pharaoh's court, adversaries have been duplicating the acts of God. And in the days of the early church outcast angels took the form of aerial spirit guides who claimed to be messengers of a new truth. Men who embraced these spirits became powerful. The spirit would perform on command, ruining their competitors, opening doors, stirring up winds, destroying, even killing. One such spirit was instructed to fly in the air over Rome and defy the teaching of Christians. The ancient world was filled with idols that spoke, came to life, and granted favors to those worshiping them.

"In a letter to the Ephesians, the Apostle Paul catalogs the Satanic forces at work in his day—principalities, powers, dominions, thrones, messengers, world powers, spiritual hosts, elemental spirits, and demons."

Abdiel gave them names. "Cybele, Hekate, Dionysus, Demeter, and Serapis. One of the most powerful at the time was Asclepius, the idol god who healed the sick and afflicted. In reality, it was the rebel Belial. You know him as the Joker Jesus."

"You discovered his identity?" the professor said.

"There is no doubt."

"Interesting," the professor said. "Toss in a little modern science and we swallow an ancient lie."

"Lucifer is the father of lies," Abdiel said. "That has not changed."

"The beauty of the deception," the professor said, "is that instead of debunking the miraculous and the resurrection, they embrace it. Had they attacked it outright, the churches would have risen up and fought them."

"But now that we know that, we can stop them," I said, getting excited. "We can get the word out. Expose them."

The professor rubbed tired eyes. "I don't think it's a coincidence that the Alexandrian manuscript was discovered now." He tested his vision with a couple of blinks. "And I don't think it was a coincidence that a young Christian girl was the one who found it. You have to ask yourself, why now? Why not a hundred years ago, or a hundred years from now?"

Abdiel nodded. "I agree. The Father directed her to the cave."

"You have access to heaven," I said. "Can't you find out?"

"It pleases me to serve the Father," Abdiel replied. "He does not report to me his every action."

"But it makes sense, doesn't it?" Sue Ling said. "God has known the manuscript was there all along. He knows what it contains. He could have orchestrated its discovery. But the question remains, why now?"

"Possibly," the professor suggested, "it has something to do with this being the first generation in thousands of years that has a Nephilim."

All three of them looked at me.

"No," I said. "No. There has to be another reason."

"It's certainly worth considering," the professor added.

"No," I said again.

"I think you're on to something," Sue Ling said. "The discovery of the manuscript triggered the arrival of the Joker Jesus, not the other way around."

"But what if Lucifer initiated the discovery?" I argued. "He could have lured the girl to the cave."

"Not likely," the professor said. "Tiffany Sproul is strong in the faith. To hear her description of the events that led up to the discovery . . . there was no temptation involved."

"Agreed," Sue Ling said.

"When Lucifer crafted this plan ages ago," Abdiel said, "he did so using conventional tactics. He did not consider the possibility of a Nephilim. That may give us an advantage."

"No," I said.

"You said it yourself, Grant," the professor said. "When the Joker Jesus encountered you at Khirbet Kana he threatened you. If you were of no concern to him, he would have ignored you."

"I will teach Grant Austin some standard tactics to prepare him," Abdiel said.

"And I'll give him a crash course on particle physics. Maybe together we can discover what other angelic abilities he has," Sue Ling said.

"No!" I said.

"We'll get started in the morning," the professor said.

"No!"

Abdiel approached me. "Grant Austin. On the Emerald Plaza tower you declared your allegiance to the Father. Now you must prove that allegiance."

"But I have a book to write," I said.

CHAPTER
10

W elcome to what has to be the biggest special of my broadcasting career."

Barbara Walters faced the camera. A slight tremor in her voice belied her characteristically calm demeanor. The camera pulled back to reveal her sitting opposite her guest.

Bearded, hair to his shoulders, wearing a white tunic, he sat with his legs casually crossed.

"To begin," Ms. Walters said, "I have to say that never in my wildest dreams did I imagine I would one day interview Jesus Christ."

"It is a pleasure to appear on your show," the Joker Jesus said.

WALTERS: Excuse me, but I have to ask this. Are you really Jesus Christ?
JESUS: I am.

WALTERS: But you don't act like the Christ we've been taught to worship. How can we be certain? Can you prove to us that you are who you say you are?

JESUS: Do you mean other than transforming water into—

WALTERS: Dr Pepper. How are we to take you seriously when you do things like that?

JESUS: You disapprove of Dr Pepper?

WALTERS: That's not my point. Why Dr Pepper and not wine?

JESUS: (grinning) Once you know me better, you'll understand. I also walked on water—

WALTERS: Tripped, fell, splashed, tap-danced on water.

JESUS: —healed a blind and deaf boy, and rose from the dead. What else would you have me do?

WALTERS: If I were to bring someone onstage who is seriously ill, could you heal them?

JESUS: A long time ago I was at the home of Simon Peter's mother-in-law. She was ill. I healed her. Word spread throughout the town, and a line of people formed at the door, all of them wanting to be healed. I healed them, one after another, until the sun went down. The next morning the line was even longer. Dozens of healings were not enough to convince the town of my identity then; healing a person on national television will not convince them now.

WALTERS: Your appearance on the Mount of Olives was certainly dramatic.

JESUS: That one was by the book.

WALTERS: Are you God?

JESUS: If you are asking me if I created the universe . . . no, I am not God.

WALTERS: (producing a Bible) Yet, according to the New Testament, Jesus Christ and God are one and the same.

JESUS: I can explain that.

WALTERS: (producing another book) Would your explanation be found in this? I have in my hand a newly published edition of the Alexandrian manuscript, which was discovered in an underwater cave.

JESUS: That manuscript explains a lot. It's a confession of sorts.

WALTERS: (flipping through the book) The manuscript has been dated by experts to the early second century.

JESUS: The dating is correct.

WALTERS: And you wrote it.

JESUS: Dictated it, actually. I had an amanuensis. I was in no condition to write.

WALTERS: Were you injured?

JESUS: I was drunk.

WALTERS: Drunk? Jesus Christ was drunk?

JESUS: It wasn't the first time. I dictated it on a dare. It wasn't one of my finer moments. Then, while I was— let's say incapacitated—my buddies hid it from me, frustrating my attempts to find and destroy it. When it didn't surface after a couple of hundred years, I figured it had been destroyed. I was wrong.

WALTERS: You say you are Jesus, but not God. You perform miracles, but you also get drunk. And you have a fondness for juvenile humor. (She leaned forward.) Who are you?

JESUS: I am not of this world.

WALTERS: You're an alien?

JESUS: I suppose I am.

WALTERS: From what planet?

JESUS: You see now, that's what makes explaining things so difficult. You have such a narrow understanding of life and the universe.

WALTERS: Who are you? And why are you here?

JESUS: You have to understand something about my race. They do not condone humor. Only a handful of us appreciate it. We are considered an aberration. There is nothing we love more than a good joke, yet all of our attempts to cultivate humor have been met with derision, lectures, and punishment. Humor is the heroin of our race. To satisfy our addiction we sought it among other races.

WALTERS: You came to earth to laugh?

JESUS: Among all the other races we visited, you have such a delightful sense of humor. You love to laugh. You appreciate a good joke.

WALTERS: Yet you're sitting here as Jesus Christ.

JESUS: (laughing) Funny story. You see, we discovered that people want to kill you when they find out you're not human. So we began passing ourselves off as humans. Sometimes traveling from place to place, sometimes living an entire lifetime in a village. If it got too boring, we went on a hunting trip and disappeared. It happened a lot back then.

This went on for centuries. We laughed ourselves silly, sometimes with you, sometimes at your expense, but it was all good. Then, while we were living in Modin during the days of the Maccabees—there was this adorable little Jewish girl there who snorted when she laughed and kept us entertained for hours—I came across all these prophecies about a coming Messiah. And I thought, wouldn't it be a hoot—

WALTERS: You mean to tell me that you masqueraded as the Messiah as a joke?

JESUS: Who would have thought anyone would take me seriously? Messiahs were a dime a dozen back then. It wasn't as though I set myself up as Caesar or the king of England or the president of the United States—though the idea has merit. Mark my words: Someday a stand-up comedian will be elected president and you'll all be singing, "Happy Days Are Here Again."

WALTERS: But Christianity has become one of the world's major religions!

JESUS: What can I say? It got out of hand. Who would have thought all of this would come from a little backwater country? When things started heating up and it wasn't fun anymore, I let them kill me, figuring that would be the end of it.

WALTERS: But you rose from the grave.

JESUS: Yeah. That was a mistake.

WALTERS: What would you say to the millions of Christians around the world who worship you?

JESUS: It was a joke, people! A joke.

WALTERS: For two thousand years, millions of people have been living a lie.

JESUS: What can I say? It got out of hand and took on a life of its own.

WALTERS: But what about salvation? What about heaven?

JESUS: The only reason we are able to do the things you consider miracles is that we have a deeper understanding of how the universe works. You're an inquisitive race. You'll get there. But, can I give you a piece of advice? You're looking in the wrong direction.

WALTERS: In what direction should we be looking?

JESUS: Certainly not space exploration, as you know it. You'll never get anywhere the way you're going. Can't you see that? The universe is hostile to you. Anywhere you go, you have to take your own planet's atmosphere with you just to survive. And then, as large as you are? It'll take you forever to get anyplace. You need to think smaller.

WALTERS: Smaller? As in subatomic?

JESUS: That's the ticket! This body? I can't begin to tell you how cumbersome and limited it is. In my natural state, I can transport across the galaxy in the blink of an electron and dance among the distant stars. And we do it without machinery of any sort.

WALTERS: We? Your race?

JESUS: Not just mine. There are thousands of races and civilizations that dwell among the atoms. I know it sounds like an oxymoron, but the smaller you are, the more the universe opens up to you. You're too large to appreciate it.

WALTERS: Your people, what do they call themselves?

JESUS: Roughly translating into your language, I am an inhabitant of Tartarus.

WALTERS: Isn't Tartarus the name of a place in Greek mythology? A place in the underworld, even lower than Hades?

JESUS: (laughing) Yeah. Funny story. We were messing with Hesiod, you know, the Greek poet? He kept going on and on about how it would take a bronze anvil nine days to fall from heaven to earth. We were ticked off at the time for being censured by our ruling council and one of us said, "That anvil would have to fall at least another nine days to reach Tartarus, a dank

and wretched pit where there is no mirth." Well, ol'
Hesiod liked that and started using it.

WALTERS: If you are who you say you are, you have completely discredited a major religion. How do we know
this isn't just another joke?

JESUS: Well, if you don't believe me, maybe you'll believe
them . . .

Four figures—three men and a woman—appeared from nowhere dressed in first-century biblical clothing. They stood
behind Jesus.

JESUS: Allow me to introduce—I believe you call them my
"partners in crime." You know them as Simon Peter,
Nicodemus, Mary Magdalene, and Lazarus. Ask them
whatever questions you have.

Chairs were brought onstage and for the next hour the five
Tartarans, draped over the chairs like rock stars, reminisced
about life in Nazareth, Bethlehem, and Jerusalem, telling hu-
morous story after story about the personalities and about the
events that took place behind the scenes of New Testament
events.

At the conclusion of the special, Barbara Walters addressed
her final comments to the camera audience.

WALTERS: It hasn't taken long for churches to embrace
this new Jesus. All across the country Christians are
rethinking the way they worship.

A video clip of a megachurch in Houston showed the pastors delivering a stand-up comedy routine that taught laughter

as the mark of true worship. The church had hired joke writers on staff. Giant screens in a converted sports arena showed clips of Jesus in Cana and splashing in the Sea of Galilee to standing ovations.

A laughing young woman leaving the church looked into the camera and said, "Hey, like I used to hang out at a bar? Now I go to church. This is a Jesus I can relate to."

CHAPTER

II

The day following the Barbara Walters special I arrived at the professor's house for my first lesson with Abdiel and Sue Ling. I didn't know what to expect. I didn't excel in these kinds of lessons. I prefer user manuals. Even as a kid, when I wanted to learn to play tennis the first thing I did was run to the library and check out a book. Of course this was different. I doubted the library had a copy of *Nephilim Skills for Dummies*.

Sue Ling answered my knock and ushered me into the living room. She was dressed casually in jeans and an oversized SDSU sweatshirt. Behind her, physics books were stacked five and six volumes deep on the coffee table.

"Change of plans. It'll just be the three of us," she said.

"The professor won't be joining us?" I asked.

"What makes you think it's the professor and not Abdiel who will be absent?"

"Because Abdiel's already here."

Sue smiled. "You've been practicing."

Abdiel materialized.

"They told me you could see angels in their spirit form," he said.

"So this was a test?"

"I wanted to see for myself," the angel replied.

"Is it second nature to you now?" Sue asked. "You didn't appear to have to concentrate."

"Easier, but not second nature."

"What else can you do?" Abdiel asked.

"I can cook, clean, and fold my own laundry."

The big angel wasn't amused. "If you're not going to take this seriously—"

I stage-whispered to Sue Ling, "I think he's a Tartaran. No sense of humor."

"So you watched the program last night?" she said. Then, turning to the angel, "Before we get started, I want to hear what Abdiel has to say about it."

"A deception," Abdiel said.

I said, "Can you be a little more specific? Like Sue, I'm anxious to hear your take on the interview."

"Deception and blasphemy."

"Abdiel has a way with words, don't you think?" I said to Sue.

Abdiel had been around me long enough to recognize sarcasm. And fear. The two come packaged together with me. Whenever I'm afraid, I get sarcastic. And having already done battle with angels once, my fear meter was off the chart.

Abdiel elaborated. "The third day's so-called miracle? The easiest to perform."

"The resurrection," Sue said.

"Of course your doctors declared him dead," Abdiel said.

"Angels have no heartbeat. Neither do they have a respiratory system."

"How about changing water to Dr Pepper?" I asked.

"A manipulation of matter."

"And the walking on water?" Sue asked.

Abdiel levitated. "Angels don't sink."

"And the boy?" I asked.

He studied me for a long moment before answering. "Why do you want to know? Are you still convinced there is good in him?"

"I just want to know how he did it."

"Healing is more difficult to perform. It requires skill and a knowledge of human anatomy. While it is still a manipulation of matter, it is more delicate. Belial is highly skilled at it."

Abdiel went on to identify the other rebel angels who appeared on the show masquerading as Jesus' disciples. He grew angry speaking of them. By the time he was finished, he was stoked to do something to stop them.

Sue instructed us to move the furniture out of the way to give ourselves some room. Abdiel moved to one end of the sofa and bent his knees.

"Can't you just levitate it out of the way?" I said.

"Put your back into it, slacker," he replied.

Sue went to the kitchen and got us coffee while we moved.

"Will the professor be joining us?" I asked.

"I told you it would be just the three of us," Sue answered.

"I thought maybe his absence was part of the hidden-angel test. He's not ill, is he?"

"He's in the back room. He said he could contribute more by praying than by sitting out here watching."

She motioned for me to sit next to her on the sofa. Abdiel

stood over us. He appeared to be ready to rap my knuckles with a ruler if I got out of line.

"The thing you need to understand about angels," Sue said, "is that they are created beings. They can do some amazing things, but they have no magical powers."

"We cannot perform miracles," Abdiel said.

"What about the deaf and blind boy?" I asked.

"Answer this for me," Abdiel replied. "Had a surgeon restored the boy's sight, would you say the surgeon performed a miracle?"

"Good example, Abdiel," Sue said. "You see, Grant, we can do many of the same things angels do, only we use tools and machines to do them."

"What about the miracles of the real Jesus, then? If we can perform the same miracles—"

Abdiel bristled, then restrained himself. He answered my question slowly, clearly, as though he were teaching a child. "The Divine Warrior used physical acts to point to a much greater power. By healing a blind man, He revealed His ability to open men's eyes spiritually. By healing the lame, He revealed He can make men whole. And by raising the dead, He revealed he could give life eternal. The Divine Warrior alone has the ability to forgive sin and heal the soul and give life."

Sue nodded her agreement.

"We can only be in one place at one time," Abdiel said, returning to the lesson plan. "We are strong, but our strength is limited. We cannot read minds. We are not omniscient. For example, we don't know the future. That is left to the Father alone."

"The biggest advantage angels have over humans," Sue said, "is their knowledge of the universe. Having assisted in its construction, they know how everything works on both subatomic

and cosmic scales, things we are only now beginning to understand."

"Lucifer has used this knowledge to torment and deceive
humans from the beginning," Abdiel said, his anger surfacing.

Sue was quick to move on. "Abdiel and I have some demon-
strations to show you what we mean."

She crossed the room and unplugged a lamp. Holding the
lamp, she nodded to Abdiel, who puckered his lips and appeared to blow on the lamp at a distance of about seven feet.
The lamp lit brightly.

Even though she knew what to expect, Sue stared at the
lamp with childlike wonder. "The same thing can be done to any
electrical appliance," she explained. "It's called witricity—turning sound waves into electricity. It's the same principle opera
singers use to break wineglasses, only this sound is beyond our
ability to hear."

She set the lamp down. Abdiel unpuckered.

"Scientists are currently developing this technology to power
cell phones without having to plug them in. It's basic physics,
really."

"Lucifer's agents use it to haunt and frighten people," Abdiel
added.

"Here's another one," Sue said.

This time there was no object involved. She simply stood
facing Abdiel. Apparently they'd prearranged the lesson plan
because the angel knew what to do without explanation.

Abdiel spoke to her. She could hear him. I couldn't.

Nodding that she'd received his message, she approached
me and slapped me.

"Ow!"

"Oh, sorry—that was harder than I'd intended."

"Why did you do that?"

"Abdiel instructed me to do it. Why didn't you stop me?"

"How was I to know you were going to hit me?"

"Didn't you hear him? He spoke in a normal voice."

I rubbed my cheek. "No, I didn't hear him."

"Sometimes painful lessons are remembered longer," Abdiel said.

Was he joking? He did it so infrequently, it was hard to tell.

"Had there been fifty people in the room," Sue said, "no one would have heard his voice except me. It's called directive sound. Now Abdiel will give you a message."

The angel looked at me. "Kiss Sue Ling. You know you want to. You may never get another chance."

I was beginning to like this demonstration. I turned to Sue, leaned close, and pressed my lips to hers.

She pulled away. Shocked. Then slapped me.

"What are you doing?" she asked.

The big angel smirked with satisfaction.

My cheek stung, but it was worth it.

Frowning at both of us, Sue touched her lips. "Like the witricity, this is basic physics."

"I thought it was basic biology," I said.

"I'd appreciate it if you'd keep your mind on the subject," Sue snapped. "Directive sound is used at the New York Museum. A person steps into a listening zone in front of a display and hears a prerecorded message. Beside him at another display, another person hears a different message. Neither of them disturbs the other."

"A man in a crowded room hears a voice," Abdiel said. "He concludes it's the voice of God. If he does not test the spirits, he may find himself doing Lucifer's bidding."

"We have one more demonstration," Sue said, picking up the television remote. She turned the set on and pressed PLAY. A prerecorded program showed a billiard table from an elevated view. The balls were racked. A cue ball struck the racked balls, scattering them across the table.

"Keep watching." She pressed the REWIND button.

The balls reversed course and reassembled themselves into the racked position with the cue ball rolling away.

"You want me to challenge the Joker Jesus to a game of billiards?" I said.

"Pay attention, funny boy," Sue replied. "Think about what you've just seen and apply it to a subatomic level."

She moved to the coffee table, poured a cup of coffee, dropped a sugar cube into the cup, and stirred. "All right, I want you to reach into the cup and pull out the sugar cube."

"Now who's being funny?" I said.

"Can't do it?" she said. "Watch."

The coffee was still swirling as Abdiel stuck his finger in the cup and stirred it the opposite direction. The swirl reversed itself. He reached into the cup and pulled out the sugar cube.

"It's the same principle you saw with the billiard balls, only on a molecular level," Sue said.

Both she and Abdiel looked at me to see if I understood.

"Impressive," I said. "Entertaining. But what does this have to do with anything? This is what you're going to teach me? These are parlor tricks. Do you really think the Joker Jesus—"

"Belial," Abdiel said.

"All right—do you really think Belial, or Semyaza, or Lucifer is going to be threatened by my pulling sugar cubes from their coffee?"

"I told you this was a waste of time," Abdiel said. "He is too dull. He has proven that the only way he can learn is by trial and error, and his errors will kill him."

"Teach me something I can use!" I insisted. "Last night Belial said that riding on a beam of light is the first step to living on a molecular level. That's something I can use."

Abdiel moved to the lamp, plugged it in, and turned it on. He looked at me, disappeared, and reappeared instantaneously on the far side of the room.

"Now that's what I'm talking about!" I said. "Is it difficult?"

"A simple process," Abdiel said. "Reduce yourself in size, step aboard a quantum of light, then step off when you've reached your destination."

"Like riding an escalator," I said. "Reduce myself. OK. How do I do that?"

"You can't."

"But you just said it was a simple process."

"It is. For me."

"OK, maybe it'll be harder for me because I'm only part angel. Show me how to do it."

"To what purpose?"

"You're kidding, right? Speed. Maneuverability. It would give me a fighting chance."

"There are more efficient ways to propel oneself. You would be outmaneuvered."

"Then show me the faster way!" I yelled in frustration.

"You're missing the point, Grant," Sue said.

"He can't be taught," Abdiel said.

"We never intended to teach you how to do these things," Sue said.

"Then why the show and tell?" I complained. "What are we doing here? Am I the only one who remembers that last time I got caught in the middle of one of Lucifer's schemes I was nearly converted into a demon condo?"

At my outburst, Sue glanced nervously toward the back of the house where the professor was praying. "Calm down, Grant.

We showed you those things so that you could understand who you're up against."

"Let me see if I understand. You want me to go up against an enemy who is stronger than me, who can go places I can't even imagine faster than the speed of light, who can generate electricity with sound, project thoughts into my head, pull sugar cubes from coffee, and, just for kicks, who could operate on my insides without a scalpel."

"I think he's got it," Abdiel said.

"Great. *Now* he gets a sense of humor," I snapped.

"Grant, this is the professor's lesson plan," Sue said.

I had a pretty good idea what was coming next. I said it before she could. "I suppose the next thing you're going to tell me is that the battle is spiritual."

"It is," Abdiel said.

"It is," Sue said.

"Yeah? Then how come every time I engage in one of these spiritual battles it's as though my body is a chew toy that's been tossed into a kennel of pit bulls?"

Abdiel bristled. "Why do you say that as though it were something unusual? Do not your Scriptures teach that the Divine Warrior suffered while in the flesh, and that you should prepare yourself to suffer as He did by the arming of your mind?"

"Yes, that is scriptural," Sue said.

"Then arm yourself with truth, Grant Austin. The best strategy is doomed if it is formulated on misinformation," Abdiel said. "The greatest warrior is neutralized if he is deceived into attacking the wrong target."

"And Satan is a master of deception," Sue added. "The first step to defeating him is not the ability to ride on a beam of light, but the ability to see through his deceptive cloak. Grant, the word for truth in the New Testament means 'not hidden.' You need to develop the ability to see through the lies, to reality."

"Reality," I said. "What is reality?"

Abdiel raised his hands in victory. "Finally! A teachable question."

Sue looked at me in earnest. "Reality is that we are living in occupied territory and Satan is in charge."

All of a sudden the world just got a little darker.

"This is not the universe as God intended it," Abdiel said. "I know because I have seen the original blueprints. This present world has been devastated by the rebellion."

"The professor described it to me this way," Sue said. "Think of Dresden, Germany, a gorgeous city known for its cultural and artistic splendor. Then it was fire-bombed, reduced to rubble. Afterward, it was still Dresden, and people walking through the charred streets could sometimes catch a glimpse of its original grandeur, but reality was that it was a gutted shell of what its designers had intended."

Familiar words surfaced in my mind. *"For our struggle is against rulers, authorities, and powers of this dark world,"* I said. "The professor used that to prepare me for my battle against Semyaza."

"Very good," Sue said. "The word for ruler is *cosmokrator,* ruler of the cosmos."

"So we're living behind enemy lines," I said.

"The Divine Warrior called Lucifer its territorial ruler," Abdiel said.

"That's what he taught the apostles," Sue added. "Paul called Satan the god of this world who blinds the minds of unbelievers, and the ruler of the air. And the Apostle John said, *'And we know the whole world is under the control of the evil one.'*"

"The offer," Abdiel prompted. "Tell him about the offer."

"What offer?" I asked.

"He's referring to Christ's temptation," Sue said. "Satan offered the world and all of its kingdoms to Jesus if Jesus would bow down to him."

"But the Divine Warrior could not be tempted," Abdiel blurted with husky pride, "and the battle was on!"

"The point is," Sue said, "it would have been a hollow temptation had the world and its kingdoms not been Satan's to give. Take Hitler, for example. At one point in the war, had he wanted to, he could have offered Paris to the Allies in exchange for concessions. He could offer it because his troops occupied the city."

"This is why we fight," Abdiel said, "to take back what Lucifer has usurped. At the end of the battle, there will be a new heaven and a new earth according to the Father's plan."

The big angel trembled with emotion, eager for battle. Then he looked at me, his present assignment, and he deflated a little. "I will train you to handle your defensive weapons first."

Weapons. That's what I wanted to hear. Offensive, defensive, what did it matter? If defense meant protecting myself from pain, I was all for it.

A broadsword appeared in Abdiel's hand. Its blade glistened, but not from reflected light. It was magnificent.

"What do you see?" he asked.

I glanced at Sue. A trick question? She, too, was waiting for my answer.

"A sword," I said. Then, to Sue, "You see it, too, don't you?" She nodded that she did.

Abdiel said, "The size and type of sword indicates a warrior's strength and intent. Lucifer's sword is similar to mine, only the blade is black."

It was clear now how Abdiel got his massive shoulders. I feared it would take everything I had just to lift such a sword.

When I glanced back, it was gone.

"What do you see now?" Abdiel asked.

"Nothing."

"Nothing? Are you certain?"

"You were holding a sword and now it's gone," I said.

"The sword is not gone," Abdiel said.

I turned to Sue. "Do you see it?"

"We think that the same ability that allows you to see concealed angels can be stretched, allowing you to see spiritual weapons," Sue said.

"*Spiritual* weapons? That sword was a spiritual weapon?"

"The sword is my spirit," Abdiel said.

"If that's true, then you have some serious spirit," I said.

"It's true. Now you understand why Lucifer's blade is black, and why a warrior's sword varies depending on the strength of his spirit and the intent of his heart."

"Look again, Grant. Concentrate like you did in Jerusalem. Try to see Abdiel's sword."

I turned toward the big angel and took a breath to relax myself. I had seen the angels in the Jerusalem clouds through a lack of concentration. I didn't try to see the sword. I simply looked past the point where it had appeared before.

Nothing.

I set myself again. Relaxed again. Stared my unfocused stare . . . and still got nothing.

"Maybe you just need some practice," Sue suggested.

"How long is Abdiel willing to stand there while I practice?"

"He doesn't understand." Abdiel sighed.

Exhibiting more patience than the angel, Sue said, "Grant, we all have a spiritual side. If you develop the ability to see a person's spiritual strength, it will appear as a sword."

"Everyone has a sword," I repeated. "Do you have one? And the professor?"

"Yes," Sue said.

Abdiel said, "It is by their swords we can identify who belongs to the Father and who does not. A believer's sword bears the seal of the Father."

"So you're not going to give me a sword?" I said.

"You already have one," Abdiel answered.

I cringed. "What does it look like?"

"See for yourself."

I stared at empty hands.

"It does not have the seal of God," he said.

"Thanks for reminding me."

"But it bears the mark of the Father, the mark that protects you from evil."

So that's where the mark was! I stared at my hands again, wishing I could see it.

"Try seeing Abdiel's sword again," Sue said. "His spirit is the strongest."

I squared my shoulders, took a deep breath, and stared, and stared, and stared.

"Nothing," I said.

"Don't give up, Grant."

Recognizing the professor's voice, I turned, expecting to see him. He wasn't there.

"Did you feel something?" Abdiel asked me.

"I thought—"

I looked again. I was positive I'd heard the professor's voice.

"I thought I heard the professor."

Abdiel nodded. He'd heard it, too. "You heard the professor's prayers."

"Really?" I chuckled self-consciously.

"What did you hear?" Sue asked.

"Seek the truth, find reality."

Then, out of the corner of my eye, I saw Abdiel's sword. But when I looked at it directly, it was gone. Out of the corner of my other eye I saw Sue Ling sitting on the sofa with an elegant sword draped across her legs. Near the hilt blazed a seal of three intertwining circles.

"You see them, don't you?" Sue asked excitedly.

I looked at my hands. They were empty.

CHAPTER

12

My laptop lay open on the desk, its screen a blank white, the cursor tapping impatiently. After leaving the professor's house I grabbed a bag of dinner at a drive-thru and came home to write. I needed to crank out at least a thousand words before bedtime, but that wasn't going to happen. I was wired, and a couple of greasy tacos were sitting heavy on my stomach.

After catching a glimpse of Abdiel's sword, I stayed thirty minutes longer, hoping to duplicate my success. That didn't happen. Neither did I hear the professor's voice again. I was beginning to fear it had all been a fluke, that I'd had some kind of spiritual hot flash.

I'd invited Sue out to eat in hopes that a casual dinner would help me unwind. She said she couldn't leave until the professor came out of his room. If it hadn't been that excuse it would have been another. So I called Jana, but she was filling in for the six-o'clock anchor. That left me and Mr. Taco.

Sitting in front of the blank computer screen, the desk still littered with fast-food wrappers and flattened hot-sauce packets, I forced myself to think about the next chapter in the book.

I closed my eyes and tried to remember my impressions and feelings during my initial visit to the Oval Office. I'd met the president earlier at a fund-raiser, but this was different. The Oval Office is the closest thing America has to a throne room. The strange part about it was that I was the center of attention. The entire staff had been assembled to meet me. The president himself introduced me, informing his staff that they were to provide me carte-blanche access to records and documents.

Of course now I know it was all a setup. The staff wasn't there to assist me. They were there to bury me with preselected information. They'd removed any need for me to research on my own. All I had to do was ask. They'd blinded me with promises and flattery.

Having assembled the memories, my hands moved to the keyboard. Fingertips poised but didn't touch down. I needed a date.

Beside me lay a stack of spiral notebooks. I shuffled through them until I found the one I needed.

Was it before or after the Massachusetts gubernatorial primary?

Glancing up in thought, I caught my reflection in a mirror. My attention leaped backward in time to swords. Was it possible to see a spiritual sword in a mirror? Not knowing didn't stop me from trying.

I relaxed the focus of my eyes and tried to see my reflected spirit.

Abdiel's sword had been so glorious, powerful, and intimidating. What I remembered about Sue Ling's sword was that it had a blue hue to it—that it was elegant.

My curiosity was getting the better of me. I had to know what my sword looked like.

Leaning close to the mirror, I backed away slowly without blinking. When that didn't work, I squinted my eyes. Then I tried opening them wide. Then I turned my head and looked out of the corner of my eye. Then I tried a series of quick glances.

Nothing.

Failure only made me more determined. I positioned my chair directly in front of the mirror and took several deep, relaxing breaths and let my eyelids fall shut. I opened them quickly.

Something moved behind me. I caught the reflection.

"You might as well materialize," I said, swiveling around. "I can see you."

There are no words to describe what it feels like to have Jesus appear suddenly in your living room, even when you know it isn't really him. However, I can describe what it feels like to see accompanying demons materialize on your ceiling.

Two words. Mind-numbing alarm.

"What are you doing here?" I demanded.

Joker Jesus spread his arms in a gesture of goodwill. Above him three transparent demons, green, slimy, bug-eyed, ridge-backed, grinning, and slobbering, became agitated when they saw me. Flashes of what it had felt like to have hundreds of them clamoring inside burned me.

"You could see me before I materialized," Joker Jesus said genially. "Impressive."

"Don't you have a show to perform somewhere?" I replied.

My afternoon training kicked in. I reached for a sword that wasn't there to protect myself. I tried the other side and grabbed air. It was infuriating. Abdiel had made it appear effortless.

"Tell me," Joker Jesus said. "Did you discover you could see the spiritual realm on your own, or did Abdiel teach you?"

"Abdiel? Who's Abdiel?" I said.

I stared at his hips, hoping to catch a glimpse of his sword. I wanted to know what I was up against.

"Is that really how you want to have this conversation? Each of us pretending we don't know about the other?"

Panic was setting in. Why couldn't I see his sword?

"Fine." I tried to sound calm. "What do you want, Belial?"

He smiled. "You know who I am."

My gaze alternated between his eyes and his hips. For a moment I thought I caught a flash of steel.

"I came because I was curious. You are the only living Nephilim. And though we met briefly in Cana, I wanted to see for—what are you looking at?"

Caught staring at his hips, I mumbled something incoherent.

"You're trying to see my sword, aren't you?" he said, figuring it out. "Interesting. You can see angels but not their weapons."

"I can see swords," I said, quick to defend myself.

"Can you? Describe mine."

"All right. I will."

I'd done it once before, hadn't I? Now would be a good time for a breakthrough. I set myself and stared at his hips.

His laughter was booming, but surprisingly inoffensive. "Would you like to see it?"

Before I could answer, his sword materialized in his hand. It was nearly as large as Abdiel's sword and, just as intimidating, black as ebony. It hummed with confidence.

"All of Lucifer's men have black blades," he said. "I prefer silver. Lucifer believes a unified appearance makes for a formidable presence on the battlefield. I can't dispute that."

The longer I stared at the sword, the blacker and more menacing it became.

"Of course, your sword bears the Father's protective mark," Belial said. "That's how I recognized you in Cana."

He hefted his sword proudly, slashing the air with it. It was an image most odd to see Jesus wielding a large black sword.

"Since we both know who you really are," I said, "how about removing the disguise?"

"Very well."

The next instant Belial, the rebel angel, stood before me in all his glory, sword in hand, levitating a foot above the floor. "Better?"

Better didn't begin to describe him. He was gorgeous, and I don't use that word to describe males. His presence was so striking, it was a greater distraction than when he appeared as Jesus.

The room grew dark, as though all the light and colors bowed before the greater glory.

Only once before had I encountered a being so beautiful I had to resist dropping to my knees in awe before him. I had fought the urge then, and I fought it now.

The sword vanished.

"You never have told me why you're here," I said.

"It's not enough that I wanted to meet you? I don't know if you realize how impressive you are."

His charm was disarming. I'd only had extended conversation with two angels in my life, Semyaza and Abdiel. The one badgered me, and the other looked down on me.

"You bested Semyaza," Belial said, amazed. "I wish I could have been there to see that. His arrogance is insufferable. I would have loved seeing his face when you turned him down, and in the presence of Lucifer!"

His laughter bounced off the walls.

"Did you really sing a nursery rhyme while standing in the center of the council?" he asked. "What did you call it: the place in the center?"

"The mush-pot," I said.

He bellowed. "I don't know what I enjoyed more—the censure Semyaza received for failing, or the humiliation he suffers for being defeated by a half-breed, no offense intended."

None was taken. I was drinking in every word. In the form of Myles Shepherd, Semyaza had tormented me through four years of high school. I watched helplessly and in horror as he coordinated the assassination of President Douglas. More than once I felt my insides ripped to pieces when he set a horde of demons on me. To hear that I'd succeeded in humiliating him was elixir to my soul.

And I loved that Belial appreciated my humor. Semyaza and Abdiel didn't. I guess when you think about it, there had to be at least one angel among millions who did.

He turned serious. "Don't let them drag you into this again," he said, sounding like a concerned father. "You've been given a chance to live a normal life, sheltered from the horrors of this eternal war. Make the most of it. Terrors await you. Believe me. I know firsthand."

He motioned to the demons above him. "These are my boys."

The bulging eyes of the demons gazed down on him fondly, their agitation somewhat soothed.

"Their mother was a brown-haired, brown-eyed beauty with a toothy smile that could charm Lucifer. Before I laid eyes on her, I used to scoff at the thought of angels being attracted to human females. One look at Kezia and all that changed. She was a cloudless spring day, a field of floral fragrance, a clear summer's night when the stars are so bright you ache with awe. Ours was a blessed union."

Belial's tone turned hard. "My boys are paying the price for our love. Would I have loved a human woman if I knew that the Father would flood the earth and condemn our Nephilim sons to eternal torment as demons?" He shook his head. "I don't know. A part of me wonders if it would have been possible for me to know Kezia and not love her."

It was difficult to imagine that the hideous creatures on my ceiling were the product of anyone's love. But Belial's anguish was real.

He looked at me with steadfast determination. "I have made my choices. I make no apologies for siding with Lucifer. I fight against injustice. My boys don't deserve this. Neither do you, Grant Austin."

I never thought I'd find myself agreeing with a soldier of Satan. But if he was looking for an argument, he would not get one from me.

"This is your destiny, Grant. You will end up like my boys, and there's nothing you can do about it. Find your Kezia. Lose yourself in her arms, the smoothness of her skin, the curve of her neck, the fragrance of her hair. Don't let Semyaza or Abdiel drag you into a war for which you are not equipped. You can't win. We've been doing this for millennia."

I mouthed the last word with him. The last time a rebel angel had told me that, I stood on the deck of the *Midway*, impotent to make the slightest change in the course of events.

"Heed my advice, son," Belial said. "I'm a warrior. And if I face you on the field of battle, I'll have no choice but to kill you."

"You can't. I have—"

"The mark of the Father? If Abdiel has told you the mark makes you immortal, he's lying. That mark protects you from evil. But if you enter into battle of your own volition, you're just another soldier."

The demons above him disappeared.

"By the way," Belial said. "Nice sword."

I looked down, then stood in front of the mirror. I wished I could see it.

After Belial vanished, I slumped into my desk chair and tried to make sense of what had just happened. Instead I wrote two chapters of my book, as crazy as that sounds. Who would have thought I could concentrate on writing after that?

It's the first time I've ever been distracted by writing. My thoughts crystallized beautifully. The images were razor-sharp. The words flowed like sweet honey. And in no time I'd written four thousand words.

I've had spurts of inspiration before. It doesn't happen often, but when it does, it's a writer's dream. Most often, though, the next day, after the fever has passed and the text has cooled, the writing is seen for what it really is: a first draft that needs polishing. Not so this time. I didn't change a word, not even a comma. These weren't sentences on the page; they were lyrics. The narrative didn't flow; it sang.

So eager was I for someone to read it, I immediately emailed the pages to my publisher before taking a shower. When I stepped out of the shower stall my phone was ringing. It was Higgins. For twenty minutes I sat on the edge of my bed with a towel wrapped around my waist and listened to my publisher sing my praises.

I was pumped. And I couldn't wait to get back to work on the book. But I'd agreed to a morning training session at the professor's house. Twice I picked up the phone to cancel.

"This is a waste of time," Abdiel complained. "He's not concentrating. He's not even making a pretense of concentrating."

"You do seem distracted, Grant," Sue said. "Is something bothering you?"

Other than wanting to get on with my life? I thought.

I'd decided not to tell them about Belial's visit. What was there to tell? He'd stopped by, that's all. He hadn't threatened me. And I knew if I said anything Abdiel would come unglued. Even now he was staring at me suspiciously.

"I made good progress on the book last night," I said truthfully. "I was in the zone, you know? And I guess my mind's still there."

"Focus is essential," Abdiel insisted. "Tell me. In which hand am I holding my sword?"

"Your left hand."

Sue looked to Abdiel. "Is that correct?"

"He's guessing," Abdiel said.

"It's in your left hand!" I said.

Abdiel shook his head. "He can't see it. He's guessing."

"I'm telling you. His sword is in his left hand," I said with confidence.

"Show us," Sue said to Abdiel.

The sword materialized in Abdiel's left hand.

"See? I told you," I boasted.

"He guessed," Abdiel insisted.

"Did you guess, Grant?" Sue asked.

Busted.

"Grant?"

"Yes," I admitted.

Sue looked away. Her disappointment hurt more than I cared to admit.

"Maybe we should move on," she suggested. "Try something else."

"Unadvisable," Abdiel said. "He needs to learn this. If he proves to be the key to unmasking Belial, he must be ready."

"I'm not suggesting we abandon the exercise, just that we try something else for a while," Sue replied.

Abdiel shook his head stubbornly. "If he doesn't learn this, it will be a waste of time for him to learn anything else. He'll be fighting blind."

But Sue wasn't backing down. "That's the second time this morning you've complained about wasting time. What difference does it make to you? You live in eternity."

"The fact that I live in eternity is irrelevant. How can he protect himself against weapons he cannot see?"

Sue turned to me. "We think you may be able to cross into different dimensions, which would allow you to transport quickly from place to place."

"Not until he can see my sword!" Abdiel insisted.

"It's faster than riding on a beam of light," Sue continued, ignoring the angel.

"I demand we speak to the professor," Abdiel said.

"No. He's praying," Sue said stubbornly.

"It will take but a moment."

"He's not to be disturbed."

"I will speak to him. You cannot stop me."

Sue Ling leveled a finger at the angelic being who was twice her size. "You stay right where you are, buster!"

Abdiel didn't know whether to be shocked or amused. Frankly, neither did I.

"If the two of you shout any louder, you'll bring down the house."

The professor wheeled himself into the room from the back

of the house. I don't think Sue and Abdiel saw it, but there was a definite smirk on his face at the sight of Sue Ling engaged in battle with an angel of the Most High.

"Grant Austin still cannot see my sword," Abdiel said.

Sue frowned. "We need a change of pace."

The professor folded his hands in his lap. I was concerned about him. He looked wrung out. His shoulders slumped. His head hung heavy.

"I spoke with President Whitson this morning," he said. "Tiffany Sproul has dropped out of school."

"Oh no!" Sue exclaimed.

"Her father's church is down to twenty members and can no longer support the family, so he's selling washing machines at Sears to make ends meet. Tiffany is waiting tables at Bruno's."

"Is there anything we can do to help?" Sue asked.

"It's not just the money," the professor replied. "Tiffany was getting threats at school. It's no longer safe for her to attend classes."

"Threats? That doesn't make sense. All she did was find a jar in an underwater cave," I said.

"Hostility needs no reason in this world," Abdiel said.

A knock at the door turned all our heads.

"That will be Jana," Sue said.

The two women embraced at the door. I hadn't seen Jana in person since Jerusalem. She looked vibrant and attractive. Confidence became her.

Setting her purse and cell phone down, she joined the group. "I just came from the Sprouls'," she said to the professor.

"They agreed to the interview?" he asked.

"They were very gracious. Thank you for arranging it."

"The world needs to know that not everyone has been taken in by this Joker Jesus."

"Neo Jesus," Jana corrected him. "We'll get fined if we call him the Joker Jesus on the air."

"On what grounds?" the professor asked.

Jana grinned. "Racial. They don't want to offend the Tartarans."

"Preposterous!" Abdiel said. "There is no race of Tartarans."

"Oh, by the way," Jana said, "I was able to get Tiffany a job at the station. Nothing glamorous, but it pays better than Bruno's."

"Grant still cannot see my sword," Abdiel said.

The professor motioned to the angel with his hand. "Patience, my friend. I wish to hear what other news Jana has for us about our adversary. Even the smallest bit of information might prove useful. Often great events swing on small hinges."

I cringed inwardly over withholding information about Belial's visit last night.

"He has appeared on all the major talk shows," Jana said. "*Oprah, Letterman, Leno, Povich, Ellen, Montel, Dr. Phil. Jerry Springer* had two other guests on his show. A Neo Nazi and a guy who is calling himself Neo Buddha."

"He is not Buddha," Abdiel said. "His name is Abner Ray. He is a carpet salesman from Fullerton."

"Really?" Jana pulled a pad from her purse and wrote it down.

"What happened on Springer's show?" I asked.

Jana grinned. "He got the Neo Nazi to cry and the Neo Buddha to laugh so hard he had a hiccup fit."

"This is a side to Belial I have not seen before," Abdiel said. "He is known for deception and torture."

The Belial I had spoken to last night appeared as neither the joker nor the sadist. I wondered if Abdiel had ever seen the genial side of him.

Jana continued her report. "Our competing network did an in-depth story on the rise and decline of churches since the discovery of the Alexandrian manuscript. Traditional churches are declining at an alarming rate. The churches that are thriving are those that are teaching what they call the doctrine of divine laughter. There are a number of variations, but the basic teaching is that laughter is a conduit of God's grace. They draw from scientific studies that prove laughter releases endorphins, which have been touted as everything from a miracle drug to holy water. Their preachers preach that sanctified laughter can cure whatever ails you, promote weight loss, and—wait for it—stimulate follicle growth."

"Men are going to church to laugh away male pattern baldness?" Sue exclaimed.

"By the millions," Jana replied. "The decline of traditional churches is but the tip of the iceberg. Bible sales are down 80 percent. And a major publisher is rumored to be close to a deal with Neo Jesus and his apostle buddies to write a Neo New Testament based on their memoirs. The new scriptures would also include the Alexandrian text, placing it between the books of Acts and Romans."

"What is KTSD doing to refute this nonsense?" the professor asked.

"You mean, 'What am I doing to refute this nonsense?'" Jana replied. "I stand alone in my point of view and my producer's patience is growing thin. He refuses to air anything negative about Neo Jesus because every time we do, the switchboard lights up with hate calls. That's why I wanted to do Tiffany Sproul's story. I know exactly what she's going through. People are leaving paper bags with dog excrement on my desk. My car tires have been sliced. And my microphone mysteriously cuts in and out when I'm doing a story that raises questions about Neo

Jesus. I have to scratch and claw for every minute of air time. In fact—" She turned to me. "In order for me to air the Sprouls' story, I had to promise my producer that I could get an exclusive interview with Neo Jesus. Have you seen him recently?"

"Um—" Her question took me by surprise. "Next time I see him, I'll ask."

"I hope it's soon," Jana replied.

"And if you can't air the Sprouls' story?" Sue asked.

"I'm putting together a documentary called *Notes from the Catacombs*. A remnant of believers have refused to abandon the faith. But they're under constant attack. I have interviews from pastors and Bible teachers who have had their family pets poisoned, swastikas spray-painted on their houses, and their children beaten up on the playground. Grocers refuse to sell their wives food, banks refuse loans or call loans due prematurely. Some have been shouted down while preaching in their own churches by Neo Jesus worshippers. Tiffany's story will be part of a larger piece that documents the story of Christians who have refused to surrender their belief in the historical Jesus. I'll try to sell it to the networks. If I can't get them to buy it, there's always the Internet."

The entire time Jana spoke the professor sat with his head bowed. When she finished, he started praying. He didn't announce it. He didn't ask us if we wanted to join him. He just started praying.

"Almighty God, strengthen the faithful, bind the wounds of the fallen, and when the day goes hard and the standard falters and heroes run from the field, may we not be found faithless, but with one voice lift our faces heavenward and shout your name, so that there is no doubt upon whose side we stand. Amen."

A long moment of silence followed.

"So, how are wonderboy's lessons going?" Jana asked.

"He still can't see my sword," Abdiel said.

"I saw it yesterday," I objected, not wanting Jana to think I was a complete failure.

The professor slapped the arms of his chair. "Sue, explain to Grant our thinking about teleportation."

To Sue's credit, she didn't gloat over this change of direction.

"Teleportation?" Jana said. "To where? For what purpose? What's your strategy?"

The professor answered. "Our strategy is as old as the Bible. Each person contributes according to his gifts. This is how every generation of Christians has fought evil since the time of Christ and we'll not depart from it now, no matter how sensational the headlines. Let the preachers preach, the teachers teach, the administrators administrate, and the encouragers encourage all to the glory of God. Our task here is to find out what Grant's gifts are. After that, it will be up to him to choose to serve according to his faith or not to serve."

Or not to serve. I latched on to those words, grateful that the professor acknowledged I had a choice in the matter. Fact was, since talking to Belial last night, my dream of a family and writing career in a small, quiet university town had been resurrected.

"And what can you do so far, Grant?" Jana asked.

"He can't see my sword," Abdiel said. "Without that ability he is useless as a warrior."

I ignored him. "As you know, since Jerusalem I can see angels even when they have not materialized. And yesterday I heard the professor praying for me while he was in the back of the house."

"You actually heard his voice? Do you hear him every time he prays for you?" Jana asked.

"Just the once."

"Have you heard anyone else praying for you?"

It's odd, but I never thought of other people praying for me. "No. Just the professor. And I have had limited success seeing spiritual weapons. Yesterday I saw Abdiel's sword briefly. I also saw Sue's sword."

Jana laughed. "You have a sword?" she asked Sue.

"Everyone does," I answered before Sue could. "A person's sword is their spirit. Sue's is elegant with a blue tint."

"That is correct," Abdiel said, glancing at Sue.

"Why a sword?" Jana asked.

It took me a moment to put it together. "Strength of spirit, and intent. A person's sword reveals their intent."

"Grant, that's wonderful! Just by looking at a person, you can determine their intent?"

"He could if he was able to see their sword," Abdiel said.

"So an elegant blue sword tells you what?" Jana asked.

This was new territory for me. I'd been so busy trying to see swords that I hadn't given much thought to interpreting them. "That her spirit is—" I pulled up an image of the sword from memory. "Elegant—that would be nobility of spirit, wouldn't it? And blue—peaceful, nonthreatening."

I looked to Abdiel for confirmation.

"Elementary, but acceptable for now," the angel said. "And what does mine tell you?"

On the off chance I might get lucky, I attempted to see his sword. When I couldn't, I relied on memory. "A strong spirit, definitely. It shimmered gold—regal, pure, reflective of the One he serves."

"An accurate assessment," Abdiel said.

High praise from the big angel. I would have reveled in my success had not the image of Belial's sword come to mind. Sinister black. Eagerly glistening. To do what? Evil. But he'd said black was Lucifer's choice. Was the black blade merely a reflection of his leader?

"Do me next!" Jana said, sounding like a little girl. "What does my sword look like?"

I looked to Abdiel for help.

His expression was unyielding rock. I was on my own.

I really wanted to do this. Maybe the incentive would be the edge I needed. I stared and focused and gazed until Jana became uncomfortable with my looking at her. I had to admit I couldn't do it.

"Teleportation," Sue said, pulling attention away from my failure. "This is going to be a two-step lesson. First, we want to see if you can move through the usual four dimensions—forward, back; side to side; up, down; and time."

"Easy," I said. "I've been doing that all my life."

"Keep it up, chuckles," Sue replied. "We'll see if you're still laughing when Abdiel shoves you through that wall."

"You're kidding, right?"

"Then, if you can move through matter, we'll see if you can take it one step further by moving through the membranes that separate dimensions. It's called degrees of freedom."

"How many dimensions are there?" Jana asked.

"Eleven. Maybe more," Sue said, looking to Abdiel. The question presented a unique opportunity. She had a chance to go where no physicist had gone before. Standing in front of her was a being who had assisted in the construction of the universe.

"You have sufficient information to proceed," he told her.

"Is this going to hurt?" I asked.

Sue shrugged. "We're going to find out."

"Great."

"What do you hope to achieve by moving Grant through other dimensions?" Jana asked. She was furiously taking notes.

"Theoretically, it will allow him to move in and out of our space and time. He'll be able to travel anywhere in the world instantaneously." To me, "That's faster than riding on a light beam."

"Theoretically?" Jana said. "Certainly Abdiel knows whether or not it's possible."

Abdiel offered no reply.

"Of course he does," the professor said. "But the Father has established guidelines to his participation. We must proceed according to our own knowledge and faith like everyone else."

"Wait a minute," I said. "I want to get one thing clear. If Sue—and I mean no offense, I think you're brilliant—leads me to the edge of some cosmic cliff and tells me to step off, Abdiel will stop me. Right?"

"I will not," Abdiel said.

"Oh . . . well . . . as long as we're clear about that," I said.

"I trust Abdiel," the professor said.

Of course you trust him, I thought. *He wouldn't let you go over a cliff. Me, he'd push.*

"Maybe it will help if you understand a little more about what you're going to do," Sue said. "Question. In space, what is there more of than anything else?"

An oral science quiz. I hated oral quizzes.

"More than anything else—" I said, buying time. "Um—emptiness."

Sue smiled. "Correct. There is more space in space than anything else. That is true among the stars *and* on the particle level. For example, if we were to construct a model of an atom on a football field, the nucleus would be the size of an orange. If we set the nucleus on the fifty-yard line, the electrons would be peas circling in the end zones. Everything in between is empty space."

"—peas in end zones," Jana said, writing it down.

Sue stood and moved to the wall that separated the living room from the hall. "And of course you know that everything is made of atoms, so things appear solid"—she rapped the wall with her knuckles—"but they aren't really solid at all."

It sounded solid to me.

"Now, theoretically," she said, "if a person were to bump into this wall often enough, there would come a time when everything would line up and he'd pass right through it."

"Is that true?" Jana looked up from her notes. "How many times would he have to bump into it for that to happen?"

"A million. Maybe a billion," Sue replied.

"You want me to bump into the wall a billion times?"

"I'll be there to help you," Abdiel said.

"I bet you will!" I replied.

"Grant, don't forget, you're different," Sue said. "It's nothing for an angel to pass through a wall."

Abdiel demonstrated. He stepped through the wall as if it were smoke. A moment later, he stepped back into the living room.

It looked easy. That's what scared me.

"How do I do it?" I asked.

Sue shrugged. "That, I can't tell you."

Trial and error. And his errors will kill him. Wasn't that what Abdiel had said?

"Why don't we start with the assumption that it's a process similar to seeing angels," Sue suggested. "Try tapping into your angel side."

"It's as easy as seeing swords," Abdiel said.

Sue pulled me to the wall and had me face it, with my toes

touching the floorboard. An inch of space separated my nose from the wall. The last time I had stood this close to a wall I was in time-out for writing on the carpet with an ink pen.

"Think expansively, Grant," Sue said. "The air separating you from the wall is no different from the wall itself. As easily as you pass through the air, you can pass through the wall."

I felt someone behind me.

"Abdiel is going to help you," Sue said.

Massive hands fell on my shoulders.

I tried to relax as I had in the Jerusalem hotel, let my eyes go unfocused, look past the—

"Ow!"

Abdiel banged my forehead against the wall.

"Don't push!" I said.

My forehead hit the wall again. And again.

"He can't do it," Abdiel said.

"Maybe you should wait until he's ready," Sue said.

Thunk.

"Ow!"

"If he could do it, he'd do it," Abdiel said.

Thunk.

I jerked out of his grip.

"Grant, were you trying?" the professor asked, doing his best not to laugh.

"I don't know if I was ready."

"There's nothing to get ready," Abdiel said.

"Why don't you try again?" Sue urged. "This time, we could count. Three, two, one."

"Counting won't help," Abdiel said. "Either he can do it, or he can't."

"Grant, give it another go," the professor said.

"Maybe this will work," Abdiel said.

He stepped through the wall. A moment later a huge angel fist came out of the wall, grabbed the front of my shirt, and yanked. The next thing I knew I was standing in the hallway with an angel.

Incredulous cheers came from the living room.

I looked back at the wall in disbelief. I did it! I actually passed through the wall! And I didn't feel a thing. Abdiel turned me around for the return journey.

Thunk. My forehead hit the wall.

"Hey!"

"It doesn't seem to work this way, does it?" Abdiel said.

Thunk. Thunk. Thunk.

"Ow! Stop it! That hurts!"

Abdiel stepped through the wall, pulling me with him. We emerged on the living-room side as easily as if we'd walked through the doorway.

Jana and Sue were on their feet clapping. The professor was beaming. I rubbed my forehead and felt a headache coming on.

"Grant, that was amazing!" Jana said. "What was it like?"

"Like Sue said. It was like stepping through air."

I glanced back at the wall, still not believing that I'd walked through it.

"Stepping from one degree of freedom to another will be more difficult," Sue said. "The membranes between dimensions are tricky things."

"Maybe I should try the wall a few more times," I said.

Abdiel had stepped across the room just inside the front door. "The membrane is thinnest here," he said, looking at something none of the rest of us could see.

He took a step and vanished.

I had to admit he had my attention. Was it really possible

that I could cross dimensions? Why not? A moment ago I didn't think I could step through a wall, but I did.

Standing where Abdiel had stood just before he vanished, I tried to see what he had seen. I didn't even know what I was looking for. A portal? A transparent skinlike substance? Was it flat, or did it undulate?

I tested the air with the flat of my hand.

"Do you see something, Grant?" Sue said.

I said, "Maybe it's my imagination, but—"

An angel hand thrust out of thin air, grabbed my shirt, and pulled me in. The last thing I remember before blacking out was hearing my own screams.

"Grant? Grant?"

My eyes fluttered open. When they focused, I was looking up at a huddle of faces.

"What happened?" I asked, as the faces blurred.

"Stay with us, Grant," the professor said.

"You blinked out," Jana said.

"Blinked out?"

"Disappeared, but only for a moment," Sue said. "Abdiel brought you right back."

"It's his physical self that resists the crossing," Abdiel said.

Resists was an understatement. It felt as though someone had tried to shove me through a sieve. Every inch of me felt burned and violated.

"That's enough for one day," the professor said.

He heard no objections from me. I didn't think I'd survive a second attempt.

"Wait . . . wait . . ." I cried.

"What is it, Grant?" Sue asked.

I laughed in triumph. "I see swords!"

It was true. Abdiel's sword shimmered gold. Jana's sword was similar to Sue's, only lavender. A formidable silver broadsword lay across the professor's lap.

My sword. What did my sword look like?

I raised my head. Blinked. The swords vanished before I had a chance to see mine.

CHAPTER
13

The professor hunched over his home office computer, sliding the mouse, clicking and dragging files. The room was larger than his office at the college but no less cluttered. Bulging bookshelves and floor-space filing was an occupational hazard.

He heard tapping on his door and looked up. Sue Ling poked her head in. Seeing he was alone, she entered the room, her purse slung over her arm.

"You're finished?" she asked.

"Abdiel left rather abruptly. You know how he can be at times, like a caged bird." The professor sat back and raised his arms over his head and stretched. "But he stayed long enough to finish."

"I'm going to the market. Do you need anything?"

"We're low on breakfast cereal."

"I have it on the list."

The professor's mind wandered back to the computer screen.

"I shouldn't be long," Sue said.

A moment later he heard the front door closing.

Inserting a memory stick labeled Grant Austin into a port, the professor transferred a large file. He then opened his email program and set the mouse to work again, clicking and dragging.

He heard the front door open.

"Sue!" he said. "I'm glad you came back. Get me some jelly beans, will you?"

"Aren't you a little old to be eating jelly beans? Do you know what they do to your teeth?"

The voice beside him startled him.

As accustomed as the professor was to having Abdiel pop in and out at all hours of the day and night, the sudden appearance of an angel never grew ordinary, especially if he was a stranger.

The angel looked over the professor's shoulder at the screen. "You've finished, I see. Abdiel was foolish to narrate our history to you. Had the Father wanted you to know it, he would have whispered it in some lonely apostle's ear."

The professor made one last mouse click, then wheeled himself back from the desk. He took a good look at the angel standing before him. "I suppose there's something poetic about Lucifer sending you to kill me."

"Irony adds a touch of beauty to death, don't you think?" Semyaza said. "Where's that muscle-brained bodyguard of yours? It's not like him to leave you unguarded."

"Abdiel still loves you, you know," the professor said.

Semyaza grinned slyly. "Is that the best you've got? Your sentimental darts have no effect on me. I know of Abdiel's feelings. I use them to my advantage." The rebel angel ambled through the room. "Lovely décor. Twenty-first-century packrat, if I'm not mistaken."

"You know that by killing me you'll only make me stronger," the professor said. "I couldn't begin to count the nights I've prayed for liberation from this blasted wheelchair." He chuckled. "That makes you an answer to my prayers, doesn't it?"

Semyaza turned on his heel. "Your insults will only make it harder for you."

The professor tossed his head back and laughed. He laughed until tears ran. "O blessed angel, O blessed day! Today I will see my Nora and Jenny and Terri again!"

"A lot of suffering still separates you from them!" Semyaza shouted in anger.

"With every passing second I am closer to see them again!"

"It is I who killed them," Semyaza said. "Theirs were sudden, but painful deaths."

"I know. When I saw a picture of you as Myles Shepherd, I recognized you from the scene of the accident. And oh, praise God, it is you who will reunite us!"

"Do not underestimate the pain you are about to suffer," Semyaza seethed.

"It will seem but a moment," the professor replied. He became serious. "And know this. Once I am free from this straitjacket of a body, once I have been liberated from the chains of this chair, I will fight you and I will not rest until the day of judgment when you and all the other apostles of hate are punished for the pain and suffering you have inflicted upon the world."

"You would challenge me?" Semyaza laughed.

The professor reflected a moment. "But why release me now, when it is you who imprisoned me in this chair in the first place? Unless—"

The professor's eyes widened in realization. "Grant! You're killing me to hurt him. He's stronger than you give him credit for. But then you know that, don't you? Grant Austin scares you."

Semyaza walked to the door. He motioned to someone in the other room. "I'm sure you're familiar with the story of Job's children."

Two men walked in. Biker types. Shirts with no sleeves. Tattoos. Looping chains. One had a nose that zigzagged down his face, a testimony to his fighting nature. His buddy pushed on a pair of brass knuckles.

"These must be the Sabeans and Chaldeans," the professor said.

"On occasion we have found it beneficial to employ local talent," Semyaza said with a grin.

The thugs wasted no time, nor did they show any conscience about beating a man in a wheelchair. They pummeled the professor's face until it was swollen and unrecognizable. Then they lifted him out of the chair and took turns holding him up while the other punched him like he would a workout bag in a gym.

"Where is your loving God now?" Semyaza taunted. "Cry out to him to save you. He won't, of course."

Through swollen lips and broken teeth, Professor J. P. Forsythe said, "Blessed Father, Almighty God, You alone are worthy of praise."

This infuriated Semyaza. "Your praise falls on deaf ears, old man! Could you stand by and watch someone you love being beaten to death and do nothing? Is your love greater than God's? Or could it be he doesn't love you as you suppose?" Semyaza yelled heavenward. "If you love him, stay the hands of the men who strike him! That is, if you can."

The thugs grunted with each blow.

Semyaza leaned close to the professor. He sneered, "You would put your faith in a God who refuses to save you?"

Through swollen eyes the professor met Semyaza's gaze. "Though He slay me Himself, yet will I trust Him."

Semyaza stepped back and levitated into the air. He grew to twice his normal size. The room grew dark as he sucked the light out of it. Colors peeled off books and walls and pictures and were absorbed by him. A wind blasted from his chest and circled the room, knocking frames from the walls and books from shelves and tossing papers into the air like frightened pigeons.

The two toughs stopped their assault and stared at him in horror. They dropped the professor into a heap and fled the house.

Semyaza continued to drain the room of light and color until he pulsed with radiance. Looking down at the professor, he taunted, "I am Semyaza. Tremble before me!"

The walls trembled at his voice. The circling wind began to howl a deafening banshee howl.

Crumpled on the floor like a pile of laundry, Professor Forsythe looked upon the counterfeit radiance. Then he looked past it, and genuine glory illuminated his face.

With whispered words so soft that not even he could hear them, he said, "Nora, darling, tell the girls Daddy's coming home."

I was at my keyboard and I was in the zone. My fingers were on fire. The screen was scrolling. The pages were flying out of me.

I'd reached the point in the story where I went to Montana to track down Doc Palmer. They'd told me he was dead, but I'd found him very much alive and none too eager to entertain visitors from D.C. I'd gotten to the part where he had me jump into a garbage pit to retrieve a copy of my book when my cell phone rang.

The ring tone indicated it was Jana.

I let it ring. I didn't want anything breaking the spell. After five cycles the phone stopped ringing. It was the right choice. She would leave a message, and I'd get back to her in a while.

I turned my attention back to Montana. *I'm standing in a garbage pit. I have eggshells and coffee grounds on my bare feet.*

The cell phone rang again. Jana again. This time I answered it.

"Grant, what's the professor's address?" she blurted.

"You're a little young for Alzheimer's, aren't you?" I joked. "You know where his house is. You've been there a hundred times."

"I know it's on Landis. What's the address?"

The urgency in her voice was a splash of cold water.

"Um—I don't know," I said, struggling to remember it. "Who pays attention after—"

"Three-one-nine-eight. Is that it?"

I could hear a police scanner crackling in the background. "I . . . I . . . don't know for sure. I know it's near—"

"Do you know where Sue is? I can't reach her."

"You've tried her cell? Of course you've tried her cell."

"It's turned off. Grant, you'd better get over there."

The panic in Jana's voice was alarm enough to get me moving. I had seen this woman stand on a bridge that was being strafed by FA-18 Hornets and remain calm.

I ran into my bedroom to get my keys. They weren't on the dresser. I always put them on the dresser. I checked my pockets. Not there. Not on the desk either. I found them on the kitchen counter but still couldn't remember putting them there.

Bounding out the door, I wished I knew how to find a dimensional membrane. Pain or no pain, I'd have used it to teleport to the professor's house.

Police. Fire. Ambulance. Jana and the news crew. All were there when I arrived. The only thing that wasn't there was the professor's house.

It was leveled. Had it not been for the rubble of what had once been a family dwelling, it would have looked like a vacant lot.

Jumping out of my car, I sprinted toward the scene. Police warned me off.

"Was anybody in the house?" I called to anybody who would listen.

Nobody knew. Or if they knew, they weren't saying.

I found Jana standing in front of the news van with a group of onlookers. They were showing her something. When she saw me coming, she broke away to intercept me.

"Oh, Grant, I'm so sorry." She flung her arms around me.

"The professor? Sue Ling? Tell me they weren't—"

"They found one body," she said, weeping.

I followed her glance to an ambulance. Emergency personnel were loading a black body bag strapped to a stretcher into the back of the ambulance.

"The professor," Jana said.

"Sue Ling? Have you found her yet?"

Jana's tears told me she hadn't.

We held each other for a long time. Neither of us wanted to let go because we knew that when we did we would have to face the awful truth. As long as we held each other, there was at least hope that Sue Ling was still alive.

"Ms. Torres, do you want my video or not? If you don't want it, Channel Six has offered to buy it."

It was one of the men she'd been standing with when I arrived.

"Of course we want it," Jana said, shrugging off her personal feelings. "Grant, take a look at this. You're going to see it eventually anyway. Brace yourself."

She instructed the man to show the clip to me. He held up a camcorder with a viewing screen and pressed the PLAY button.

The video began with a three-year-old boy swatting at a ball with one of those Flintstone-sized plastic baseball bats. An off-camera female voice went from yelling encouragements to the batter to—

"Jeff! Jeff! Look at that!"

The picture on the screen dipped to show grass, then raised to an overcast sky that was beginning to swirl.

"Have you ever seen anything like it?" the female voice said.

A pause, then, "Sybil, get Mikey into the house."

"What? You don't think it's a—"

"Get Mikey into the house!" the cameraman screamed, shaking the camera. "Into the bathtub. Pull a mattress over you."

A blurred head passed in front of the camera, coaxing Mikey to put down the bat. "I'm taking him to Mother's," the female voice said.

"There's no time."

"You're crazy if you think—"

"Don't argue with me, Sybil! Get into the tub! Now!"

Off camera, Mikey was crying. His mother consoled him, her voice fading until the slam of a screen door cut it off altogether.

Standing next to Jana, Jeff the cameraman said, "I almost ran at this point."

"Why didn't you?" Jana asked.

"The video. Crazy, isn't it? All I could think was that if I stayed and got the shot, maybe I could win one of those family video show awards, you know? Here's where it gets hairy—"

A funnel formed in the clouds and slithered earthward, as though someone had summoned it. The instant it touched the roof of his neighbor's house, the structure exploded. The view on the video screen went wild as the cameraman ducked, cursed, ran, then framed the scene again. Debris filled the air hundreds of feet high.

"Would you look at that?" Jeff's camera voice said. "I don't believe it."

The video recorded the funnel retracting into the clouds. The screen went blank.

Jeff lowered the camera. "Is that prime-time news video, or what? How much do you think I'll get for it?"

"The producer makes those decisions," Jana said.

I compared what I had just watched on video with the live scene. No other house on the block had been damaged. Just the professor's.

"I barely knew the guy who lived there," Jeff said. "Saw him coming and going mostly. He was a cripple. Had one of those ramps up to the porch. Tell you one thing, though, he musta done something bad to tick God off like that. You saw it. It's like the finger of the Almighty reached down and, boom! Sayonara, Charlie. My wife says she doesn't think anyone deserved what he got. Me? I think God drilled him on account of he was shackin' up with this Oriental babe."

Just as my knuckles were about to make an impression on Jeff the cameraman's face, a scream startled us all.

Sue Ling had managed two steps from her car before collapsing, her face contorted in horror. A bag of groceries lay on its side, breakfast cereal, deodorant, a stalk of celery, and a bag of jelly beans spilling onto the street.

Two police officers reached her before we did. Jana pushed them aside and held her friend in her arms. I made a couple of futile gestures, including righting the grocery bag and replacing the items.

On the verge of hysteria, Sue Ling moaned that she never should have left him. Nothing we said consoled her.

I felt helpless. Relieved. Hurt. Angry. But mostly helpless.

The rage would come later.

I stayed with Sue Ling at Jana's house until Jana got off work. We didn't want her to be alone.

Mostly she sat and stared into space as I answered her questions with what little information I had. I told her about Jana's call, arriving at the scene, and the video clip. The police called it a freak accident. Sue Ling and I knew better.

"He was working on Abdiel's narration when I left," she told me. "His computer—"

"Destroyed," I said.

"The hard drive, do you think—"

"It was smashed up pretty good."

That was an understatement. Everything had been obliterated. Totally and completely obliterated. Not a piece of furniture, not a book, not a sheet of paper had been left intact.

After the police had finished with the scene they had let me sift through the rubble. With nothing to identify I did fine until I lifted a piece of what looked like part of a desk and found a twisted wheelchair wheel beneath it.

"What about backups?" I asked her.

"He had a backup of Abdiel's narration on a memory stick. He kept it in his pocket. He was going to make a copy for you when he was done."

"How far along was it?"

Fresh tears fell. "They had just finished it as I was leaving for the store."

I offered to have supper delivered. Sue went into Jana's bedroom and lay down instead. I checked on her after a few minutes and she was asleep.

Just as well. I wouldn't have watched the news had Sue Ling been awake. The destruction of the house on Landis Street was the top story. The male anchor handed it over to the reporter at the scene.

Jana's face filled the screen.

"In what the insurance company is calling an Act of God, a single-family dwelling on Landis Street was leveled by a powerful tornado that touched down briefly in North Park. Inexplicably, no other house was damaged."

She told me later she fought to keep the phrase Act of God out of the report. Her producer insisted on it.

Neighbor Jeff's video clip played.

"The owner of the house, Professor John Patrick Forsythe, was the only person in the dwelling at the time. He did not survive."

Jana interviewed the first officer on the scene and went on to tell of the professor's connection to Heritage College. Her words barely registered. I was screaming into a sofa pillow.

I left Sue with Jana and drove to La Jolla Shores. The thought of going home was too suffocating. My condo was too small to hold my rage.

It was midnight. I kicked off my shoes and walked barefoot on the wet sand. A full moon painted the beach with silvery brushstrokes. White waves crashed and slid up the sloping shoreline, splashing my feet with bubbly foam.

The sea has always had a calming effect on me. Here I can walk and meditate and relax. But it had no calming effect on me tonight. The rage that churned within me was deeper than the deep blue sea.

I screamed at the stars. "Abdiel! Abdiel, show yourself! Abdiel!"

A half hour of this and I barely had a voice left. I searched futilely for a dimensional membrane. No matter how much it hurt, if I found one I was going to pop into Abdiel's bedroom uninvited, as he was so fond of popping into mine.

"Abdiel!" I yelled.

Each unanswered cry only made me angrier until I was a madman. Ranting. Kicking the surf. Throwing punches at the heavens. But so far all I'd succeeded in doing was scaring away two couples who had come to sit under the stars and neck.

"You are distraught."

I recognized the voice. My hair disheveled, my eyes charged, I swung around in fury. "Where have you been?"

"I have walked every step with you," Abdiel replied. "Had your anger not blinded you, you would have seen me."

The stretch of beach behind him showed only one set of footprints.

"You just let me scream myself hoarse?"

"Is that the question you really want to ask me?"

He was right. Insufferable, but right. I pointed an accusatory finger at him, my hand shaking with intensity, but the words weren't coming. My mind was crammed with questions, threats, and accusations. They log-jammed in my throat.

"You want to know where I was when the professor was attacked," Abdiel said for me.

"For starters."

"I was watching."

"Watching! Watching? You were watching?"

"You heard me correctly."

"What . . . how—you were *watching*?"

"I was not alone."

In my mind I saw an arena of angels entertaining themselves with the professor's death. What really ignited me was that I knew what it was like to be the man in the middle. I had once been in a battle for my life, surrounded by heavenly spectators.

"You watched and did nothing?" This was unbelievable. Beyond my comprehension. "Are you a sadist? I thought you were his friend. Why didn't you rescue him?"

"We are pleased to serve the Father," Abdiel said.

"That's it? That's your explanation? Or is it your excuse? Do you know what I think? I think you were afraid. For all your self-righteous, holier-than-thou snobbery, I think you're just using God as an excuse to hide your cowardice!"

Abdiel's chest heaved. His eyes blazed. His sword appeared and burst into flame, knocking me off my feet. I sailed through the air and landed on my backside in the sand.

I'd never felt a hit like it before. It wasn't like a punch to the chin or gut. The blow passed completely through me. It didn't knock the wind out of me, but it certainly knocked some of the fight out of me.

On my back I stared up at a glowing, levitating, angry angel.

"Any further questions, Grant Austin?"

"Yeah. Did he suffer?"

I scored a blow of my own. Abdiel's shoulders fell. His glow wasn't nearly as fierce.

"I have witnessed the deaths of hundreds of Christian martyrs. I have seen no finer example of faith. The professor remained steadfast. Unyielding."

I envisioned the professor's final moments. The wheelchair warrior.

"Regardless of what you think, Grant Austin, it never gets easier for us. The valiant death of a believer reminds us of the darkest day, when heaven was helpless."

I shook my head. "I still don't understand how you can just stand by and watch someone be murdered."

"It pleases us—"

"Yeah, I know—to serve the Father. But if you ask me, the battle plan stinks. How can you expect to enlist human support for the cause if you abandon them when they're attacked?"

"You labor under a misconception," Abdiel said. "One that the professor did not share."

"And what misconception is that? That human lives are as valuable to God as angels?"

Abdiel's anger flared. I flinched.

"Do not speak blasphemy, Grant Austin. Even in pain. I will not tolerate it. You cannot begin to fathom the depths of the Father's love for you."

I knew I'd gone too far and wasn't proud of it. In my attempt to defend the professor I was dishonoring him.

"The misconception," Abdiel said with forced restraint, "is that death is the end of life. It was my honor to escort the professor through death's door to a higher realm of existence. I wish you could see him. He is healed. He is with his wife and daughters. He is happy. And he is most eager to continue the fight against Lucifer."

The angel's words shamed me. What kind of friend was I to

wish the professor continued pain and sorrow in this life for my sake?

"He has fought the good fight," I muttered.

"Indeed."

"You said there were others with you. Who?"

"You will see them. They will be at the professor's funeral."

My backside was getting cold. I could feel the water soaking through my pants. "Can I get up now?"

Abdiel made no attempt to stop me, so I climbed to my feet and tried to brush wet sand from my hands and clothes, which is always a futile effort. My anger had not ceased. It had merely been redirected.

"Who did this to the professor?" I asked. "And why?"

"While I cannot say with certainty, it is safe to assume the order came from Lucifer."

"You don't know for sure?"

"We are not omniscient."

"But God is."

"The Father is not in the habit of informing us what another is thinking."

"But you're on His side. I thought it was different with angels."

"You are on His side as well. In some ways our walk is no different from yours. We, too, face challenges. We, too, must choose how we will respond."

"But you said you were there. You saw who killed the professor."

"Correct," Abdiel said.

"Who? Not Belial."

My comment intrigued Abdiel. "Why would you dismiss Belial? He is your enemy."

After meeting him, I couldn't bring myself to believe that

Belial had anything to do with the professor's death, but this wasn't the time to get into it with Abdiel.

"Just tell me who did it," I said.

"If I tell you, what will you do?"

"Like you, I'll face the challenge and choose how to respond."

My answer pleased him. "He is indeed our common enemy," Abdiel said.

That's all I needed to hear.

"Semyaza!" I muttered.

But there was no choice to make. Now that I knew, a single path lay before me.

Revenge.

Had we ordered a day for the funeral, we couldn't have selected a better one. The sky was a brilliant, blue-vaulted dome. A sweet ocean air blew off the Pacific, softly rustling the leaves of the trees. Patches of flowers splashed color here and there—ruby red, sun yellow, pure white.

Greenwood Mortuary is a patch of green paradise in an asphalt city. Grassy hills stretch luxuriously across the terrain. Shaded alcoves provide protection from the sun on warm days. Even the chapel hints of a more peaceful age with its stone walls, stained-glass windows, and waterfall gardens.

The small turnout surprised me until I thought of the number of funerals I had attended for college professors. You hear about their deaths. You remember fondly the influence they've had on your life. You might even send a card. But they're a part of the past and you've moved on, and nostalgia isn't a high priority in a hyperactive world.

The media were there, taping a follow-up to one of the more bizarre stories in San Diego's weather history. That's what the incident had become for the media. A freak weather story. Only a few of us knew that it was a surgical strike in a vicious cosmic war that threatened every man, woman, and child.

Dr. Marvin Whitson, president of the college, performed the service. He gave the professor a good send-off, balancing his academic achievements with testaments to his character. There were no brothers or sisters to mention. The professor's parents had both died when he was young. His wife and daughter had been his only family.

Sue Ling attended in the role of grieving widow. I don't know what else to call her. She loved the professor as deeply as any woman has loved a husband.

Jana stood to one side of her, wearing a broad-rimmed black hat and veil. She attended as a friend, not a news reporter. I stood on Sue's other side.

Abdiel attended in human form, his broad shoulders and thick neck barely contained by a suit and tie. His appearance as a human was a gesture of respect to the professor, one that Sue and Jana and I appreciated.

As Dr. Whitson said a final prayer, Sue took my arm. She whispered, "How many?"

"Thousands," I said.

And there were. A short distance above us thousands upon thousands of angels circled the professor's casket, their heads bowed in honor of a fallen warrior.

Following the ceremony, Abdiel approached me. "The professor continues to intercede for you."

Somehow that didn't surprise me. "The next time you see him, thank him for me. And tell him I miss him."

"He has every confidence in you," Abdiel replied. "I don't know what he sees in you."

I gave a half-smile in response. "I never know when you're joking."

"You think I'm joking?"

CHAPTER
14

Following the funeral, Heritage College held a reception to honor the professor. Sue, Jana, and I made an appearance, then went to Jana's house, where Sue had been living. She didn't want to be alone.

The girls changed into comfortable clothes, and I removed my tie and coat. We sat and reminisced. Then all of a sudden Sue jumped up. She wanted to go to the professor's house. Jana and I indulged her. People mourn in different ways.

We followed Sue into the rubble that had once been a house and began sifting aimlessly, looking for anything salvageable. It soon became evident that Sue's sifting had purpose. It focused on the professor's study.

"Look for discs, floppy drives, memory sticks—anything that might contain computer files," she said when we asked what she was looking for.

"Abdiel's narration?" I asked.

Holding a cabinet door in her hand, Sue straightened up. "That's why they killed him."

"Oh, honey, are you sure?" Jana exclaimed. "We don't know that, do we?"

Sue offered no explanation. She tossed the door aside and continued digging.

"Found something," Jana said after a while.

She held up a broken piece of plastic with a metal tip. A memory stick with my name on it.

"Do you think we might be able to—" Jana said hopefully.

Sue took the memory stick from her, examined it, and tossed it.

Two hours of rummaging yielded three CDs and a half-dozen floppies. None of them were usable. I also found a photograph of Sue and the professor on a cruise. Both were wearing brightly colored leis and holding a tropical drink with an umbrella.

"A Bible cruise to Ensenada," Sue told us. "This was taken as we were boarding. It was the last time he smiled the entire cruise. He didn't take to sailing."

Eight o'clock that evening, back at Jana's house, I said good night and drove home. I'd agreed to take Sue to the college the next day to help her clear out the professor's office. She expressed hope of finding a backup copy of the angel history there.

I had mixed feelings about it. Like Sue, I hoped to find a backup copy of the angel history. I had a couple of chapters the professor had printed out for me, but that was all. What I wasn't looking forward to was packing up the professor's personal belongings. Going through the professor's belongings would take an emotional toll on both of us.

Maybe I'd feel better about doing it in the morning. It had

been a long day, and my emotions were depleted, leaving a hollow feeling in my gut. It was going to take time for me to adjust to a world without the professor.

I couldn't help thinking that had I been there with him, things would have turned out differently. I'd gone head to head with angels before and survived, hadn't I? I couldn't help thinking that had I been there to face Semyaza, I would have figured out some way to save the professor.

Reaching into my pocket for the house keys, I noticed that the porch light had gone out. I was tired. Maybe I'd wait until morning to replace the bulb.

Keys in hand, I froze when I realized I wouldn't be needing them. The front door was ajar. The doorjamb splintered.

I looked around. No one was in the courtyard. I'd seen no one in the parking lot.

Using the tip of the key, I slowly pushed the door open and peered inside. My heart was racing. The only light was what spilled into the room from behind me.

I flipped on the light switch next to the door. Nothing happened. I flipped it repeatedly, as if to goad the lamp into lighting. As my eyes adjusted, I saw the lamp lying on its side on the floor. So was the table upon which it had sat. And the sofa and recliner. Everything in the room had been upended.

Having spent the afternoon stepping over rubble, I felt practiced at it. I cautiously made my way to the kitchen and tried that light switch. The room burst into view. As in the living room, everything not nailed down had been tipped over, including the refrigerator. Its door gaped open and frozen packages of meat and containers and ice cubes splayed across the tiles. I took note of the fact that the ice cubes were half-melted.

With trembling hands I opened my cell phone and dialed 911 and reported the break-in. While waiting for the police I stood in the lighted kitchen, not wanting to venture into the back of the house until they arrived.

When I was closing the phone, I noticed I had messages and remembered that I'd turned the phone off for the funeral. All five recorded messages were from my publisher, each one more frantic than the last.

"Call me," the final message said. "I don't care what time it is." He included his home phone number. I closed the phone and stuck it in my pocket.

The police walked me through the house. They assigned an officer to make a list of what was missing. The big items were all there; the television, stereo, my bicycle. My laptop was missing.

"Work-related?" a female officer asked me.

"Yeah."

"Any sensitive material? Account numbers?"

"Um—just personal banking records."

"What company do you work for?"

"I'm a writer. Self-employed."

"Oh. So nothing anyone could use."

I'd like to think whoever stole the laptop would read my chapters, recognize the quality of writing, and be tempted to sell the material to a publisher, passing themselves off as the author.

"No," I said to the officer. "Nothing anyone could use. My backup drive is also missing."

"Do you keep a copy off site?" she asked.

"Just the backup."

"Printout copy?"

"Just the backup."

"You know, sir, you really should have an off-site copy of all your important files. Do you have the serial number of your laptop?"

It took me a while to find it. It was stapled to a receipt in last year's income tax file. The officer wasn't optimistic the laptop would be recovered.

My emotions, which had bottomed out before I returned home, went subterranean. It was nearly eleven o'clock—2:00 A.M. New York time—when I called my New York publisher.

"Grant," the half-asleep voice said on the other line.

"I was going to wait until morning," I said.

"No . . . no . . . I needed to talk to you before 8:00 A.M. my time."

That can't be good.

"Where are my chapters?" he said.

I scanned the mess that was my condo. "Um—see, here's the thing—"

"Grant, it's 2:00 A.M. Do you have my chapters, or don't you?"

"I had a break-in," I explained. "The police just left. Someone stole my laptop."

Silence. Then, "Did you have a backup?"

"They stole that, too."

"Hard copy?"

"Look, Paul, I can rewrite the chapters."

Even as I said it, I felt doubtful. I could write new chapters, but how do you re-create the inspiration? The stolen chapters were the best writing I'd ever done.

I could hear Paul Higgins breathing on the other end of the line and could only wonder what Mrs. Higgins was thinking of me right about now.

"That won't be necessary, Grant," Higgins said.

"Paul—Mr. Higgins, I can get the chapters to you. Believe me, it's some of my best writing, better than—"

"Did someone really break into your house and steal your laptop?" Higgins asked.

"You think I made that up as an excuse?"

"Grant, I've worked with writers for thirty years. It wouldn't be the first time."

It angered me that he thought I was lying. "I can send you a copy of the police report."

"No, it's just as well. Grant, we're canceling your contract."

"What? No! Paul—"

"I was going to make the decision in the morning anyway," Higgins said. "I just thought if you had the book nearly finished—"

"But why?"

There was a rustling as Higgins repositioned himself in bed. "It's a marketing decision. So much has happened since the assassination. The coming of Neo Jesus. The filing of impeachment papers against President Rossi."

"Wait . . . what was that? Rossi is being impeached?"

"What hole have you had your head stuck in all day, Grant? It's been all over the news. The *Washington Post* broke the story this morning. Rossi has been linked to gambling and the New York mafia."

"He'll resign," I said, more to myself than Higgins.

"Not likely," Higgins exclaimed. "They'll find a workaround. Nobody wants Lamott to become president."

No humans maybe. Semyaza had predicted this scenario while we stood on the deck of the *Midway* and watched Douglas's assassination. Lamott was the rebel angels' man. I tried to remember exactly what Semyaza had said. With Lamott as president, in the absence of real leadership, special interest groups will tear the nation apart.

"Anyway, between Rossi and this Neo Jesus creature calling for a worldwide scientific summit—"

"He what?"

"For crying out loud, Grant. Turn on the television."

"I've been at a funeral all day."

"Sorry. A close friend?"

"Yeah," I said, surprised at how close the professor was to me.

Higgins swore. "Now I feel like a jerk giving you this news today. But it came down to this, Grant. No one could have foreseen it, but the world has moved on. President Douglas's assassination is ancient history. Marketing insists they won't be able to move the books. Maybe we can try it again in twenty or twenty-five years, to coincide with an anniversary of the assassination. So keep your notes."

"They were on the computer, too," I said.

My cell phone rang moments after I closed it. It was Jana.

"Grant? Did you know about this summit of scientists in Geneva?"

"Yeah, I—"

"Why didn't you tell me? I thought we had an agreement. Ostermann has been all over my producer to send him. If I don't get some kind of interview with Neo Jesus soon—"

"I just found out myself," I said.

"He's . . . he's there with you right now?"

"From my publisher."

"Your publisher? What's he doing calling you in the middle of the night?"

"Canceling my contract."

"Oh, Grant, I'm so sorry. Are you all right? Sue's asleep. Do you want me to come over?"

"Thanks, but this wouldn't be a good time. The place is a mess."

I figured I'd tell her tomorrow about the break-in. She apologized again and said good night, but not before reminding me that I'd promised to get her an interview with Neo Jesus.

With mattresses on opposite sides of the room and the floor of my bedroom a display for the contents of my bureau, I had plenty to do before I could sleep. But the bedroom would have to wait. If I didn't get the chicken and meat and frozen dinners back in the freezer, I'd regret it in the morning.

Walking out of the bedroom, my heart nearly leaped out of my chest. I wasn't alone.

"You should consider hiring a maid."

Jesus stood in the middle of my living room. Rather, Belial impersonating Jesus.

"Is there a heavenly equivalent to the cowbell?" I asked him.

"To what purpose? If we wore bells, people would know we were here. Oh, a joke. Sarcasm. I'm more of a slapstick humorist myself."

"So I've noticed."

Belial wandered around freely, glancing into each room. "This was . . . unnecessary."

"You know . . . Semyaza!"

"He doesn't want Abdiel's foolishness to become public," Belial said.

"That's what this is about?"

I went over to the cabinet where I keep my files. That's where I'd put the printouts of the angel history. They were gone.

"All this to get a couple of chapters?"

"No. All of this to get to you. He knew where the chapters were."

Enraged, I picked up the closest object within reach, my own book, and flung it across the room, shattering the lamp on the floor.

Belial sighed sympathetically. "Semyaza has that effect on people . . . and angels. He will do anything to hurt you. And since he can't hurt you directly, he'll hurt those closest to you."

"The professor."

"An unnecessary death."

"Abdiel said Lucifer ordered it."

Belial laughed. "Abdiel? You don't know how funny that is. Do you really think Abdiel knows the decisions made in Lucifer's council? Semyaza alone planned and executed the professor's death. His purpose was twofold: to prevent the dissemination of the angel narrative, and to hurt you. Mostly, to hurt you."

If that was his plan, he'd succeeded gloriously. I thought of Sue Ling and Jana, and Christina in Washington. They were in danger for no other reason than that their deaths would injure me.

"And your role in this is what?" I said, trying to remain calm. "Report back to Semyaza and tell him he succeeded?"

Belial frowned. "You wound me. I am not Semyaza's man. There are many of us who grow increasingly disgusted with his tactics. Does that surprise you? Give it time, Grant, and you will learn that we are not the united horde you make us out to be."

"Then why are you here?"

He appeared hurt by my tone. "No reason," he said, shrugging it off. "I've said what I came to say. I'll take my leave."

"Wait!"

He looked at me suspiciously. "I like you, Grant. But I draw the line at helping you clean up."

"I have a friend who . . . well, it would mean a lot to me if you could give her an interview."

"Your reporter friend? Jana Torres?"

I didn't like that he remembered her name.

Belial grinned. "I can think of worse ways to spend thirty minutes. Tell her it can be arranged."

CHAPTER

15

"You have to respect a man with this many books," I said, loading my twelfth cardboard box. Sue and I stood waist-deep in boxes in the professor's college office. I held up a small blue volume. "I have just one question for you. What's a Polyglot?"

Sue studied the word on the book spine. "It's a book about parrot languages."

"Parrot languages?"

"Polyglot a cracker?"

We laughed. Of course it was silly, but silly felt good and it became the tone for the day. Along with polyglot jokes.

"What's a polyglot?"

"Anything he can hold in his claws."

We didn't care that our jokes made no sense.

"What should I do with this?"

"Polyglot it."

It felt good to laugh. Even better to see Sue Ling laughing.

Ever since the professor's death she'd appeared smaller, frail and vulnerable. It hurt to see her this way.

I hadn't told her about my book contract being canceled or the break-in. I didn't want to add to her sadness right now. If silly wordplay lifted her spirits, I was all for it.

With the books packed, I turned to the walls, taking down diplomas, awards, pictures. All the photos were school-related except for three framed portraits on the desk. One of the professor with his wife's arms around his neck. One of his daughters. And one of Sue Ling.

"Look at this." I removed a plaque from the wall. The professor's coat of arms. "Forsythe is Scottish. It means, 'a man of peace.' The family motto is: *Instaurator ruinac.*"

I stopped short of the translation, wishing I'd read it before saying it.

"Repairer of ruin," Sue translated.

"Yeah."

Having spent yesterday tramping through the rubble that had once been the professor's house, I feared the motto would dampen Sue's spirit. I was grateful that it didn't.

I found a scratchpad square of paper taped to the wall so that it could be seen while sitting at the desk. It was a quotation from Dante, supposedly given to him by his hero, the poet Virgil:

> *Whatever plot these fiends may lay against us, we will go on. This insolence of theirs is nothing new.*

"Can I have this?" I asked.

"A piece of notepad paper, Grant?"

I showed it to her.

"That's his handwriting," she said. "Take it."

She turned away, and as she did all the silliness left her. The quotation did what I feared the coat of arms would do. It reminded her that the professor was a casualty of war.

"I've decided to work on my dissertation," she said. "It will take a while to get back into it, but I think I can finish it in a year."

"Dr. Sue," I said with a grin. "That sounds better than Sue the doctor, doesn't it?"

She didn't laugh. The good times were gone.

"If you need help with research on your book," she said, "or want me to proof the pages for you, let me know. It would look good on my resume to say I assisted Grant Austin with his second Pulitzer Prize–winning book."

That stung. I thanked her for the offer and let it pass.

"I'm moving back to my apartment tonight," she said. "I've imposed on Jana long enough, though it has seemed like old times living together again. It's going to take a while adjusting to living at my apartment. I usually only sleep there." A pause, then, "You can come visit me."

"You know I will. Besides, it's not like we won't be seeing each other. We still have the training sessions."

She'd been pulling files from a cabinet. She stopped. "You're still going through with the training?"

"Of course I am. I'm not going to let Semyaza get away with this."

She became smaller just standing there. Her head bowed. Her shoulders sagged. Fear glazed her eyes. Was she frightened for me, or for herself?

"You'll help me, won't you?" I said. "I need someone on my side. All Abdiel does is yell at me."

"Abdiel's continuing your training?" she asked.

"Why wouldn't he?"

"Why would he?"

She had a point. I had just assumed Abdiel would continue training me. But he had always participated at the professor's request, hadn't he? And even then he often acted as though he didn't want to be there.

Without Sue and Abdiel, I was sunk.

I placed the pictures on the desk and went to her. She didn't look up. As often as I'd felt the sting of her sharp tongue, the heat of her fiery gaze, and the painful jab of her wit, I preferred them to the defeated woman standing before me. I wanted to take her in my arms, press her to my chest, rest my cheek against her head, and assure her that everything would all right. But if I made a move toward her and she recoiled, the damage between us would be irreparable.

"Sue, I need you. Your knowledge. Your encouragement. Your friendship. Nobody understands me like you do. If I get Abdiel to agree to continue the training, will you help me?"

For a long time she said nothing. I gave her the time she needed. The longer she took, the more I convinced myself she was searching for the words to turn me down.

"I'll help you if you answer one question to my satisfaction."

"OK," I replied hesitantly.

"How many glots has a polyglot got if a polyglot could glot polys?" She looked up at me with an impish grin.

I laughed. "How long have you been cooking up that one?"

"Most of the morning," she said with a smirk.

Abdiel agreed to continue my training with reluctance. What he disapproved of most was that I had badgered him for two days to get him to appear. I called to him in my apartment, at the beach, on the patio at Heritage College (the librarian complained and security asked me to leave), and standing in the rubble on the professor's property. I even called out to him in the shower, since he appeared to enjoy popping in at inconvenient moments.

"I'm not your genie in a bottle," he complained.

"Fine. Get a cell phone and I'll text you."

My training resumed three days after the professor's funeral in my condominium's recreation room. My place was still a mess, and Sue's apartment was too small. The rec room seemed the logical choice. It was large and people rarely used it during the day.

The room had a billiard table, a Ping-Pong table, a wet bar, and a wall lined with video arcade games, including Ms. Pac-Man, Asteroids, Golden Tee Golf, and a Spiderman pinball machine. A bulletin board was plastered with notices from the association, lost-animal flyers, and appliances for sale. In other words, it was a perfect location for spiritual warfare tactics.

Sue sat at a table on a folding chair, a stack of physics textbooks beside her. Abdiel and I stood facing each other in the center of the room. Two things united us: devotion to the professor and the common goal of finding a way to unmask Belial and thwart this worldwide deception. For some reason he'd taken a liking to me. Maybe we could take advantage of that.

"If he can't see swords, he can't defend himself!" Abdiel insisted.

"Maybe he's incapable of seeing swords. Did you ever think of that?" Sue said.

My training had picked up right where it left off.

"If he can see angels, he can see swords," Abdiel insisted.

"Are you accusing Grant of lying?" Sue challenged.

Sue had been disagreeable ever since Abdiel appeared. I

should have realized she would hold him accountable for the professor's death. And she was miffed at me for having to hear about my canceled book contract and condo break-in from Jana.

I was equally frustrated. No matter how hard I tried I could not see Abdiel's sword unless he showed it to me. If it was as easy as he said it was, why couldn't I do it?

"Let's try the teleportation again," I suggested.

"How can I make you understand?" Abdiel said. "If you cannot see an enemy's sword—"

"We'll come back to it. You have my word."

That seemed to satisfy him. It placated Sue. And it gave me a chance to succeed at something. I didn't want to admit it, but I was getting discouraged. If I was able to see my sword right now, I was afraid it would look like a limp spear of asparagus.

"Try taking it one step at a time again," Sue suggested. "Try the wall."

With Abdiel beside me, I put my toes against the wall. He raised a hand and I fended it off. "You're not going to smash my head into the wall again, are you?"

"It seemed to knock some sense into you last time," Abdiel replied.

Sue reminded me of the physics. Theoretically, given the vast amount of space in the universe even on the tiniest level, a normal person could do this given enough attempts. Being part angel, I had an advantage.

"I'm ready," I said.

With Abdiel's hand on my shoulder, side by side we stepped through the wall, emerging poolside. I felt some resistance going through the wall, but it wasn't difficult and, more important, it didn't hurt. Coming back through was even easier.

"Now try it on your own," Abdiel said.

"Wait!" Sue jumped out of her chair. "Grant, do you think you should?"

The latent junior-high kid inside me was shouting, *"Are you kidding? This is so cool!"* The adult Grant was worried that I might get stuck halfway through.

"If that happens, I'll pull you out," Abdiel said.

"I'm going to do it," I said.

Sue folded her arms and took a step back.

I stood with my nose to the wall and took a deep breath. Closing my eyes, I thought about what it felt like to pass through the wall. I leaned forward.

My forehead felt a cool pressure from the drywall. I felt resistance, like walking into a stiff breeze. Leaning into it, I took a step. It felt like the molecules of the wall were trying to congeal around me. I pressed harder.

I cleared the outer edge. The resistance gave way, and I stumbled onto the deck just as one of my neighbors was walking past the pool, looking at his mail.

My sudden appearance startled him. Envelopes went flying. He jumped away, found the edge of the pool, did the windmill thing with his arms, and splashed into the water.

I jumped back through the wall before he surfaced.

"Grant, you did it!" Sue gave me a congratulatory hug.

Abdiel was proud of me. I was proud of me.

"I think I'm ready to try that dimension thing again," I said.

"Grant, are you sure?" Sue had hold of my arm.

"I've completed step one. Step two is the logical next . . . well, step."

Abdiel was already looking for a thinning of the dimensional membrane. "Over here," he said, motioning me to a spot in front of Ms. Pac-Man.

"Grant . . ." Sue said.

"I really want to do this, Sue. One of Semyaza's strategic advantages is his ability to choose where and when our confrontations take place. If I can do this, I'll be able to escape if necessary, or follow him and confront him at a time and place of my choosing."

I didn't say it, but I thought that if the professor had had this ability, he'd still be alive.

"Besides," I said, "think of the money I'll save on airfare."

Abdiel positioned me in front of the membrane. I couldn't see it, but this time I could feel something there. Cold. Gelatinous. Abdiel put his hand on my shoulder.

"We'll try it slower this time," Abdiel said.

I nodded. My heart hammered. I thought I could feel my breath bouncing back into my face. Something was definitely there.

I prepared myself the same way I had with the wall. Eyes closed. Imagining myself going through it.

Following Abdiel's lead, I took a step.

The next thing I remember was moaning with the cool tile floor pressing against my back. Sue was on her knees bending over me. I heard her voice echoing down a long tunnel.

"Grant? Grant!"

"Is it possible to bruise atoms?" I asked. "Because every atom in my body aches."

She helped me into a chair.

"You progressed farther than last time," Abdiel said.

"And you were unconscious longer!" Sue added.

"I suppose we're done for the day," Abdiel said. "I will take my leave."

"Wait," Sue said. "I want to try something else."

"I would have thought you'd be the first one wanting to quit," I said.

"As would I," Abdiel added, also taken aback.

"Sue, if you want me to try to fly, I'm afraid my wings are a little tired."

She wasn't listening. Neither was she smiling.

"I've been thinking," she said, "about the mark. Exactly what does it protect Grant from, and more important, what does it not protect him from?"

"It doesn't make me impervious to pain," I said, my head still spinning. "And it doesn't make me immortal."

"Are you certain of that?" Sue said. "I mean, for at least while you have the mark?"

"The mark protects me from Lucifer and Semyaza," I said. "I don't think it protects me if I step off a cliff."

"Or force your body through a dimensional membrane," Sue said.

"Abdiel's there to pull me out," I said.

"But will he always be there for you?" Sue asked.

I saw what she was getting at.

"The mark protects Grant from being possessed by demons," Abdiel said. "It is a mark of God's favor."

"But he's still vulnerable," she said. "What happens if he dies?"

We all knew the answer to that. I was destined to be a demon.

"That's what I've been thinking about," Sue said. "What can we do to change that?"

"His fate is sealed," Abdiel said.

"Is it?" Sue challenged him. "How do you know?"

"Since the time of the deluge, all Nephilim share the same fate," he replied. "Grant is Nephilim."

"He's also human," Sue said.

"His Nephilim blood condemns him."

"Maybe his human blood can save him," Sue said. "Has anyone tried? Hear me out. I've been thinking a lot about this. The Nephilim lived mainly in the Old Testament, right? There have been just a handful of Nephilim who have lived on this side of the cross. Have any of them tried to be saved? Have they prayed for salvation?"

"To what purpose?" Abdiel said. "Salvation is not for Nephilim."

"But we don't know that until someone tries, do we?" Sue insisted.

I liked her thinking. "Abdiel, do you know of any Nephilim praying for salvation?"

"And remember, Grant's *grandfather* is an angel," Sue added. "That makes Grant only one-quarter angel, three-quarters human. It's worth trying, isn't it?"

"But if I am saved," I said, "will I lose the mark?"

"You'll have the seal of God on you," Sue said. "That will protect you from demons, and from becoming a demon."

I looked to Abdiel. "What do you think?"

"It pleases me to serve the Father," he said. And when I started to say something, he added, "It is His decision to make."

"But you'll be able to tell whether or not it works?" I asked.

"I am able to see who belongs to the Father," he said.

"Well then, let's ask Him to make a decision," I said. "Sue, what do I need to do?"

"You must humble yourself before God, and agree with Him that your sins make you unfit to dwell in His holy kingdom, and that nothing you say or do can change that. Then you acknowledge that Jesus, His sinless son, took the penalty for your sins upon Himself on the cross. You accept His sacrifice on your behalf and pledge to live your life acknowledging Him as your savior and Lord."

"At which point the Spirit enters you," Abdiel said.

"Any words I need to recite?" I asked.

"The Father knows the intentions of your heart," Abdiel re-plied before Sue could.

I stood on shaky legs. "All right, let's do this," I said, ner-vously, fully aware that my destiny hung in the balance. "If you don't mind, I think I'd like to do this alone."

There was a supply-and-game closet on the opposite side of the room. I crossed the tile floor and shut the door behind me.

Stacks of board games filled the shelves, along with billiard supplies, Ping-Pong paddles and balls, and cleaning supplies. It struck me as odd that the course of my eternity would be deter-mined in a game closet.

I got down on my knees and prayed, remembering Sue's in-structions. But it was Abdiel's comment that I relied on most. *"The Father knows the intentions of your heart."*

I closed my eyes in prayer and let my intentions be known.

When I opened them, I tried to assess if I could tell if it took or not. I felt good for making the decision, as I did when I de-clared my intentions to serve the Father on top of the Emerald Plaza. Other than that—

There was only one way to find out for sure. I stood and opened the supply closet door.

Sue looked expectantly at me, then at Abdiel. "Well?" she said to me.

"I did it."

She turned to Abdiel. "Well?"

The big angel didn't appear to hear her. His eyes were stead-fastly on me.

"I was as sincere as I can be," I told him.

He gazed at me with deep sorrow. "I'm sorry, Grant. The Spirit is not within you."

I thought I was ready for it, but the news hit me hard. "As you said, it's the Father's decision. It was worth a try."

Abdiel left a short time after that. Sue and I sat at the table. She took my hand.

"It's not you, Grant. You didn't choose to be born Nephilim. Don't take it personally."

I chuckled. "Why would I take it personally? All I did was ask God to save me and he refused."

CHAPTER
16

That night, following my failed salvation attempt, I fought off a gnawing sensation of doom by keeping myself busy restoring order to my condo. Sue offered to help me. I thanked her, but I wanted to be alone. My condo wasn't the only thing in a shambles. I had a career to resurrect. At least I had a measure of control over it, unlike my eternal destiny, over which I had no control.

I hated to admit it but, having been reminded that I was a demon-in-waiting, I shared the same hopeless desperation. And—this was even harder to admit—I believed I knew how Lucifer and his crew felt as well. Being doomed without hope of reprieve colors a person's perspective. You can't face a destiny of hellish eternity with no exit and not have it affect your thoughts and decisions.

Once the bedroom and kitchen were livable again, I turned my attention to the living room. That's when I noticed I wasn't alone.

I wasn't frightened this time. I guess I was getting used to angels popping in and out of my private space.

"I don't suppose you're bringing me glad tidings of great joy," I said.

Abdiel appeared more subdued than usual.

"When the professor first asked me to meet you," he said without greeting, "I resisted."

"Yeah, I remember. You made a comment about me being a half-breed."

"At the time I figured you were Semyaza's man."

"You figured wrong."

"You surprised me."

Abdiel got down on his knees next to me and helped me gather up DVDs and arrange them on a shelf. He hovered. Neither his knees nor his feet touched the carpet.

"I couldn't understand why the professor spoke highly of you," Abdiel said. "He believed in you. He still does."

Although it wasn't news, the comment set me back. The professor was still pulling for me. The thought was a much-needed tonic.

"I don't like working with humans," Abdiel said softly.

"Not exactly a newsflash."

He registered the sarcasm, then let it pass. "What might not be as obvious are my reasons for feeling this way. I keep my distance because I have become overly fond of you."

I laughed. "You're fond of me? You certainly hide it well."

"Humans. Creation in general, humans specifically."

I grinned. "You're fond of me!" I said, rubbing it in.

"You misunderstand what I am saying."

Irritated, he set a handful of DVDs on the shelf and stood. I smiled up at him sweetly, stopping short of batting my eyelashes.

"You are the crown of creation," he snapped.

"I thought you'd never notice!" I gushed.

He let out an angry grunt. "I can see I'm wasting my time on you. I will take my leave."

"No . . . wait." I stood up. "I'd like to hear what you have to say. I apologize. I tend to get spiteful whenever I'm turned down for salvation."

"You have a touch of Lucifer in you," he said.

"Now that's just mean."

"You forget. I loved Lucifer. His ambition and bitterness warped him. It will do the same to you if you give in to it."

"You were about to tell me of your fondness for creation," I prompted. I figured that since I'd been the one to knock us off topic, I should be the one to pull us back on.

For a moment Abdiel's gaze drifted away from the present to past memories. "I cannot begin to describe to you the eloquence of pristine creation. Neither can I do justice to the depth of longing within us to interact with this new race of beings. You must understand, we loved you at first sight. With eager anticipation we looked forward to introducing you to the wonders of the cosmos. Then Lucifer poisoned the waters with sin. It worked as a catalyst, moving ever outward, and so it will continue until every molecule of creation is utterly corrupt."

A sadness fell over Abdiel such as I had never seen. His ache was so powerful I could feel it.

"It had never occurred to us that Lucifer would deface the Father's creation. By us, I mean the whole angelic realm. Of course the Father knew. I can remember a time when all Lucifer could talk about was the Father's plans for a new created order. He looked forward to it as much as any of us. And then for us to see it disfigured by sin—" Abdiel's voice trailed off.

Then he added, "To see the crown of creation disfigured by sin."

It struck me that this was no longer the confession of an angel who didn't like me, but an eyewitness account of the beginning of cosmic history. I wished I was recording it.

"Our fondness for you explains our eagerness to dispatch the Father's messages to you."

"But you said you don't like working with humans," I reminded him.

"That is true."

"How can you love humans and not like working with them?"

He looked at me quizzically. "Of all people, I thought you would understand."

"Why me?"

"You love Sue Ling."

I started to deny it, but knew I could never make a convincing argument.

"But because of who you are, your love puts her in danger."

"She would be better off if she didn't know me."

"Lucifer and Semyaza know how I feel about humans. Down through the centuries they have attacked those to whom I ministered."

"Including the professor," I said.

"Semyaza struck a threefold blow when he killed Professor Forsythe."

"Sue, me . . . and you."

"Now you understand why I do not wish to work with you, even though the professor has pleaded to the Father that I do so."

"And you are pleased to serve the Father."

Abdiel liked my answer. "So, you can be taught."

"I still can't see swords."

"How do you expect to—" He stopped midsentence. "I am certain that in time you will develop the skill."

Several seconds passed with neither of us speaking, and neither of us wanting the conversation to end.

"Do I have a say in this?" I asked him.

"Less than you think."

"What if I petitioned the Father in prayer? He still listens to my prayers, doesn't He?"

"He is the Father."

"I'll take that as a yes. You see, the way I figure it, Semyaza already has it in for me. So it's not like you're putting me in danger."

"My association with you would increase his incentive."

"Let's say that's true. I still have the mark of the Father protecting me, right? The other people you've hung out with can't say that."

"Angels of the Most High don't hang out."

"So, you'll do it?"

"It pleases me to—"

"Yeah, I know. It's up to the Father."

"What would you have me teach you?" Abdiel asked.

"To see swords, for one thing."

"I fear that is a lost cause."

"But you just said—oh, I get it. Very good. You're catching on."

Abdiel appeared pleased with himself.

"And you can explain to me why you never touch the ground. What is that all about?"

"We will save that explanation for another time," Abdiel said.

"One thing more."

"Yes?"

"I want you to dictate to me the angel history. The more I know about angels, the better equipped I'll be to do battle against those who rebelled."

Abdiel's brow furrowed. "Semyaza killed the professor to keep that history out of human hands."

"That's why I want it."

"You did what?" Sue Ling cried. "What were you thinking?"

She held two breakfast plates in her hands. She set one down at her place and dropped mine in front of me. At impact a biscuit jumped and a bit of scrambled egg and a sausage leaped off the plate. The sausage rolled over the edge of the table before I could catch it.

Sue turned away and walked to the sink.

I should have waited until after breakfast to tell her I'd asked Abdiel to dictate the angel history to me.

Sue had called early this morning to tell me she was coming over to fix me breakfast. It was her way of checking up on me to see if I was all right after yesterday's disappointment in the rec room.

"What kind of breakfast do you want?" she'd asked. "My breakfast—or the professor's breakfast?"

"What's your breakfast?"

"Lowfat yogurt on cereal and orange juice."

"And the professor's?"

"Eggs, sausage, biscuit, and coffee."

"With gravy?"

"I draw the line at gravy."

When she'd arrived, she'd arrived with a smile. The smile made up for the gravy. It was good to see Sue Ling happy again.

Thanks to me, that didn't last long.

Pushing away from the table, I approached her. Her head was bowed. Her hands clenched the side of the sink.

"I thought you'd be pleased," I said to the back of her head.

She wheeled around. "Pleased?" Her eyes were brimming with fury and tears. "Pleased? Why don't you just stand in the middle of what's left of the professor's house and curse Semyaza until he kills you, too?"

"He can't touch me. I have—"

"Oh, well, that's just great," Sue snapped. "They can't touch you. But what about me? Or Jana? Or Christina? Have you thought about anyone but yourself? What's to keep them from leveling the entire city of El Cajon just to get back at you? You saw what they did to the Bay Bridge. That's just a fraction of what they can do. Firestorm. Hurricane. Earthquake. Grant, these are the forces at their command."

Until now I hadn't realized how deep Sue Ling's fear was.

"Why do you think I wanted to find all the copies of that blasted history?" she said.

"I thought you were trying to recover the professor's last project."

As soon as the words were out, I knew I should have phrased it differently. Her tears came freely now. She turned her head in a futile attempt to stop them.

"I wanted to make sure any remaining pages, any remaining media, any remaining data was destroyed," she said through her tears.

"And this morning—" I said, sensing the real reason for breakfast.

"I came to get the chapters Jana and I delivered to you. Do you have them?"

It was my turn to get angry. "You should have just told me

what you wanted. You could have saved yourself a trip, and a breakfast. Semyaza beat you to them."

For several moments we glared at each other. Then she gathered her things and stormed out.

"And thanks for your underwhelming concern for me," I yelled at her back. When she didn't respond to that, I added, "If the professor wanted it, you would have made him gravy!"

Her answer was to slam the front door.

I moved to the table and looked down at the ruins of breakfast. Picking up a link of sausage with my fingers I bit it in half. It was cold.

Bent over the back of the sofa, I fumbled with the electrical cord. It took me several attempts before I hit the outlet. I was thinking about Sue. Was I signing her death warrant by doing this?

"You appear troubled," Abdiel said.

"I've never interviewed an angel," I replied.

"You fear that this will jeopardize your friends. Do you wish to reconsider?"

I plugged the other end of the cord into a microdigital recorder. "I hope you don't mind if I record this."

Whenever it was available I used outlet current. That way I didn't have to worry about the batteries wearing down midinterview.

"I do not mind," Abdiel said.

I spoke into the recorder. "Test, test, test. This is Grant Austin, and I am interviewing—"

I motioned for Abdiel to speak into the recorder. He leaned toward it.

"Abdiel, servant of the Most High God."

I clicked the recorder off to check the levels. The recorder picked up my voice clearly, but for some reason, not a single word Abdiel spoke had been recorded.

"That's odd," I said. "Let's try it again."

"The results will be the same. An angel's voice cannot be recorded. I would have to take on human form to generate the required sound waves."

"Why didn't you say that earlier?"

"You asked if I minded being recorded. I don't mind."

"How much trouble would it be—"

"You want me to expend tremendous amounts of energy just so you don't have to apply yourself?"

"Fine." I set the recorder aside. "We'll do this the old-fashioned way."

Which wasn't too far from the truth. With no laptop I was reduced to a yellow legal pad and a pen.

The angel launched into his narrative.

"How do I, Abdiel, Seraph of the heavens, describe to humans clothed in flesh the horrors of celestial war? How do I explain countless dimensions to beings—"

"Um—wait."

"Did you run out of ink already?"

"Ink's fine," I said. "Before we get to the narrative, I want you to tell me about—"

I pointed with my pen to his feet, which were two inches above the carpet.

"What is your fascination with angel feet?"

"What is your reluctance to tell me? I want to know why angels' feet don't touch the ground."

Abdiel stood motionless for so long I thought he was going to refuse.

"It is to our shame that we do not," he said, "for there was a time when we walked the earth freely."

"In the beginning," I said, "before Lucifer poisoned it with sin."

Abdiel nodded. "Very perceptive. We are accustomed to walking on fiery stones on heaven's mount in the midst of the eternal sea. To touch something that has been corrupted by sin—"

"Is repulsive to you."

"You understand."

"Semyaza once told me it was repulsive for him to take the form of a human."

"Centuries ago, during the time you call the Middle Ages, I ministered to a man who told me he had once been sewn up in the carcass of a rotting, maggot-filled moose. He had an elementary understanding of what it is like for us to touch a sinful cosmos. The effect on us is more deeply corrosive. The sight alone is painful."

"It hurts you to look at us?"

"Like a mother looking at her mangled child."

"But where is the shame? There's no shame in turning aside from something unpleasant."

Abdiel looked down, troubled. While I didn't yet understand it, his disgrace was obviously real.

"When Lucifer's rebellion was put down, a series of punishments were enacted. Some of the rebels were thrown into a dark dimension, where they are being held until the day of judgment. Others, along with Lucifer, were denied residency in heaven. However, they were allowed to attend the heavenly council."

"Why didn't the Father throw all of them into the dark dimension?" I asked.

"The Father is merciful. He gave Lucifer an opportunity to repent. From the beginning, Lucifer had been enamored of God's cosmic creation. By giving Lucifer continued access to it, he could have chosen to fulfill his original role and administer his responsibilities to the glory of the Son."

"Instead, he poisoned it."

"Not only poisoned it, but terrorized it. Of course, his most reprehensible act was attacking the Son when He came to earth. For that, following his defeat at the cross, Lucifer and his followers have been forever denied heaven. They will never again walk the fiery stones."

"So he's trapped in the very creation he poisoned," I said.

"Lucifer has petitioned the Father repeatedly, arguing that this punishment is too cruel."

"You still haven't explained how this brings shame to the angelic realm."

We had arrived at the moment of truth and Abdiel was reluctant to continue.

"Lucifer uses our refusal to touch the cosmos as the capstone of his argument that his punishment is unbearable."

"And the Father's response?" I asked.

"*Behold, my Son.*"

At last I understood. "*And the Son became flesh and dwelt among us.*"

"When He walked on the earth He left footprints," Abdiel said. "Something Lucifer would never do."

As I wrote this down, I formulated my next question. I had done my homework for this interview. Humiliated by the fiasco of the presidential biography, I had made myself a pledge that I would never again take an interview or a bit of research at face value. I would corroborate it with further research.

On the sofa next to me were three books. One of them was the Bible. I opened it to a place I'd marked.

"It says here—"

> *And there was a war in heaven. Michael and his angels fought against the dragon, and the dragon and his angels fought back. But he was not strong enough and they lost their place in heaven. The great dragon was hurled down—that ancient serpent called the devil or Satan, who leads the whole world astray. He was hurled to the earth and his angels with him. . . . Therefore, rejoice you heavens and you who dwell in them! But woe to the earth and the sea, because the devil has gone down to you! He is filled with fury, because he knows that his time is short.*

"The revelation to John," Abdiel said, identifying the source. I wasn't finished. I selected a second passage I'd marked. "And it says here—"

> *. . . God did not spare angels when they sinned, but sent them to Tartarus, putting them in gloomy dungeons to be held for judgment . . .*

"The revelation to Peter," Abdiel said.

I looked up. "So, Lucifer and those who rebelled have been cast out of heaven and are awaiting judgment."

"Correct."

"Cast down to the earth."

"The cosmos. Correct."

"But this second passage says God sent them to Tartarus. Some translations interpret that as hell."

"*Gehenna* is hell. The word given to Peter is *Tartarus*."

"This is the place Belial is using in his scam. Only, according to him, Tartarus is an inhabited world on a subatomic scale."

Abdiel stiffened. "Belial is using the name deceptively."

"So, these two passages—"

"Say the same thing."

"Which makes Tartarus—"

"The cosmos," Abdiel said.

"Gloomy dungeons?"

"Once you walk on heaven's fiery stones, this world of sin will appear to you as a gloomy dungeon. Its chains are space and time, a severe prison for beings who were created for eternity and limitless dimensions."

Abdiel must have forgotten who he was talking to, because I would never have a chance to walk on heaven's fiery stones. And since this is the only world I have ever known, I found it difficult to think of it as a gloomy dungeon, what with its sunsets and majestic peaks and oceans and panoramic skies. Yet, for all its beauty, this was the corrupted version.

One thing was certain, though. I took pleasure in the thought that, for Lucifer and Semyaza, it was a gloomy dungeon and that they were imprisoned and doing time for their crimes while awaiting sentencing.

CHAPTER

17

Sue phoned and asked me to meet her at La Jolla Cove.

When she called, I was reviewing the notes of my first session with Abdiel. Replaying it in my head. Jotting down comments in the margins. The conversation with Sue was short. I sensed no residual anger from this morning.

As I approached the coast the sun was lowering itself into the water like a weary traveler easing into a hot tub. Orange and yellow hues splashed brilliantly across the horizon against a deep blue sea.

If this was a gloomy dungeon, heaven had to be beyond magnificent. But then, I'll never know, will I? Like a dogged companion, doom accompanied me down the hill. I shoved him out the door. Three's company, and I didn't want any foreboding feelings around during this rendezvous with Sue Ling.

I was in luck. The parking gods smiled on me. I found a space within a block of the cove. Sue was waiting for me beside a low, whitewashed wall. She gazed down at the cove, watching the carefree activity of the beachgoers.

On the drive there I'd formulated a strategy. Apologize quickly. Apologize profusely.

"Sue, I—"

She placed a hand over my mouth, and I saw something in her eyes I'd never seen from her before. Affection. The hand over my mouth was unnecessary. The look in her eyes struck me dumb.

Taking me by the hand, she led me along the walkway. We came to a path leading down to the tide pools. She sat on the wall, swung her legs over, and pulled me after her. We helped each other down a steep slope to a massive rock-staging area for sea activity. Waves crashed against the far edge, launching sprays of water twenty feet high. Tide pools dotted the surface. Deep fissures were narrow windows to the tidal forces below.

Hand in hand we peered into the tide pools, jumped the fissures, and ran to avoid the downpour of crashing waves, giggling like little kids. We mistimed a wave and paid the price with drenched hair and clothes.

Sue's laughing eyes sparkled brighter than the emerging stars. Drops of seawater freckled her cheeks.

In the dimming light people flattened into silhouettes against a rosy, pale, western sky. The rocks turned glossy black. The occasional flash of a tourist camera stamped postcard images in my mind.

Shivering, Sue pulled me by the hand up the slope. We nested on top of the wall and shared the panorama of a darkening ocean.

It had been years since I felt this happy. Her hands in her lap, Sue leaned against me for warmth. I had to remind myself that she was vulnerable. While this was a fantasy come true for me, it was therapeutic for her. Tonight she needed a friend, not a complication.

We sat in silence under night's canopy, enjoying the breeze, the scenery . . . and each other's company.

"This morning—" Sue said.

"Is past and forgotten," I replied.

She leaned back and grinned at me with incredulity. "The past is forgotten? That's an odd statement for a historian to make."

I grinned, too, though I didn't like being called a historian. I was a writer who did historical research when a project required it. But the moon was rising and—well, right now, who cared?

But Sue was ready to talk. "A physicist and a historian sat on a wall—"

I laughed. "Sounds like a joke. What's the punch line?"

"You tell me. Is it a joke? Or is it the beginning of a different kind of story?"

If she could have seen how my heart leaped at that moment, words would have been unnecessary.

"I hope it's not a joke," I said, keeping the tone light. "But if we're going to tell it, we need to rewrite the first line. How about, 'A physicist and a Nephilim sat on a wall—'"

The distance between us increased, though neither of us had moved.

I apologized. "I'm sorry, Sue Ling. I shouldn't have said that."

"No," she said softly. "You're right."

It did need to be said, but did it need to be said tonight? Right now? If I could have, I would have taken it back.

The silence stretched to a point where I thought the conversation was over. We would sit here a while longer, then we'd stumble over good-byes and she'd go home and I'd go home and tomorrow it would be as though tonight had never happened.

"Have you thought about having children?" Sue Ling said.

I laughed in spite of myself. "Whoa! Where did that come from?"

She smiled. "It's a logical queston, your being Nephilim."

"I did bring that up, didn't I?" I muttered. "Um—well, yeah, I've thought about it. How can I bring a life into this world, knowing that it's a future demon, that it's hopelessly doomed for eternity?"

"Have you come to terms with that for yourself?"

"No, not really. I tell myself I have, but there will always be part of me that hopes for a miracle or an escape clause. Some nights I pray that I'll wake up and realize it was all a bad dream and I'm just like everybody else."

Her hand squeezed mine; with the other hand she stroked my forearm. "I don't need children, Grant."

She didn't explain. She didn't have to. Her relationship with the professor would have raised the question of children long before now.

"Sue . . . this is too soon. I don't want to—"

"Take advantage of me?" She smiled seductively. "Did you ever think that I might be the one taking advantage of you?"

It was a delicious thought. I cautioned myself not to put too much stock in the images that conjured.

"This morning, when I came over to your condo, I didn't come just to get the manuscript. I came to try to talk you into moving away with me."

"Moving? Where?"

I knew it. I was going to lose her.

"Does it matter? Neither of us has roots here. You can write anywhere. All I need is a university within commuting distance.

I'll finish my Ph.D. and teach. You can write another Pulitzer Prize book."

"Book? Singular?"

"My, aren't we ambitious."

After a shared laugh we returned to the topic.

"We can't hide from them," I said. "It's not like they're the local mafia. No matter where we go, they'll find us."

"Don't you see? Moving is a symbolic gesture. It shows them you don't want anything to do with them and their war. There will be no reason for them to bother us."

"And since I have the protective mark . . ." I added.

"Exactly! You're no threat to them, and they can't touch you. We could live in a quiet little university town and make the most of the years given us."

A quiet, normal life with Sue Ling. What more could I hope for?

"When I met the professor," I said, "he told me to find a big hole and crawl into it. When I went to see Doc Palmer, he told me to disappear. He said that once the rebel angels saw I was no threat to them, they'd leave me alone."

"Isn't it time you realized they're right?" Sue said.

But there was something else to consider. Thoughts of the professor conjured up images of Semyaza summoning deadly winds to kill him. A part of me didn't want to slip quietly into the night with Sue Ling. It wanted to fight. It wanted revenge.

"Grant?" Sue said tentatively, sensing something was wrong. She stroked my fisted hand.

"I vowed to avenge the professor," I said.

"How?"

Her defiance was instant. Explosive.

"How, Grant?" she repeated. "Are you going to wrestle him

to the ground, cuff him, and turn him over to the authorities? Shoot him? As if that would do any good. Grant, you can't even give Semyaza a bloody nose."

"I've got to do something," I said stubbornly.

"Grant, I've seen you train, remember? You can see him coming, but then what? You might even be able to chase him through a wall without help. But all he would have to do is flip into a different dimension, something that comes naturally for him. Even then, why would he? What threat do you pose to him? I know I side with you when Abdiel's around, but he's right and you know it. How can you defend yourself against weapons you can't see? We're talking about seasoned warriors. This is Semyaza, not Myles Shepherd. He's toying with you. He knows how to get to you, to make you keep coming back for more. And—" Tears came furiously. "I can't take it anymore, Grant. I lost the professor, and I can't stand the thought of losing you, too."

She buried her head against my chest and sobbed. I put my arm around her.

"They've been doing this for millennia," I said softly, more to me than to her.

She was right, of course. Semyaza would like nothing better than for me to come after him, assuming that I could. Was that why he killed the professor? To lure me into coming after him? Did he know something about my protective mark I didn't know? Would it protect me if I was the aggressor?

"When I think of the professor," Sue said, her voice muffled against my chest, "God forgive me, Grant . . . but I hate him."

"Sue! Why?"

"I try not to. But I can't help myself. When I think of him, I see him with his wife and his daughters and he's happy, and I'm miserable and alone. He doesn't need me anymore, Grant. I was just someone he was passing time with until he could be with her again."

"Don't say that, Sue. I'm sure it isn't true."

She lifted her head. "Do you think he's told his wife about me? And what happens when I die? Do you really think she's going to share her husband with me?"

The sudden twist in the conversation had me befuddled. But then, even if I'd seen it coming, I still would have been ill-equipped to comment.

Sue laughed bitterly. "I'm sure she's amused at the silly schoolgirl who fell in love with her professor husband."

I'd never seen this side of Sue Ling before. She'd always been confident, efficient, professional. She'd always been strong for the professor.

Since I didn't know what to say, I just held her and let her cry.

"Grant, I don't want to lose you." She sobbed. "I don't want to lose you."

"Shhh. You're not going to lose me," I said, rocking her.

"Your mind is wandering, Grant Austin. Do you not wish to hear this?" Abdiel asked.

"Oh . . . um . . . right." I adjusted the yellow pad on my lap. "Sorry. Where were we?"

"I was describing Lucifer's plan to thwart the Father's redemptive strategy," Abdiel said. "You were with Sue Ling, I believe."

He was guessing. He'd guessed right, but I wasn't going to admit it. I was thinking about last night at the cove. Sue and I talked until well past midnight. I walked her to the car, and there was an awkward moment when we didn't kiss. I promised her I'd make a list of places other than San Diego I'd like to live. She was going to do the same.

I didn't tell her about my sessions with Abdiel. It would only upset her.

Soon after Abdiel arrived, he began as he had before, reciting the official angel version. He hadn't gotten far when I interrupted him again.

"Can I ask you a question? You were there, right? At creation. In the early days with the Watchers and the Nephilim. When Jesus walked the earth."

"I was present on many occasions. I was among those selected to minister to the Divine Warrior following His temptation in the wilderness."

"That's what I want."

"You want me to minister to you?"

"I want you to tell me what it was like to be there."

"Is that not what I'm doing?"

"No. You're giving me a classroom recitation. You were an eyewitness. I want to interview you."

It was rocky at first, but I've worked with people who are unaccustomed to being interviewed. I know how to draw them out. How to help them recall details they thought they'd forgotten or thought were unimportant.

With Abdiel, I got him to talk about his prior friendship with Lucifer, and the downward spiral of emotions he felt as he watched his mentor slip from an exalted position to enemy rebel and terrorist, from an ardent enthusiast of the Father's creation to its saboteur, from devoted leader to spurned lover, from joy and faithfulness to bitterness and rumors of insurrection that polarized the angel nation.

I learned that heaven's war erupted when the council was

between sessions as Lucifer and his men marched on the throne room. There they encountered archangels Michael, Gabriel, Uriel, Raphael, and Abdiel, who had been alerted to the plan.

Lucifer had made it clear he felt his rightful place was on the throne to the right of the Father's throne, the one that had been given to the Son. It was this throne the loyal archangels defended.

However, as Lucifer advanced, he did not approach the throne of the Son. He strode toward the Father's throne.

As often happens during cataclysmic moments in history, no one could recall who struck the initial blow. Abdiel recalled that his attention was on Lucifer, whom he said he barely recognized, so changed was he by his bitterness and hate. The next thing Abdiel knew he was fighting for his life.

Lucifer believed that once the fighting started, a groundswell of angelic support would surge to his side. It was a fatal error. Barely a third of heaven's angels sided with him and the rebellion was quickly put down.

"So then," I said, "after the rebellion was put down, and Lucifer and his leaders were confined to the created order of space and time—"

"Tartarus," Abdiel reminded me.

"—Lucifer set about sabotaging creation. What exactly did he do?"

Abdiel thought a moment. "Your limited knowledge of the cosmos makes it difficult to describe to you his actions. There is a parable the Divine Warrior told that might be useful. Think of the cosmos as a large field of grain. After the grain was planted Lucifer scattered tares among the wheat. As the wheat grows, so do the weeds. Your scientists have registered the destructive effect on the cosmos with their observation that matter tends toward disorder and decay."

"That was not part of the Father's original creation?" I asked.

"Why would the Father create disorder and decay?"

"So you're saying that had not Lucifer sown tares among the cosmos, the universe would be—"

"Ever-changing, from glory to glory."

I felt the seconds ticking as I wrote as fast as I could, hoping that I'd be able to read my own writing later. I needed to get another laptop. I could type a lot faster than I could write.

"All right," I said, catching up. "What next?"

"You are familiar with Lucifer's deception of the first man and woman."

"The Book of Genesis."

"I have nothing to add to that account," he said. "You are also familiar with the passage regarding the Watchers and their cohabitation with women, also in Genesis. I have nothing to add to that account."

"Wait," I said. "I have some questions here."

"I will not answer them."

"What? Why not?"

"You are hoping that through my narration you will learn of the abilities of the ancient Nephilim. I told you previously I will not reveal that information to you."

I'd hoped he'd forgotten about that.

"Fair enough, but there are still some questions I'd like to ask. For example, why were the angels called Watchers?"

"From the beginning it was the Father's intention that angels and mankind interact freely. Watchers were appointed to guide humans in their understanding of the spiritual realm. Among those appointed were Semyaza and Azazel, with whom you are acquainted. This was their chance to return to the Father by exercising their role as good shepherds."

"The cohabitation with human women. Was it simply uncontrolled desire, or was it a strategy of Lucifer's rebellion?"

Abdiel appeared impressed with the question. "Very good, Grant Austin. While your birth was the result of unbridled lust—"

"Thanks for reminding me."

"—the action of the Watchers was a strategy that backfired. That said, it would be wrong to characterize what happened purely as a military act. Some of the Watchers genuinely loved their wives and children. But that did not make their actions any less of a violation of duty."

"What did Lucifer hope to gain by the strategy?"

"By combining the angelic and human races through intermarriage, he hoped to combine their destinies. Lucifer was convinced the Father would not condemn His pet creation (Lucifer's term for humans). By producing mixed families he thought the Father would have no other choice but to relent. And, if He didn't issue an outright pardon to the rebels, at least He'd ease the burden of their sentence."

"Cleansing the earth never occurred to Lucifer?"

"The Flood was a devastating blow to him. Not only did it thwart his plan, but it created dissension in his ranks that exists to this day."

I'd sensed the anger Belial felt over the failed strategy when he brought his Nephilim sons, now demons, with him on his first visit.

"After the Flood, the Father began revealing His plan to redeem the world, beginning with a prophecy that the enmity between a serpent and a woman was a foreshadowing of a day when the son of a woman would crush the head of the serpent."

I jotted a side note to myself. I knew the reference was in Genesis. I'd check it later.

"The Father then chose a race of humans from which this deliverer would come, the race of Abraham. From the race of Abraham He chose a tribe, Judah. And from among the tribe of Judah, he chose a family. The deliverer would be born of the family of David. Once a family was chosen, Lucifer launched a full-scale assault."

Abraham . . . Judah . . . David . . . I wrote furiously while Sue Ling's voice played in my head. *Grant Austin! Didn't you learn this in Sunday school?*

"Lucifer knew that if he could find a way to cut off this blood-line, he would thwart the Father's redemptive plan. The history of the kingly line of David, along with their temptations, is well documented, culminating in Lucifer's ultimate success—Jehoiachim and his son, Johoiachin, though I would add Nehushta, wife and mother, for she was an evil-hearted woman. These kings were oppressive, cowardly, selfish, and thoroughly godless.

"The prophet described the family as a despised and broken pot, an object no one wants, to be cast aside. The Father agreed. He pronounced the end of the David line. As for Jehoiachim, the record was to show him childless. None of his offspring would prosper. No offspring from this man would sit on the throne of David or rule in the house of Judah. The family line was cut off. Lucifer had won."

My cell phone rang. It continued to ring as I raced to write down the last of Abdiel's words. For a moment I considered asking Abdiel to answer it for me, but didn't like any of the resulting scenarios that flashed through my mind.

Punching the final period I lunged for the phone. It was Sue Ling.

"Do you mind?" I said to Abdiel.

He didn't object, so I flipped open the phone.

"Where are you?" I asked.

"At the library," she whispered from her end. "What do you think about Chapel Hill, North Carolina?"

I glanced at Abdiel. I didn't want Sue Ling to know he was here.

"This isn't a good time for me," I told her. "Can we meet later? How about lunch?"

"Grant? Are you having second thoughts? You sound funny."

"No. Not at all," I said, keeping my comments general. I didn't want Abdiel to know what Sue Ling and I were discussing. "I just . . . this isn't a good time."

We arranged a lunch date and I closed the phone.

"When you saw Sue Ling's sword," Abdiel said, "the image of her spirit, you described it as elegant and blue."

"That's what I saw," I said, unsure where this was going. "Did you see something different?"

"We saw the same thing," he replied. "Only what you described as elegant, I would describe as frail."

"What are you saying? That Sue Ling is weak?"

"She has taken the professor's death hard," Abdiel said.

"We all have."

"It has caused her to doubt."

"Your point?"

"Have you considered that Sue Ling might be part of Semyaza's plan to eliminate you as a threat to Lucifer?"

My anger flashed. I was on my feet. "Sue Ling would never side with Semyaza."

"She would never knowingly conspire with Semyaza, that is true. However, this wouldn't be the first time Semyaza has used a beloved person as a vessel of doubt and fear."

I hated that what he was saying made deceptive sense. Semyaza knew that the professor's death would enrage me . . . that I'd want revenge.

"If you had the ability," Abdiel said, "I would instruct you to keep an eye on her sword. It will reveal her intent. But since you cannot do that, test her spirit. When you are with her, does your spirit thrive—or does it diminish? Test her spirit, Grant."

CHAPTER
18

S ue Ling chose an upscale Italian restaurant on Main
Street, which turned out to be a great place for good
food at luncheon prices. We shared a plate of angel-hair
pasta and shrimp and a piece of tiramisu and drank espresso
while we discussed moving to Chapel Hill, which had quickly
become our favorite choice for its university atmosphere. We
looked at downloaded pictures of Chapel Hill on her laptop
while we ate.

Sitting shoulder to shoulder in the booth with her, eating,
talking, laughing, planning, was better than my best Sue Ling
fantasy, which had always been tempered by reality. She still intimidated me with her intellect at times and by her ability to
marshal facts and figures. At other times she sent me soaring
with an affectionate glance or playful touch.

After lunch we went to the mall. Sue had seen a shoe sale
advertisement in the morning paper. Since I was without a book
contract and basically unemployed, I tagged along. While she

shopped for shoes I browsed the mall bookstore. A mistake. My
anxiety level rose significantly when I learned they no longer
carried my book. While I'd made good money from the biography, it wasn't enough to make me comfortable, especially when
I figured in the cost of an upcoming relocation.

Everywhere we walked in the mall we saw posters and T-
shirts of Neo Jesus. One T-shirt had a picture of him laughing
on the back, with a quotation on the front: "It was a joke,
people!" A poster in a window featured two stone tablets resembling the Ten Commandments, only these were the Top Ten
Reasons Not to Take Christianity Seriously. The number one
reason was, "It was a joke, people!"

Leaving the mall we spent the afternoon strolling hand in
hand through Balboa Park, shared an artichoke salad and
French roll for dinner, and attended a free outdoor performance
of *Much Ado About Nothing*.

Sue kissed me on the cheek when we said good night.

As I fell onto the sofa in my living room and reached for the
remote, I reflected on this most incredible day. I remembered
what Abdiel had told me.

Test her spirit, Grant.

Well, I'd done that, too. At the restaurant and again at the
mall I had tried to see Sue Ling's sword with no success. The
rest of the day I didn't even think about it. I was preoccupied
watching the way her hair tossed when she turned her head; letting my eyes, which until now, had had to steal glances, linger
on her; drinking in her affection like an expensive wine I never
thought I'd taste.

Now that we were apart and I wasn't distracted by her physical presence, as much as I hated to admit it, my spirit was troubled. I had an underlying feeling that her attraction to me
wasn't what it appeared to be on the surface, or what I wanted

it to be. Not that she was attempting to deceive me, at least not intentionally. But I feared she was acting out of need, not love.

And I couldn't shake the feeling that she was diverting me from something important.

I clicked on the television to distract myself from this unwelcome thought by watching the news. Jana greeted me, along with all the other viewers. She was filling in for the anchor again.

Local news led with a report of another burst underground water pipe, this one flooding several downtown blocks. The San Diego infrastructure was aging, and pipes were bursting at the rate of two or three a week.

The third story was an interview of a sociologist at the University of California, San Diego. He'd written a book, *The Post-Christian World,* in which he identified two emerging philosophies that were developing as a result of the discovery of the Alexandrian manuscript and the appearance of Neo Jesus. One philosophy was rejecting all authority and structure. A video clip featured a barefoot Berkeley street preacher who wore a T-shirt with the message, *Whoever said life was to be taken seriously?* He preached a free and open society without marriage, laws, or government.

The second emerging philosophy was being taught by academics who were furious that there were civilizations in the universe that were laughing at us. They advocated the scrapping of NASA and all outer space activities in order to redirect our energies to the exploration of inner space. A critic of their philosophy characterized their efforts as, "One eentsy-teensy step for man, one giant blunder for mankind."

Related news stories included support groups of former evangelicals who were "mad as hell for being terrorized by hell" all these years; of missionaries stranded in foreign countries for lack of funds; and of charitable giving at an all-time low.

Meanwhile, scientists from all over the world were gathering in Geneva in anticipation of the conference with Neo Jesus.

After listening to the sports scores, I turned off the television and prepared for bed. Teeth brushed and standing in my pajama bottoms, for some reason I had a sudden urge to walk through a wall. I hadn't done it since my last training session with Abdiel present.

Having never soloed, I was hesitant. What if I got halfway through the wall and got stuck? I picked up my cell phone. I could call maintenance if I got stuck, couldn't I? But, how would I dial? I put the cell phone down.

When I was deciding which wall to walk through, my gaze fell on the front door. It was thinner than a wall. A training wall.

I walked over to it. I liked my chances.

Before stepping through the door I looked out the peephole door viewer. I didn't want to scare anyone. The hallway was clear. I readied myself.

Laughing, I stepped back. I'd forgotten to unlock the door. My luck, I'd pass through to the other side and not be able to get back, and I certainly didn't want to get caught in the hallway in my pajama bottoms. I unlocked the door.

Now I was ready. I took a deep breath. Relaxed. I reminded myself that matter was more space than anything else. That all I had to do was align my elements with the door elements and slide through with room to spare.

"All right," I told myself, my nose less than an inch from the door.

I stood there.

"You can do it," I assured myself.

I stood there.

"You did it before."

After a couple of minutes of smelling the paint on my door, I backed away. Why was I afraid to do this?

"OK," I said, not ready to give up. For some reason a children's riddle came to mind: *How do you eat an elephant? One bite at a time.*

So why are you trying to push the entire elephant through the door all at once? I asked myself. *Why not a piece at a time? That makes sense, doesn't it?*

I was talking gibberish. A good indication I was scared and about to chicken out.

"No! I'm going to do this!"

I placed my hand on the door.

"All right. A hand, then an arm, and the rest of me follows. That's the plan. Smooth as silk."

Again, I prepared myself. I relaxed. I envisioned myself doing it. Closed my eyes. I felt my hand slide through the door to the other side. Then my wrist. My arm. My elbow.

"Ha! I'm doing it!"

My face hit the door hard and I lost momentum. When I tried continuing forward, my toes and knees and nose hit the inside of the front door with a *thunk!*

As I blinked back the pain, my predicament became chillingly clear. My arm was sticking through the front door up to the shoulder.

"All right," I told myself, trying to sound positive. "It was a good first try. Let's just back away and try again."

I pulled back. The door clenched tight. It wouldn't give me back my arm.

"Don't panic," I said, knowing full well that when people say, "Don't panic," it's already too late.

Nothing I did could free my arm. I tried relaxing. I tried a sudden jerk, but only once because it hurt something fierce. I tried opening the door and reaching around to the other side. All I managed to do was play with my own fingers.

It was cold outside so I closed the door while I considered my options. My cell phone was out of reach. I could holler until help came, but what would I say to explain how my arm got through the door in the first place? I could shout for Abdiel, but I really didn't want to do that. He was already unimpressed with my abilities. This would only make it worse.

I was beginning to lose sensation in my arm and fingers. From the cold? Or was the door cutting off my circulation? Either way, my fingers were getting stiff.

I looked for something to wrap around my hand and arm. There was absolutely nothing within reach. The only material within reach was my pajama bottoms.

My hand and fingers were so cold now I was beginning to shiver. The tips were numb. I looked at my hand through the peephole. No amount of flexing could restore the circulation. I'd run out of choices.

Slipping my pajama bottoms off, I checked the hallway, then opened the front door and managed to wrap them around my hand and arm. Already my arm was feeling better from the warmth when I heard a front door close.

Stepping back inside, I closed my door.

I could hear someone humming. A woman's voice.

Peering through the peephole at my pajama-covered arm I prayed that she wouldn't come this direction. The humming turned to singing. It was getting louder. Now I prayed she would mistake my arm for some sort of flagpole and just walk past it without a second thought.

The singing stopped just as she came into peeping view. I kept my hand as rigid as possible.

It's a flagpole. A flagpole. A flagpole, I told her with my mind.

But Jedi mind tricks work only in the movies. She examined the pajamas with curiosity. She looked at the front door and I ducked out of the way. Why, I don't know.

When I looked through the peephole again, she was reaching toward the pajamas.

No . . . no . . . no . . .

She began unwrapping my arm.

. . . no . . . no . . .

Getting down to the last layer, she pulled the pajama bottoms off my arm and gasped. I couldn't keep my hand still any longer. I flexed my fingers. She screamed. She couldn't take her eyes off my hand. She screamed and screamed, then began hitting it, first with my pajama bottoms, then with her hand.

I opened the door. "Stop it! That hurts!"

For a moment she froze, staring at me, pajama-bottomless, in horror. She looked at my arm through the door, then back at me, and began to scream again, this time putting legs to her screams. She ran down the hallway.

I knew it was just a matter of time before people started coming. I retrieved my pajama bottoms with my toes, passed them to my free hand, and shut the door.

Wouldn't you know it? Just when I was standing there with one hand stuck through a door and another hand holding my pajama bottoms, an angel appears.

"If Semyaza could only see you now," Belial said with a smirk. At least he had the decency to appear as himself and not Jesus.

One-handed, I pulled on my pajama bottoms, hopping on

one foot, then the other. I was beyond embarrassment or pride. All I wanted was to get my arm out of the door.

"Can you—" I said. "I was trying something, and—"

Belial walked up to me and looked at my arm in the door. "Have you done this before?"

"Once by myself. The other times I had help."

He nodded. He didn't ask who had helped me. He didn't need to.

Belial placed his hand on my shoulder, and my arm slid out of the door as smoothly and easily as if it was moving through a wall of mist.

"Thanks." I flexed my hand. Already the circulation was returning.

Within a few minutes I had company. Police. Firemen. Paramedics. The landlord. The association handyman. The woman and her boyfriend. A dozen of my neighbors.

I felt sorry for the lady. She came across as a lunatic, telling everyone how she came across my pajama-draped arm sticking out of the door. The police were suspicious, believing me to be some sort of prankster. But the evidence showed no hole in my door, both of my arms attached, and me wearing my pajama bottoms.

"Is this what you do for fun?" Belial asked when we were alone. He'd kept himself from view while the authorities were questioning me. He was here, though. I could see him.

I'd put on a robe and was tying it. "This little amusement? Amateur stuff compared to the fun you're having with your Neo Jesus scam."

Belial waved my comment aside. "I don't want talk about that now."

He did appear preoccupied.

"Grant Austin, I'm not sure you appreciate your unique position."

"I'm one of a kind," I quipped. "Who else can get their arm stuck in a door like that?"

Despite his genial appearance, Belial made me nervous. I hadn't forgotten he was the enemy. And the fact that he was nervous made me even more nervous. His eyes kept darting this way and that, as though he expected someone to appear at any moment.

"I'm not referring only to your being Nephilim," he said. "But to your favor with God."

My hand rose to my forehead. How long was I going to do that? I knew the mark wasn't there.

"What do you want, Belial?" I said.

"Grant Austin, I want you to consider petitioning the Father for grace for all Nephilim."

It took a moment for me to comprehend what he was saying. Of all the things I'd imagined he might say, this wasn't one of them.

"Consider your unique position," Belial said, "and your shared destiny. You alone can speak for the Nephilim. You can be their champion. The Father has shown you favor. He will listen to you."

Of course the idea intrigued me. I'd already failed to receive salvation as a human. This was a chance to receive it as Nephilim. Why hadn't I thought of it earlier?

"I wish you could meet my oldest boy," Belial said, "the way he was. You remind me of him."

"Do you really think the Father will consider my petition?"

"Look at the lengths to which he went to redeem humans and creation," Belial said. "He has promised them a new heaven and a new earth. Upon death they are clothed in redeemed bodies. This he has done, though they have sinned. Why should you and the offspring of angels be punished for sin that is not yours? Despite your destiny, you have chosen to serve the Father. Should not all Nephilim be given a chance to make the same choice? Do you really believe the Father would damn those who choose to worship him?"

He'd get no argument from me. "How do I—I don't know where to begin. Do I just pray? But then, how would I—?"

Belial became agitated; not because of what I said, but because of something I couldn't see, or sense. His eyes darted around the room.

"What are you—"

"Shhhh!"

He disappeared.

I stood in the center of my living room, fearing that my ceiling was about to erupt with demons, or that rebel angels would at any moment storm through the walls.

Belial reappeared so suddenly, it made me jump.

He spoke in a conspiratorial tone. "There are some who would be furious if they knew about this, Semyaza among them."

All the more reason to give Belial a hearing, I thought.

Returning to my question, he said, "It would be better if you petitioned the Father face to face."

"Is that possible?"

"You could present your petition to the Father in the throne room during one of the council sessions."

"Heaven's throne room?" I said. "You're not serious."

"It offers you the greatest chance of success," Belial said. "I can prepare you."

I looked at him skeptically.

"You have every reason not to trust me. But I'm doing this for my boys and the offspring of my brothers who dwell in perpetual torment."

As I will someday, I thought. If there was a chance I could escape that fate, wasn't it worth the risk? "How would you prepare me?"

"There are some things Nephilim can do that Abdiel won't show you," Belial said.

"Such as?"

Belial shook his head. "This isn't the time. And we need a place where we can prepare without fear of discovery. Once it becomes known what you are attempting to do, believe me, all the forces of hell will try to stop you."

"Why? What threat is this to anybody?"

Belial studied me as he would a naïve child. "The fate of Nephilim is evidence in Lucifer's argument that the Father's punishments are too severe. Should the Father favor your petition, it would be a severe blow to Lucifer."

"Where can we meet?" I said.

"There is a place, but after what I witnessed tonight"—he glanced at the door—"I fear it might be painful for you to go there."

"We would have to pass through a dimensional membrane."

Belial was surprised. "Abdiel has taught you about dimensional portals?"

"I have not successfully passed through one, even with his assistance."

Belial thought about this a moment. "The membrane that separates this world from Sheol is the thinnest and easiest to traverse."

"Sheol! You want to take me to hell?"

Belial shook his head. "Sheol isn't hell. It's the realm of the dead. It is deserted now. Following the Son's victory over death, it was emptied, and all the inhabitants were paraded into heaven. It is safe for us because those of us in the rebellion avoid it. It is the site of Lucifer's humiliation and our greatest defeat."

"Sheol," I repeated. "You want to take me to Sheol."

"If you want to present your petition, it is the only way, Grant Austin. Once there I can train you, shielded from the eyes and ears of Lucifer. It also has a portal to the King's Highway. It is guarded, so I would be unable to accompany you any further. But I see no reason why you would not be granted passage to present your petition to the Father."

"Sheol. Heaven. King's Highway," I muttered. "This is . . . too much. I'll have to think about it."

Belial scrutinized me, probably wondering if I'd run to Abdiel with the news the first chance I got.

"Give it serious thought, Grant Austin, and I am certain you will agree with me that this is a chance that may never come again. Not only your fate, but the fate of my boys and all Nephilim rests in your hands. I will take my leave of you now."

"Wait," I said, remembering something. "You promised to give Jana Torres an interview."

"Make the necessary arrangements."

After Belial left, I lay in my bed and stared at the dark ceiling, my future home along with all the other oozing, slimy, pointed-tooth demons. Unless—

"Sheol!" I said to the darkness. "Heaven's throne room! Is it really possible? And to think there was a time when I thought getting invited to the Oval Office was a big deal."

CHAPTER
19

Sheol.

Had Belial warned me not to tell anyone of our plans, I would have suspected a scam. He gave me no such warning. Was he really on the level?

Sheol. The courts of heaven.

I couldn't get them out of my mind. Abdiel had described heaven as walking on fiery stones. Do you wear dress shoes for that, or are tennis shoes OK?

Me. Standing on fiery stones before the throne of the Almighty God. Presenting a petition for mercy on behalf of all Nephilim. Hard to believe.

Passing through the dimensional membrane was no small concern. It wasn't hard to imagine. The memory of my earlier failures was quite vivid.

One other thing bothered me. What if the Father turned down my petition as He had my salvation? Would the brief memories of heaven's glory add to my eternal torment?

But—and this was what kept drawing me back to it—what if the Father granted my petition?

"Your mind has wandered again, Grant Austin," Abdiel said, pausing in his narration.

He'd arrived as scheduled for our third session.

"Clearly you are of two minds this morning," he said. "I will return after you have resolved your conflict with Sue Ling."

He thought I was preoccupied with Sue. If I was going to tell him about the petition, now was the time.

"Stay," I said. "Yesterday you told me how Lucifer spoiled the lineage of David and how the Father cut it off as the promised bloodline of the Redeemer. What happened next?"

"Lucifer and the rebels rejoiced."

I smiled. "But not for long."

Abdiel reflected my smile. "No, not for long."

"What were your thoughts at the time? You and Michael and Gabriel and the others. It appeared Lucifer had won a major victory. Did you know how the Father would counter it?"

"Angels are not told the future, Grant Austin. We were unaware of the Father's plan until He implemented it."

"But weren't you a little concerned? Your former commander was celebrating."

Abdiel thought for a moment. "The circumstances were of no consequence to us."

"How can you say that? The Messianic bloodline had been cut off!"

Abdiel stood, serene and confident, two inches above the carpet in my living room. "Only a fool would believe he could outsmart God."

"You think Lucifer is a fool?"

"He cannot win, yet he persists in his rebellion. He has set a course of destruction, yet he believes it will result in good. How can anyone think him wise?"

"So . . . what happened? What did the Father do?"

"He outwitted Lucifer."

I flexed my fingers, the ones that had been stuck outside the door last night. They were stiff and it hurt to write, but I wanted to get this down.

"In fulfillment of the Messianic prophecy, the promised Redeemer, the Divine Warrior, was born to a carpenter in Nazareth, to a man named Joseph who was of David's bloodline."

"But that line had been cut off."

Abdiel held up a hand, signaling me to be patient. "The Father, the King of Kings, provided a worthy royal bloodline himself by sending His Son. The Spirit of the Most High came upon Mary, and she conceived and bore a son, the promised Redeemer. Lucifer never saw it coming.

"It was a bold and brilliant offensive move. On the night of the birth, the Son of the Most High invaded Lucifer's territory. The tactic stripped Lucifer of his oft-repeated argument that the limitations of the cosmos were a cruel punishment for beings created for heaven. For on that night the Son of God became flesh and dwelled among humans. Every footprint He made was a witness against Lucifer."

"The battle was on," I said.

"Yes, Grant Austin. The battle was on."

A scene flashed in my mind of Lucifer and Semyaza and the others in total disarray for not having anticipated the Father's move, furiously hurling blame and accusations at each other.

I couldn't help but wonder what Lucifer thought. In a way, he got his wish. He got to go head to head with the Son. This was his chance to prove himself. I wondered if he had prefight jitters.

"You are familiar with the Gospel accounts?" Abdiel asked.

"I have read them. The quiet courage of Jesus recorded in them was my inspiration in the days preceding my decision to reject Semyaza's offer," I told him.

"Ask me about an incident, and I will relate to you my memories of the spiritual battle."

"If it's all the same to you," I said, "I'd rather you choose the incidents. Which ones are most memorable to you?"

I thought I'd get an argument from him. I didn't.

"Capernaum," he said. "Simon Peter's mother-in-law was ill with the burning fever. When the Divine Warrior arrived, they were tying an iron knife by a braid of hair to a thornbush."

"Why?"

"That was the local remedy for burning fever. However, the Divine Warrior recognized the fever as an attack. The rebels often attacked Peter. He was the most volatile."

"Are you telling me that all sickness is a form of spiritual attack?"

"How did you arrive at such an obvious error?" Abdiel said. "Lucifer uses biological weapons when it suits his purpose. Neither is every storm a rebel attack, though angels can summon the winds and command the waves. A person whose eyes are open spiritually can see the difference between a natural occurrence and a spiritual attack."

"It keeps coming back to seeing swords, doesn't it?" I said testily. I was thinking he'd chosen this incident just to hammer me again.

His puzzled expression argued otherwise. "If you were blind and I were a physician, would you be as angry at me for trying to help you see?"

"You're right. Sorry. So the woman's fever was an attack. What did the Divine Warrior do?"

"He rebuked the fever and the demon who brought it, and she was healed. But it is what happened next that makes the incident memorable. It was a trap."

"A trap?"

"The rebel forces launched an attack on Capernaum, terrorizing its people with infirmity and possessing them with demons."

I squirmed uncomfortably, remembering what that felt like.

"When word got out about the healing, the townspeople lined up at the woman's door, begging the Divine Warrior to heal them. He healed many of them, late into the night. The next morning, the line was even longer, but the Divine Warrior was no longer in the house.

"His disciples found him in a solitary place, praying. When they told him about the line of people, he informed them they would not be returning to Capernaum."

"He turned his back on all those people?"

"I told you. It was a trap. He alone could heal them. Lucifer's strategy was to use the Divine Warrior's compassion against him."

"But—"

"Physical healing is temporary, Grant Austin. The temptation was to divert the Divine Warrior's attention from His mission with things that are temporary. Had He spent all His days healing people who would eventually die, what then? He turned His back on their physical needs to provide for their eternal needs."

Abdiel then related the time the Divine Warrior single-handedly defeated a legion of demons who had tormented a man most of his life, and the time rebel agents attempted to sink the boat he was in by summoning a storm.

"Bracing himself against the forces, the Divine Warrior

spoke, and the winds and the waves recognized the voice of their creator and obeyed him," Abdiel said. "Day after day, for three years he walked the land, forcefully advancing the Kingdom of God, reclaiming occupied territory."

He spoke of the victories with a subdued tone, as though he was dreading what was coming next.

"Had Lucifer understood the mystery of the Father's strategy, he never would have sought to kill the Divine Warrior when he did. He made a huge tactical mistake in believing that by becoming human, the Son had put himself in a vulnerable position."

"Lucifer holds the power of death," I said.

"Not only the Gospels; you have been reading the Epistles, too," Abdiel said.

While that was true, my statement was born of feelings of personal vulnerability in spiritual battle.

"You are aware of the earthly events leading up to the Divine Warrior's death," Abdiel said. "Lucifer entering Judas. The flowering of the spirit of corruption that the rebels had cultivated in the Sanhedrin and the courts of Pilate and Herod. What was not recorded in the Gospel accounts is the assemblage of angels in heaven, a company of warriors prepared to battle against the forces that had arrayed themselves against the Son, both angel and human.

"The empty throne at the Father's right hand was all the motivation we needed. We knew our objective. Rescue the Son and return him to his rightful place. The Father had a different plan. He shut heaven's gates." Abdiel's face was marked with lines of pain as he relived the memory.

Giving him time to gather himself, I wrote at the top of a new sheet of paper, *When Heaven Was Helpless*. I recalled his telling me how wrenching it was to witness the professor's death and do nothing. How much more difficult it must have been to watch Lucifer abuse and crucify the Son and do nothing to intercede.

"The method Lucifer chose for the Divine Warrior's death was symbolic. The prince of the air had the Son suspended between heaven and earth as a trophy of his victory. All the forces of hell surrounded the cross in anticipation of a rescue attempt that never came. When the Divine Warrior breathed his last breath, Lucifer himself transported his captive to Sheol, the realm of the dead."

The pain of the memory made Abdiel pause. His words weighed heavy when he continued.

"Surely now, we thought, the Father would send us to storm Sheol and free His Son. But He didn't. Heaven's gates remained locked. What we didn't know was that the Divine Warrior was exactly where He intended to be. He preached to the captives of that netherworld—those who had died in times past.

"And then heaven's gates were opened. And Gabriel's trumpet blew. We were ordered to Sheol to assist the Son. When we arrived, instead of finding huddled masses of defeated souls, we came upon a battle in progress with the Divine Warrior's sword flashing furiously.

"Lucifer did not surrender Sheol without a fight. Michael battled him personally to free Moses. But the tide of the battle turned quickly, and the Divine Warrior stood victorious over Lucifer and the power of sin and death.

"Once again the Father had used Lucifer's strategy against him, and what Lucifer thought was his greatest victory became his greatest defeat, and the capstone that sealed his fate.

"Oh, I wish you could have seen it, Grant Austin. We lined the King's Highway on both sides as the triumphant Son led his captives and the saints of the past—Abraham, Moses, David, Solomon—into the courts of heaven and presented them to the Father. At that time He, however, did not take His rightful throne, instead returning to earth to deliver a message of hope to the hopeless who were still grieving His death."

"When Jesus ascended—" I said.

"Yes?" Abdiel smiled, anticipating my answer.

"Suspended between earth and heaven, occupying the territory of the prince of the air, this time victorious. We call that an in-your-face statement."

"The Divine Warrior will return in similar fashion," Abdiel said.

"As Belial did," I said.

"Only when the Divine Warrior returns," Abdiel said, "Lucifer and Belial's time will be up."

Christus Victor.

After Abdiel took his leave of me, I tried to imagine what it had been like in Sheol, when the Son of God showed up escorted by Lucifer and his thugs. Lucifer must have been busting his buttons. At what point did he realize he'd made a grave mistake?

Good, Grant, I thought, wincing at my unintended pun.

I tried to imagine Lucifer's horror when the Divine Warrior drew his sword and made his intentions known. That must have been something to see.

Drawing from the skirmish I'd witnessed over the Bay Bridge the day the president was assassinated, I had some idea what Sheol was like in the midst of an all-out battle. Assaults at the speed of light. Explosions of brilliance as combatants engaged. The darkening light of angel death. Abdiel and the reinforcements bursting onto the scene to find the Divine Warrior victorious. They'd arrived just in time for the parade along the

King's Highway. I sure hoped they had some kind of video play-back in heaven, because that was something I definitely wanted to see.

I glanced at the clock and began gathering up my notes. Sue Ling would be here soon. It would be easier for everyone if she didn't know that Abdiel had been here.

My eyes fell on the phrase, "Lucifer himself transported his captive to Sheol . . ." Wasn't that what Belial was offering to do for me? I'm sure it wouldn't be his first time to play escort. But the people he normally escorted were already dead, weren't they?

I slumped against the couch at the thought. I had to be crazy to be considering doing this.

The doorbell rang. I stacked the pages hastily on top of the notepad. Where to put them? The bedroom? Even there I'd have to put them away, its being the passage to the bathroom. My dresser drawer.

The doorbell rang again.

"Grant?"

Sue's muffled voice came through the door. She tried the door. It began to open. I'd forgotten I'd left it unlocked for her.

Getting up, I lifted the sofa cushion, threw the notes under it, and slammed the cushion back down, making a pretense of smoothing it as Sue walked in the door.

"Grant! You're cleaning up for me? How sweet."

She kissed me on the cheek and I caught a whiff of her perfume. I didn't have a clue what it was called. I knew it as Sue Ling's scent and it drove me to distraction.

She carried a black leather valise that I had seen at the college. How many times had she pulled papers from it to hand to the professor? She was reaching into it as she crossed the room.

She sat on the sofa, on the cushion that hid my angel narrative notes.

"We need to make a decision about Chapel Hill sooner than we thought," she said.

"Um—"

Alarms were going off in my head. It was probably nothing. It was not as though she were a princess and I was hiding a pea. Still, I'd feel a lot safer if she were sitting somewhere else. Anywhere else.

"I have an idea. How about if we discuss this at Howard's over tea and pastry?"

I opened the door, inviting her to accompany me.

"If it's all the same to you, I'd prefer staying here," Sue said. She settled back against the sofa and, with a slight frown, repositioned herself to get comfortable. "However, tea sounds good."

"Tea," I said, closing the door. "Great idea. How about if you fix us both a cup?"

She cocked her head. "Grant! Is something wrong?"

"What? No. I was just kidding. I'll fix us the tea."

Sue turned her attention to the papers she'd pulled from the valise.

I raced into the kitchen, filled the kettle with water, and threw it on the stove, turning the burner on high, then raced back to the doorway that connected the two rooms.

Without looking up, Sue said, "The enrollment deadline at the University of North Carolina is earlier than I thought. I called the professor of the department of theoretical physics and he's willing to review my coursework and thesis. Of course, he can't guarantee I can keep my thesis subject—professors are funny that way—but he seemed to like it and said he'd present it to the advisory board."

As she told me her impressions of the theoretical physics department, she spoke positively and with animation for the first time since the professor's death. She was getting on with her life.

The teapot began to whistle. As I turned back into the kitchen, she raised her voice so I could still hear her.

"I went to UCSD and talked to a couple of my professors. They're impressed with the program at UNC. Professor Ledbetter put me in contact with a student who just transferred from there."

Throwing open cabinet doors and drawers, I grabbed two cups, two spoons, a box of teabags, and a handful of sugar packets and threw them onto a serving tray. Lunging for the kettle, I poured hot water into the cups a little too fast. Scalding water leaped out of one cup and onto my hand.

Replacing the kettle on the stove, I did a silent dance of pain. After a second or two I realized Sue was no longer talking. Forcing my voice into a normal tone, I said, "Have you talked with her? Or was it a him?"

Sue didn't answer me. When I carried the tray into the living room I discovered why. Sue was standing beside the sofa. The cushion was raised. She was reading my notes.

"What's this?" She held the papers between us.

"I thought it best you didn't know."

"In spite of last night, you did this behind my back." Tears and pain filled her eyes.

There was no use lying to her. I'd dated the pages.

I'd hoped I'd have more time to come to a decision. But I really didn't need more time. It would only delay the inevitable. Word of my petition would get out. If the Father granted it, Lucifer would retaliate. He'd go after those who were closest to me.

"Sue—"

Setting the tray down, I took the notes from her and set them aside as well. I reached for her. She backed away.

"As much as I want to," I said, "I can't walk away from this. I'm sorry. There's too much at stake."

She folded her arms, raising one hand to her mouth to hold in the sobs.

I touched her shoulder. She shrugged it off.

"You should go to Chapel Hill," I said. "It sounds like the right place for you to finish your work. I wish I could go with you, but I can't. It's because I care for you too much to put you in danger. Once they see we've split up, they'll leave you alone."

"Split up?" Sue spat. "The only time we were together was in your dreams."

It was her pain talking, but that didn't make it hurt any less. I turned aside, fighting my own emotions. I'd adored Sue Ling from a distance too long to give her up now. Sending her away was the right thing to do, but I didn't want to do it.

I felt her hand touch my cheek.

"Grant, I'm sorry," she said softly. "I didn't mean that."

She turned my head. Her face was close to mine. Her eyes were brimming with emotion. She took me by the hand and pulled me onto the sofa. She cuddled up next to me, her arms around me, her head on my chest.

"You're a good man, Grant. I know this is hard for you. You want to be Superman and save the world, and I adore you for it. So few men are noble anymore. But Grant, can't you see? You've been dealt a losing hand from the beginning. I love that you're noble, but right now you have to be realistic. God has given you a chance for happiness in this life. Don't throw it away."

She looked up at me invitingly, just as she did in my fantasies. Our lips brushed. I held her gaze. It drew me in. I pulled her to me, our lips pressed together in a long-awaited kiss. Her eyes closed. I kept mine open. I'd spent too much time with my eyes closed imagining Sue Ling; now that I had her in my arms I didn't want to squander a moment of it.

The kiss on the sofa wasn't our first kiss, but it was the first passionate embrace. If I could have stretched that moment into forever, it would have been heaven.

"What did you do to Sue Ling?" Jana said, pulling me aside by the arm.

Her news crew paid no attention to us as they carried cameras and sound equipment into my apartment. This was Belial's choice of location for the interview. My guess was that he chose this location over the studio so that he could talk to me afterward.

"What? I didn't do anything to Sue," I protested. "What makes you think I did?"

"We talked until two last night at a coffee shop," Jana said. "She wouldn't tell me what happened, but she was clearly upset. I've never seen her like that before."

"Like what?"

"Like some lovesick teenager. 'I think he loves me . . . he doesn't love me . . . do you think he loves me?' That sort of thing."

I tried not to smile. The thought of Sue Ling as a lovesick teenager was the best news Jana could have reported. Sue Ling loved me. My head swam with the thought.

When we'd parted yesterday she'd begged me to reconsider my decision and move with her to Chapel Hill. I made no promises. We agreed to talk about it again later.

"Miss Torres," one of her crew interrupted. "The sofa OK?"

"No," Jana said. She began pointing and directing. "Pull those two chairs together against that wall. Put that end table between them. Grant, do you have something tasteful that we can put on the table?"

"How about my book?" I quipped.

She gave me the grimace I'd played for.

We settled on an ornate desktop clock President Douglas gave me one Christmas. It came with papers and a photograph documenting that the clock had sat on the desk in the office of former secretary of state William Jennings Bryan.

Belial chose that moment to arrive with his usual suddenness, startling a member of the crew, who knocked over a studio light. He ran to the truck to get a replacement bulb.

The room that had bustled with the noise and voices of pre-taping preparations became hushed. Whenever Jesus enters a room he commands attention, even if he is an impostor. After hearing the stories of the Divine Warrior, seeing Belial dressed as the Joker Jesus grated on my nerves. But then, they were calling him Neo Jesus now, weren't they?

"Grant!" Belial said, all smiles. "And who is this lovely daughter of Eve standing beside you?"

I introduced him to Jana though he'd met her before. Belial was all charm. Jana wasn't impressed. She returned his fawning approach with courteous professionalism. But I knew, given the chance, she'd kick him where it hurt.

That thought led to another. An alarming one.

"Can you excuse us a moment?" I said to Belial, pulling Jana aside. I whispered, "You're not going to make him angry, are you?"

"What do you mean?"

"You're not going to try to expose him."

She looked at me suspiciously. "Why do you ask?"

Before I could answer Belial interrupted us. "Grant, have you come to a decision about my offer?"

Jana glared at me. "What offer?"

"WHAT'S HE DOING HERE?"

Abdiel's voice reverberated off the walls. He appeared just as the crew member, carrying two replacement bulbs, returned from the truck. He dropped them both.

"WHAT'S HE DOING HERE?" Abdiel repeated. "AND WHAT OFFER?"

"What offer?" Jana echoed, equally furious.

Sue Ling appeared at the front door. "Grant, I was driving by and saw the news trucks . . . Oh!"

"What is this?" Belial bellowed. "Some sort of trap?"

"Grant Austin," Abdiel yelled, "answer my question. What is he doing here?"

"What offer?" Jana asked.

"Grant? What's going on here?" Sue said.

Those members of the news crew who hadn't already run out the front door stood with their backs pressed against the wall.

Sue was giving hurt looks to Jana and me.

Jana, ever the professional, saw a newsworthy event in the making. She was motioning to her cameraman to start shooting. But it wasn't her regular guy, and the cameraman fumbled with the equipment as the two angels squared off against each other in the center of the room.

I moved in front of Sue, protecting her. She grabbed my arm from behind and clung to it. "What are they doing here, Grant? And what offer?"

The two angels circled each other, their jaws set, their fists clenched. Belial's sandals had come off. Neither of the angels was touching the floor.

"Sue, stay back," I said.

"What offer?" she repeated.

The next instant swords flashed. Abdiel's silver broadsword. Belial's intimidating black-bladed broadsword. As the two combatants circled, they gripped and regripped their swords.

The first blow struck like lightning and cracked like thunder. Twin arcs, sweeping upward, clashing overhead. The gleam of the swords burst into sparks at impact. I not only saw it and heard it . . . I felt it. The blow knocked me back a step.

Sue whimpered. "Grant? Are you all right?"

Twin arcs appeared again, clashing over the warrior angels' heads with force, showering the room with sparks that painted everything with a harsh white light and cast frightening black shadows. This time I anticipated the force from the blow and held my ground.

A short distance to my right Jana was standing perilously close. She seemed mesmerized by the blows. Oblivious to the danger.

Abdiel and Belial drew their swords back for another blow. I didn't want to leave Sue unprotected, but Jana was within striking range of the swords.

"Jana, back away!" I warned.

She glanced at me, perplexed. Could she not hear me?

The angels swung their swords.

I moved instinctively. "No!" I stepped between the combatants.

Looking back on it, what I did was stupid. For some reason I thought maybe I could grab their weapon arms and force them to lower their weapons.

Instead, a third broadsword appeared.

Mine.

It was gleaming silver, and it flashed with a righteous radiance.

Overhead the swords of Abdiel and Belial clashed. Standing in a shower of sparks I swung with all my might in an upward arc. My blade hit theirs at the point of impact, separating them.

The convergence of three swords produced a shower of sparks that fell so heavily I ducked my head and closed my eyes. When I opened them again, everyone was staring at me.

The room appeared as it did on any ordinary day, except for the cables and lights and soundboard and general clutter of the news crew.

Abdiel looked down at me with controlled amusement. Belial appeared troubled.

"Grant, are you all right?" Sue said.

Jana's eyes asked the same question.

I looked at them. "I see swords."

It was just Jana and me in the living room. She played the video on a monitor and for the first time I saw what she and Sue and the crew members had seen. It was quite unremarkable.

Abdiel and Neo Jesus squared off against each other in the center of my living room. They eyed each other. The recording showed me yelling at Jana to get back. She looked at me as if I were crazy. I lunged between the two angels, separating them.

That was it. No swords. No lightning. No thunder. No sparks. No heroics.

"I like my version better," I said.

"What did your sword look like?"

I shrugged. "A guy doesn't like to brag."

"Yeah? Since when?"

She gathered up her things, throwing cords into her bag.

"Are you angry?" I asked.

Looping her bag over an arm, she hefted the monitor. "Why would I be angry? I get to go back to work and tell my producer I didn't get the interview. And that now I'll probably never get it."

I felt bad. Shortly after my lunge, Belial departed suddenly. He didn't act as if he would accept another invitation soon.

"Let me carry that for you," I offered.

"Just get the door, Grant."

As I held the door open for her, she paused long enough to say, "You really blew it with Sue Ling."

"Yeah. I should have told her."

"About what, Grant? The sessions with Abdiel? The interview? Or Belial's offer?"

Following my not-so-courageous intervention, Sue and Abdiel stayed long enough for me to tell them about Belial's offer. They both left in a huff.

"That's three good women, Grant," Jana said. "Me. Christina. And now Sue Ling. For being such a smart guy, you just don't know a good thing when you see it, do you?"

She was wrong. I knew a good thing when I saw it. I just didn't know what to do with it.

I leaned against the door in thought after closing it.

I could see swords.

CHAPTER

20

The reaction to Belial's plan was unanimous. Jana said even if she could, she wouldn't cover it, and she was in the business of reporting disasters. Sue wept, kissed me on the cheek, and turned away as though I were dying. At times like this I missed the professor.

Abdiel was angrier than I'd ever seen him. "You don't know who you're dealing with! You don't make deals with the devil."

I laughed at the irony. "It's not as though I can sell my soul to him. He already owns it."

"All the same, this isn't a Make-A-Wish program, Grant. Belial either wants something from you . . . or he's using you."

"Yes, he's using me. He's using me to free his sons from a thousand years of torment. You said it yourself. Some of the angels developed genuine feelings for the women they married. Is it so inconceivable to believe that Belial might have feelings for his offspring?"

"He is evil!"

"What if he's acting on his own as he claims?" I countered. "What if he's taking as much of a risk as I am?"

"You would be foolish to proceed."

"All right, I won't. I'll turn Belial down, on one condition. That you agree to help me present my petition to the Father."

"I can't do that," Abdiel said.

"Can't, or won't? I know you know about these things. Is it possible for me to enter Sheol? Are there membrane passages linking Sheol with heaven? What about the King's Highway, is it still open? Will I be allowed access? And if I do get to heaven, will it be possible for me to stand on those fiery stones and present my petition to the Father? What day does the Father hold council, Abdiel? Thursdays? Do I need to make an appointment?"

He let me rant. When I was finished, he said, "I can't answer your questions, Grant Austin."

"Then I'll just have to find the answers elsewhere."

"I will take my leave of you."

"Yeah. I think that's a good idea."

I was furious. They didn't know. They weren't Nephilim. Who were they to tell me not to risk my own life? They had the hope of salvation. None of them faced an eternity of suffering. Why couldn't they understand that? If a man is given a chance to avoid eternal torment, he'd be a fool not to take it.

For a week I stewed over my choice. And since stewing is best done alone I didn't talk to anyone.

Abdiel was a no-show for our next scheduled session. I'd been looking forward to the topic. He was going to narrate his recollections of the apostles.

Apparently Lucifer went crazy after the Resurrection. The Divine Warrior had taken the fear out of death and Lucifer was livid over the loss of one of his favorite weapons. He tried to recover it with a reign of terror on the early church, personally orchestrating the painful deaths of the leaders of the church. His strategy backfired. Word of the courageous deaths of the martyrs was carried on the four winds. Christian faith spread like a prairie fire.

I stuck the notes from our previous sessions in a box and shelved them. Maybe I'd find a use for them someday. Or maybe someday I'd come home and find my apartment had been plucked off the face of the earth by Semyaza. You'd think after all these millennia the guy would learn how to use a paper shredder.

Seven days of mourning Sue Ling's absence was an unspeakable torture. She was in my thoughts when I woke; she was in my thoughts every moment I was awake; and she was in my thoughts when I went to bed. Then I dreamed about her.

Even though I knew it would be painful for both of us, I had to see her again. I told myself we needed a proper good-bye, but the truth was, I just had to see her again. I bought some pastries and went to her apartment. A man wearing boxer shorts and a T-shirt opened the door.

"Who are you?" I blurted.

"I don't know what you're selling, fella, but your sales pitch needs some work," he said with a rakish grin. "Come back when you've come up with a better opening line."

He started to close the door. I stopped him, my hand hitting the door just below the number. Sue Ling's apartment number.

"Hey, buddy. What's your damage?" the guy yelled.

Behind him the bedroom door slammed shut, but not before I caught a glimpse of jet-black hair.

At times like this the brain of the human male short-circuits.

I shoved the bag of pastries in the guy's face and pushed my way past him. He stumbled backward, fell against the wall, and slid to the floor.

"Sue Ling!" I said, storming the door. "I'm coming in!"

I was bursting through the bedroom door before the guy in the boxer shorts could recover. A frightened Asian woman was hurriedly pulling on a bathrobe.

Not Sue Ling, but this was still her apartment. Her bed. Her dresser. All the furniture in the living room.

"What are you doing in this apartment?" I demanded. "Where's Sue Ling?"

The guy in the boxer shorts grabbed me, swung me around, and was just about to flatten me when something sparked behind his angry eyes. He broke into a grin. "You're Grant Austin! I got your book!"

The woman in the robe said a few things in a language I didn't understand. She communicated well enough, though, punctuating her remarks with a couple of pitched shoes.

The guy in the boxer shorts pulled the door shut just in time to save us from injury. "I have a letter for you from Sue Ling. She told me you'd probably come around someday."

He eagerly unburied an envelope from a pile of letters and receipts and telephone books and socks still in their packaging and car keys and handed it to me. My name was written on it in Sue Ling's handwriting.

"We swapped apartments," the guy said happily. "I just transferred out here from UNC."

"Professor Ledbetter introduced you," I said, recalling the comment Sue made about a student from Chapel Hill.

"That's right. He linked us up. Anyway, we got to talking and figured, why spend all that money shipping furniture and looking for new apartments? Why not just swap?"

From the looks of Sue Ling's apartment after only a few days of residency, the guy in the boxer shorts came out ahead on this deal.

Rummaging in stacks of boxes in the living room he found a copy of my book. It was the first time I'd ever autographed a book for a guy in boxer shorts.

"Oh . . . your bag," he said, as I was leaving.

"You can have it."

He looked inside. "Cool! Pastries! Thanks. What a pal!"

I turned to leave.

"Um . . . Grant? Would you mind autographing the bag?"

For ten minutes I sat in the apartment parking lot staring at the unopened envelope. I didn't have to open it to know what it said. I might as well be holding a dagger, deciding whether I wanted to stick it in my heart.

I opened the envelope.

You understand, don't you? It has to be this way.

Sue

P.S. You can see swords!

I dialed her cell phone number and got a recording. Her phone was no longer in service.

I called Jana.

"Seven days, Grant?" she said. "It took you seven days before going over there to see her?"

"Not now, Jana. You can yell at me some other time."

The life had gone out of me.

Jana apologized. "She doesn't want you following her, Grant."

"I know. Did your producer give you a lot of grief over the interview?"

"No more than usual, though he brings it up every time we run a story on the Geneva conference. 'Wish we had that interview. Timing couldn't be better.' That sort of thing."

"Yeah."

"You haven't seen him again, have you? Belial?"

"No."

"You'd tell me if you had, wouldn't you, Grant? And if you do see him again, could you at least ask him if he'd be willing to . . ." Her voice trailed off.

"Yeah. I'll ask him."

We said good-bye and I sat in the car with no place to go. Christina came to mind. I'd just stormed into one girlfriend's apartment and talked with another old girlfriend. It seemed only natural to call a third old girlfriend.

"Grant!" Christina called cheerfully. "Long time!"

"How are things in D.C.?"

"I'm in Geneva, Switzerland, for the conference. Senator Vogler is the head of the U.S. delegation. Don't you read the newspapers, Grant?"

"I thought it was just a bunch of scientists."

"That's how it started, but with everything happening—you did hear that President Rossi is being impeached, didn't you?"

"I heard something about it."

"Grant, you really need to get back to D.C. Anyway, with the impeachment and the stock market the way it is and the on-going Middle East crisis, everyone's open to new directions. All the major powers have sent delegations. It's so exciting! The timing couldn't be better! Grant, everyone is talking about a new world order. You should be here. History is being made."

"Christina, you know that Neo Jesus is—"

"Grant? Sorry, but I have to go. Word of advice? Get on a plane and get over here. The whole world is watching."

The connection lost, I closed my phone and tossed it on the passenger's seat. It was hard to fault Christina. I remembered what it was like living and working in D.C. Everything happened in great surges that had little to do with truth or reality. It was easy to get swept up in the tide.

Driving home I stopped at Starbucks on a whim. Their café mocha was calling to me. Comfort coffee.

As I walked in the door I saw five men wearing three-piece business suits sitting at a table in the back of the shop. All five of them had gleaming silver swords.

Angels drink Starbucks. Who knew?

Their conversation ceased when they saw me. Five pair of angel eyes followed me as I walked to the counter and placed my drink order. They watched me as I drummed my fingers on the counter, waiting for the order to be filled.

"Join us?" one of them said.

"Thanks, guys," I said, "but I need to be—"

I was thankful they didn't insist. Paying for my drink, I turned to leave just as another business suit walked into the shop. He had a black sword.

He looked at me. His eyes flashed recognition. I'd never seen him before. Then he looked past me and saw the five angels in the back. They glared at him.

Getting caught in a crossfire came to mind. Should I hit the floor? Seemed like a waste of a perfectly good café mocha.

The suit with the black sword backed out of the shop. Conversation at the table resumed.

As I walked out the door, one of the angels called after me. "Take it easy, Grant."

Now that I could see swords, I was seeing them everywhere. And not just angels. On my way to the car I saw two men across the street walking on the sidewalk. The taller man was smiling and doing most of the talking while patting the other man on the back. They looked like friends. However, I saw that the pats were stabs in the back.

On the street corner a woman had her arm around her schoolboy son. She was pointing at a couple of toughs crossing the street. They didn't want to mess with this woman. She leveled a silver sword at them as she warned them to stay away from her boy.

On my way home I stopped by the professor's house. I parked across the street. I didn't get out. The lot had been cleaned and leveled. Builders were erecting a new frame structure. There was nothing left on the property to remind people that a godly man had once lived there.

I had walked through a wall in the house that had once been on that lot. And I had seen swords for the first time in that house, though briefly.

Abdiel had been right about Sue's sword. I saw elegance. He saw frailty. Her spirit just wasn't strong enough for the battle. Had she depended all these years on the professor's strength?

After a week of worry and a day of anguish my own sword wasn't looking nearly as impressive as it had when it flashed between Abdiel and Belial. I noticed a continuous deterioration as the day went on and began to check it regularly. Each time I looked—I was wrong to think a person's sword could be seen in a mirror; it couldn't—it became a little duller.

I went to bed that night determined to get on with my life. Until I learned otherwise, I was going to assume Belial had withdrawn his offer.

There were a couple of book ideas I'd mulled over in the past. Tomorrow morning I'd go to San Diego State University and do some initial research. Maybe if I lost myself in work the pain of losing the professor and Sue Ling would ease up a bit.

With the dawn of a new day I was up, showered, and shaved. Fueled by a bagel and orange juice, I'd dressed in a casual suit and had my briefcase equipped with pens and legal pads. This morning I'd reacquaint myself with the unconventional research librarian at SDSU, and this afternoon I'd go shopping for a new laptop.

It felt good to be Grant Austin, writer, again. With briefcase in hand I headed toward the front door wondering, now that I could see swords, if it was possible to stop seeing them. Maybe if I put everything of a spiritual nature out of my mind, I'd eventually lose the knack. It was worth a try. Today I would make a conscious effort not to be spiritual. It would be carnal Thursday, the first day of the rest of my—

Abdiel appeared in front of me so suddenly I nearly ran into him. Wouldn't you know it? The moment I decide to be carnal, an angel appears. He appeared more glorious than normal.

"Wearing your Sunday suit?" I asked.

"Be not afraid, Grant Austin," Abdiel said.

"Why? Are you going to bang my head against the wall again?"

Abdiel's radiance increased. It was a fearful glory. Its weight fell heavily on me.

"I bring to you a message from the Father," Abdiel said. "You are placing the mark of God's favor in jeopardy. Should you choose to enter Sheol, you will enter without the protective mark of the Father, for you will enter it as a warrior."

"A warrior? I'm no warrior. All I want to do is present a petition. Can't I enter Sheol as a diplomat?"

Abdiel offered no reply. Several moments passed before I realized he was waiting for an answer.

"Oh—" I said. "If given the chance, I choose to enter."

"So be it," he said.

He lingered, his glorious glow softening until he was the angel I was accustomed to seeing. He spoke quickly and in earnest. "Think, Grant. Think on these things."

He disappeared.

I looked down at my sword. The mark of favor was gone. I yelled at the ceiling, "I thought angels were supposed to deliver good news!"

A voice behind me said, "How about a good joke?"

I turned to see Belial. My carnal Thursday wasn't off to a good start.

"Don't you have a conference to attend?" I said.

"The conference starts tomorrow. Don't you read the newspapers, Grant?"

"I've been a little preoccupied."

I glanced at the ceiling, wondering if Belial had brought his boys with him. Without the mark I was vulnerable to demon possession. Not an attractive thought.

Belial saw where I was looking. "They're in Orange County. I won't lie to you, Grant. They're doing what demons do. But if things go according to plan, they won't have to do that anymore, will they?"

"Aren't you afraid this is some sort of trap?" I said.

"Don't you feel naked without the Father's mark on your sword?" he countered.

It didn't take him long to notice.

"Look, Grant, I was wrong the other day. After I left, I felt foolish about it. Please give my apologies to Jana and tell her I'll be glad to reschedule the interview. But I'm more concerned about us. If this is going to work, we're going to have to do it together. Frankly, you're my last hope. Do you still want to go through with it?"

My first impulse was to tell him I needed time to think about it. But I didn't, did I? I'd paid dearly to get to this point.

"I'm in," I said. "When do we start?"

"Right now."

"Now?"

"With all the attention in Geneva tempting and seducing the delegates in anticipation for the weekend, I was able to slip away unnoticed."

"OK. What do we do first?"

"I take you to Sheol. We'll look around. I'll show you the portals to heaven. Once we get you there, we'll have a better idea what we're up against."

My blood chilled. I'd planned to go to SDSU and a computer store today. Sheol wasn't on the itinerary.

"What do you need me to do?" I asked.

"I need your consent."

"Do you want me to sign my name in blood?"

Belial laughed. "All I need is your word."

I laughed. "I can't buy a used car on my word."

"We're more trusting than used-car dealers."

I hesitated. Was I really going to do this? I thought of all the Nephilim who shared my fate. They were once like me. I was the only one left. The only one able to speak for all of us.

In fatherly tones Belial said, "I'm not going to downplay the dangers. It's a rotten deal, it really is. You asked for none of this. And if there weren't so many lives on the line, I'd tell you to forget it. The outcome of heaven's war is not going to hinge on Grant Austin. But you can bring good out of it. You have an opportunity to rescue innocents caught in the crossfire."

"Take me to Sheol," I said.

"That's your choice?"

"That's my choice."

Belial sighed heavily. "Very well."

He held out his hand, not to shake, but the offering hand of someone who is going to take you on a journey. I grasped it.

"Lesson number one, Grant Austin."

His eyes blazed with black fire. He laughed.

"Never trust the devil."

CHAPTER 21

Hitting the membrane portal felt like running through a screen door at sixty miles per hour. The molecules of my body were ripped apart, their cohesiveness snapping like rubber bands stretched beyond their elasticity.

Belial ignored my screams. The louder I yelled, the harder he yanked. My screams turned to moans, then childlike whimpering as I begged for the pain to stop. The physical force of transit hammered my eyes and clawed at my cheeks and neck. Liquid fire poured down my throat. It was too much for me. Too much. My body's only defense was to shut down. The last thing I remembered was tumbling onto a gritty, rocklike surface.

Voices, distant and unintelligible, roused me. My eyelids fluttered. Memories flashed, all of them painful. Fear and panic stirred within me. I willed my eyes to stay open. Shards of light stabbed them shut. Shielding my eyes with my hand, I forced myself to keep looking.

The light came from two sources a short distance away. They had human shape and stood against the deepest black I'd ever seen. Angels. Too bright to identify.

Rolling to my side I raised my head to get a better look. A mistake. The effort set off a series of blinding white explosions in my head. For a time all I could do was lie there, breathing heavily. Gradually, the pain subsided and I tried again.

My initial thought was that I was in a massive cavern. Its limits stretched beyond available light. However, there was enough light to illuminate a vaulted ceiling that appeared to be made of red rock, the same material upon which I'd landed.

A thick coat of dust—red like the rock and powdery—covered everything. The slightest movement stirred it. I could feel it on my skin. It covered my clothes. The air was saturated with it. I could taste it. Gritty. Bitter, like ashes.

Some of the dust had been scraped away where I'd landed, revealing the surface. It was rock unlike anything I'd seen before. Translucent. Beneath the surface, lightning flashed, yet without giving off any light. With each spark of lightning I felt energy go out of me. Weakening me.

Between the acrid atmosphere, which made breathing difficult, and the energy-draining rock, it was clear I wouldn't last long here. I had to get out, and quickly.

"He survived the passage," a voice said.

Belial? Possibly. It sounded like his voice but different. Harder.

"Fortunate for us, not for him."

That voice I recognized. There was no mistaking it.

"Semyaza," I croaked.

The face of my nemesis shone over me. "Welcome to Sheol, Grant."

There's nothing like the presence of a rival to get one's blood stirring. I wrestled myself into a half-seated position, propping up on my elbows.

"Forget to pay the light bill, Myles?" I said. "Nice place, from what I can see of it. My compliments to your decorator. He's captured the barrenness of your soul."

"Spare me your adolescent sarcasm. And you will address me as Semyaza."

I chuckled. "Can't do that. You'll always be little pimple-faced Myles Shepherd to me."

With a grunt, he kicked my arm out from beneath me. My head hit hard.

His reaction was worth it. In high school Myles Shepherd had been the only kid on campus with a perfect complexion. Not until recently did I know why. Lucifer's vain lieutenant wouldn't stoop so low as to be seen with a common human zit.

Belial appeared behind him. I could see it was him now. All traces of the genial Joker Jesus were gone. They walked a short distance away and spoke to each other in whispers.

I struggled to my feet, my hands and clothes covered with the sticky, powdery dirt. Was this really Sheol, the realm of the dead? Despite the peril of my situation, the historian within me stirred. If this really was Sheol, King David had dwelt here after death. So had Abraham, Isaac, Jacob, and Noah. Abel had been its first resident, joined later by his parents, Adam and Eve. The dead population of the entire world until the cross!

To paraphrase a saying, "Oh, if these rocks could talk! The stories they'd tell!"

The place was vacant now. I tried to imagine what it must have been like for them to dwell here with no sun or moon to mark the passage of time. That is, if time even existed here. And I tried to imagine the day the Divine Warrior arrived. Fresh from the cross. A dead man among the dead. With one difference. He hadn't come to be death's victim, but its conqueror.

What a battle that must have been! Lucifer wouldn't have given up his trophies without a fight. Man, what I wouldn't give to be permitted to research that day and write an account of it. The shouts that must have echoed through this dreary place . . . the excitement as the Divine Warrior led them out of here to heaven!

Semyaza's laugh cut into my reverie. The two rebel angels peered over their shoulders at me.

I didn't have time to waste on imagining the past. The present demanded my full attention if I was to survive. Just standing here, my arms and legs felt as if they were filled with sand. I needed to implement a strategy.

Wait.

I didn't have a strategy.

OK, it was time to formulate one.

Wait.

There was nothing to formulate.

My situation could be summed up in one sentence. I was toast. I'd been hoodwinked, bamboozled, swindled, tricked, and flummoxed. All that was left was to fold, spindle, and mutilate me.

It had been a setup from the beginning. They'd cut me off from my world. No one on earth knew I was here. How long would it take for someone to miss me? Weeks? Months? I'd managed to alienate everyone who cared for me. And even if they knew I was in Sheol, what could they do? I was on my own, left to my own resources. Somehow I had to find a way to escape. But how? Even if I could find the membrane portal, I didn't know if I could summon the courage to step through it. I feared I wouldn't survive another crossing.

Belial befriending me. All that sentimental talk of petitioning the Father on behalf of his sons. It had been a setup from the beginning. They had played me perfectly. And why not? They'd been doing this kind of thing for millennia.

Despair seeped into my heart. It wasn't as though I hadn't been warned. *"The greatest evil comes with a smile."* Those were the professor's words. All the time I'd been scoffing at the world for believing the lies of the Joker Jesus, I'd been swallowing a different lie, one custom-made for me. I felt like a chump.

If I ran, where would I go? Darkness surrounded me. The air burned my throat. The rocks sapped my strength. Besides, how do you outrun beings who travel at the speed of thought? That left fighting. But was that really an option? It was two against one, and both of them had superhuman strength—not to mention an arsenal of weapons that defied imagination. I'd seen them knock a helicopter out of the sky with a blast of light. Had not friendly angels caught the chopper, everyone on it would have perished. Did I dare hope that friendly angels would rescue me?

The last time I faced Semyaza, Abdiel had been there with some of his buddies. They weren't much help, but they didn't like me then. Now Abdiel was on my side. At least I thought he was on my side. Sometimes it was hard to tell.

The only sure thing I had was my sword, and it had seen better days. I examined it. The blade was cloudy gray and the edges were dull and growing more blunt by the second as the hopelessness of the situation took root in my mind. It was no match for Semyaza's and Belial's swords, which were intimidatingly long, impressively thick, razor sharp, and black as the ace of spades.

"I'm a dead man," I muttered.

Under different circumstances, being a dead man in Sheol would have struck me as funny.

I lifted my face heavenward—at least I thought it was heavenward. Who knew what direction heaven was in relation to Sheol? I was desperate for a glimmer of inspiration.

"If you're praying for the cavalry," Semyaza said, "it's a wasted effort. Contrary to what you've been led to believe, good angels don't frequent Sheol."

A lie? Not likely. Semyaza enjoyed telling the truth when he could hurt you with it.

Standing beside him, Belial smirked. "Only once have the Father's forces entered Sheol, and that was to assist the Son. You're just not worth their effort."

"Then what are you waiting for?" I taunted. "Reinforcements? Are you that afraid of me?"

Semyaza scoffed. "If bluster were a weapon, Grant Austin, you would be a formidable opponent. Forgive us if we are not intimidated by your witty expulsion of hot air."

"So why the delay?"

"Even a minor spectacle such as this deserves an audience."

Rebel angels began appearing out of nothingness. Hundreds of them. Thousands. Encircling us. Positioning themselves in layers until it appeared as though I was standing in the center of a grand coliseum.

If this was a coliseum, then two ferocious lions were in the arena with me. That made me the featured martyr.

The strange thing about the gathering was that I had never seen so much beauty assembled in one place. Every face was striking. If I lingered on any one of them, my jaw dropped in awe. The fact that they all wore black swords kept things in perspective. What struck me most was that the sheer number of attractive beings with weapons of evil went a long way in explaining the amount of wickedness in the world.

Before the arena was completely formed, the increased light from additional angels afforded me a better look at Sheol.

The red-rock sky stretched for as far as the eye could see, hanging there without pillars or support of any kind as effortlessly as earth's blue sky. The terrain consisted solely of rock. There were no trees. No vegetation of any kind. No streams or lakes. Neither were there any buildings. About a half-mile distant there was an outcropping of craggy hills and cliffs pocked with dark recesses. Caves? Passageways? Or just shadows? I couldn't tell from this distance.

With rebel angels in the vicinity, demons couldn't be far behind, I figured. And I was right. The demons began arriving, taking up position overhead, packing themselves tightly together. They were wriggling, hideous, green ridge-backed creatures with jagged teeth. They snapped at each other unceasingly, stopping only long enough to leer at me in anticipation of what was to come.

I wondered if they were aware that I'd come to Sheol to present a petition to the Father on their behalf? If they were, none of them appeared to be eternally grateful.

The growing number of rebel angels grew restless with the clamor of a preshow audience.

"What, no concessions?" I asked Semyaza. "No peanuts? Popcorn? Cotton candy? No Lucifer bobble-head dolls?"

If he heard me, he ignored me. He had his game face on, his attention on the assembled force of hell.

Then the ground beneath my feet began to tremble, building in intensity. My knees buckled and I went down.

All around me, the ground fell away. No, it wasn't falling. I was rising. I found myself atop a pillar roughly four feet in diameter thrusting upward ten, fifteen, twenty, thirty feet into the air.

Semyaza and Belial rose with me, one on each side. Only they didn't need pedestals. They stood on air.

There were no preliminaries.

"Behold!" Semyaza said, his voice filling the chamber effortlessly. "The last Nephilim!"

You would expect the crowd to roar at this point, as they did in the Roman Coliseum when the Christians were led out in chains. But these former residents of heaven were eerily silent. What they lacked in noise, they made up for with expressions of loathing. The gaze of thousands of rebel angels bore into me as though they were examining something disgusting they'd scraped off the bottom of their sandals.

Their unblinking scrutiny chilled me when I realized that compared to the slimy, wriggling demons overhead, I was considered the repulsive one.

"You've all heard," Semyaza continued, "how this despicable worm mocked Lucifer at an angelic tribunal, refusing to acknowledge his allegiance despite our impressive enlistment effort. How he chose instead to side with the Father, who would damn him for no other reason than that he is part angel."

At this, the spectators became agitated.

"In my defense," I said, my voice puny compared to Semyaza's, "it should be pointed out that—"

An invisible hand clutched my throat, severing the sentence. Belial's eyes flamed in warning. With a final squeeze for emphasis, he released me. I rubbed my throat and coughed.

"An injustice occurred at that tribunal," Semyaza said. "In an act most capricious, the Father granted this Nephilim protected status, giving him license to flaunt his traitorous ways in our faces without fear of consequence or reprisal."

The crowd became raucous. Their faces twisted with outrage. I had to give it to Semyaza; he knew how to work the crowd.

Semyaza spoke with the cadence of a revival preacher. "That which we have believed from the beginning, that which we have clung to with unswerving hope, that which we have fought for against superior odds, has today, at last, born fruit! Justice has won the day against a Father God who would play favorites!"

He motioned to me dramatically. "Behold the Nephilim!" he exclaimed in triumph. "Stripped of the Father's protective mark!"

Sheol rocked with angelic cheers.

"That which the Father gave so arbitrarily, we have taken away!"

The pillar beneath me shook with the noise of the celebration as the assembled rebel angels rejoiced at the expense of my foolishness. Never before had I felt so low and ashamed.

Semyaza drank it all in. His moment of triumph. My humiliation. What angered me most was the ease with which he'd bested me. Within a matter of weeks after I received the Father's protective mark, he'd conned me into surrendering it.

The demons celebrated in their own way, anxious for the command that would loose them. How long would Semyaza let them feed on me before he turned me into one of them? Weeks? Months? Years? A sheen of perspiration coated my skin as I remembered the last time I'd been possessed by demons.

The flash of a black blade caught my attention. Semyaza drew near, his sword leveled at me. "Did you really think this would end any other way?"

He punctuated the comment with the tip of his blade. It sliced my arm with ease.

"Hey!" I cried, grabbing the wound.

My hand felt wet. I lifted it in disbelief.

At the sight of blood the crowd hushed. Semyaza and Belial shared the crowd's muted astonishment as they gawked at the sword's red tip. The weapon that had been created to wound the spirit had wounded the flesh.

Semyaza grinned. He jabbed my other arm.

"Ow, that hurts!" I howled, backing away. The thirty-foot drop behind me limited my retreat.

"There's never been a living human in Sheol," Belial mused, equally thrilled.

"An interesting development, wouldn't you say?" Semyaza added.

With a sweeping swish of his blade he sliced my chest. A superficial wound, but it had a stinging bite.

The spectators roared with delight.

Licking his lips, Belial drew his sword, eager to give his blade a taste of blood. He and Semyaza began circling me like a couple of jackals.

I moved to the center of my space, turning with them, trying to keep both of them in front of me. My own sword, pitiful as it was, appeared in my hands. With weary and bleeding arms I raised it defensively, biting back the pain.

I swung at them wildly, my blade finding nothing but air. I was a writer, not a swordsman. What did I know of dueling? But I knew not to lunge too far. While the physics of Sheol might be different from earth in some respects, gravity was a constant.

They toyed with me. When I faced one of them, the other would feign attack. They seemed to be content to wear me down. The tactic was working. My arms and legs grew increasingly heavy. The atmosphere and strength-sapping rock were taking a toll. My breathing was labored, and I was getting dizzy from circling.

Time was on their side. I had to take the offensive. Were

angels vulnerable to the sword in Sheol? Could I give as good as I got? I was about to find out.

I lunged at Belial. Then, pivoting suddenly, anticipating Semyaza's attack from behind, I swung with all my might. It worked. I caught Semyaza by surprise. The expression on his face was priceless as he realized his error. But it was too late. My blade caught him at the waist.

And passed right through him without harm.

Now the surprise was mine. Expecting resistance and finding none, the momentum of my swing spun me around and I nearly toppled from the tower. I stared at my sword in disbelief. It had betrayed me.

The crowd erupted with laughter.

"Imbecile." Semyaza laughed. "As an opponent, you have always been a disappointment. A disposable pawn. A hack who fancied himself a bestselling writer. And now a warrior with an imaginary sword." He played to the crowd. "Behold! The student of a human cripple and a pompous archangel!"

The quip about Abdiel went over big with the crowd. As Semyaza reveled in the applause, I tested my blade against my own leg. I had a ghost sword. It passed right through me.

The physics of Sheol made no sense.

Belial attacked. I reacted instinctively, positioning my sword to block. But instead of a clanging of swords, Belial's sword passed through my blade and made a sickening thud against my leg just above my knee.

With a howl, I collapsed into the dust.

The crowd cheered. Belial raised his sword in triumph.

With my chest heaving, tears blurring my vision, and the cut on my leg feeling as though I'd been burned with a fireplace poker, I fought a trio of rebel allies that rose up from within me—pain, nausea, and panic.

Clearly, I had to find a different weapon. A ghost sword was worse than no sword at all. But what else was there? Alone atop a thirty-foot tower, the sword was the only weapon available. If I was going to keep myself from being filleted, somehow, I had to figure out a way to make it solid like theirs.

I began by assembling every fact I knew about spiritual swords. I knew that it had taken me a long time to learn how to see them. That was no longer a problem. Not only could I see them, I could feel them.

What else?

"Stand and fight, Grant Austin," Semyaza said. "Your wounds are not that grievous."

I ignored him. I was busy.

What else did I know about spiritual swords?

I knew they reflected a person's spiritual strength and that their appearance varied as the person's strength of spirit varied.

I had mistaken Sue's thin sword for elegant when in reality it was fragile. But there was no mistaking my current spiritual state. My sword was functioning well in that regard. It was a pitiful, dull gray and the blade was chipped. Just like me. Dull and definitely chipped.

What else? There had to be something I was missing.

The crowd took up a chant for me to stand.

What about faith? Did the sword's consistency vary according to a person's faith? But that didn't make sense, did it? Rebel angels had long ago abandoned the faith, yet their swords were in fine shape.

"I'll not tell you again, Grant Austin," Semyaza said. "Stand and fight. If you do not, I'll loose a legion of demons upon you."

Favoring my good leg, I struggled to get up. I had to delay the demons for as long as possible. It's difficult to reason with a thousand demons screaming inside your head. I'd have to buy time by dodging sword thrusts.

I faced my attackers, my arms hanging heavy at my sides. They felt like stone. What difference did it make anyway? Even if I could wield my sword, it couldn't protect me.

My mind was racing. *Swords. Swords. Spiritual swords.* What else did I know about them?

The circling began again with Semyaza and Belial eager to resume the spectacle. I tried to counter their moves, but every time I placed weight on my wounded leg, it felt as though another sword thrust had found its mark.

Belial lunged. I dodged. Semyaza swung. I ducked. The crowd didn't care that I was defenseless. They weren't looking for a good fight. My pain was their entertainment. My death would be the climax.

My only hope was that there was something in my training that could save me. A piece of information . . . the significance of which I didn't comprehend at the time.

I remembered a training session in the professor's living room when he quoted a Scripture passage to me about swords. Something about doing battle with the sword of the spirit, which was the Word of God. And there was another passage. Something about that Word being sharper than a two-edged sword.

Looking at my own blade, I agreed that sharper was good, but what I really needed right now was solid.

Just then Semyaza and Belial lunged at the same time. I pulled back at the last second, and their swords clanged inches in front of me. I thrust my sword upward to break them apart. It passed effortlessly through their blades.

Frustration welled up inside of me. I gave it voice.

Think. Think! Double-edged sword . . . what else? Piercing to the dividing of soul and spirit, of joints and marrow.

Piercing! Yes! Piercing was good. What I wouldn't give to do a little piercing of my own right now.

Another swing by Semyaza swished under my chin.

Belial's sword caught my shirt just under my arm and cut a nice flap.

Joints and marrow. Joints and marrow. What else? Think, Grant. Think! There was some kind of link between a person's words and a person's sword. The passage said something about thoughts and intents. God's Word, the sword of his spirit, was . . . was . . . was what?

I dodged another thrust. Semyaza was aiming for my good leg.

What was the final phrase of the Scripture passage? God's Word was what in relation to thoughts and intents?

I had it—God's Word was able to discern a person's thoughts and intentions because it suited his purpose. A spiritual weapon for a spiritual task. A judge needed a discerning sword. But here in Sheol, the separation between spiritual and physical didn't seem to be as great as it was on earth.

Put it together, Grant. Put it together!

There was a link between a person's words, his thoughts, his intentions, and his sword. Here in Sheol that link became phys-ical reality. Semyaza and Belial had brought me here, intent on killing me. Their swords had taken on a form that could accom-plish that task. On the other hand, since my arrival, my inten-tion had been to flee, to find a way out of here. What if I *chose* to stay and fight? What if I *chose* to do injury to angel flesh?

I looked at Semyaza.

Not a problem.

Gripping my sword with new hope and determination, I abandoned all thoughts of escape. I resolved to do battle.

My sword shimmered in my hand.

Semyaza swung at my midsection. I made no attempt to back away. Instead, with a two-handed grip I swung with all my might. Our swords clashed with force. Sparks flew at the point of impact.

Out of the corner of my eye I saw Belial react in surprise. He'd become careless. He was dangerously close.

Do angels bleed? I intended to find out.

Whirling around, I slashed at Belial, knocking his sword aside. He pulled back, but not fast enough. The tip of my sword caught his cheek. His hand flew to the cut. His eyes registered astonishment, then rage. There was no blood, but I'd hurt him.

"Yes!" I exclaimed. I hadn't felt this good since arriving in Sheol.

The blade of my sword had become razor sharp. It was also a darker shade of gray.

I hurled myself at Semyaza, hoping to catch him off guard. He blocked my blow inches from his face.

Seething with fury at the turn of events, Semyaza and Belial backed away. The crowd grew quiet.

"Cowards!" I taunted. "Things are different now that I have a fighting chance, aren't they?"

I flailed wildly at them, desperately wanting to land at least one solid blow for the professor. With each swing my sword grew darker and darker.

"Come on!" I taunted. "I'm just getting started."

If anyone ever tells you that devils fight fair, don't believe them.

Semyaza spat a curse at me. It took form in the shape of a fiery dart and hit me in the chest with a stinging blow. He spat again and stung my hand.

The crowd was back in it.

Staying well outside my reach Semyaza and Belial took turns

spitting fiery darts at me. With each hit the initial sting was sharp, then the pain lingered and burned. I took a hit in the cheek, and my left eye began to swell shut.

Using my sword like a baseball bat, I swung at the darts, hitting some of them aside. But for every one I knocked aside, three struck me. They were coming too fast.

I dropped to one knee, jerking from the sting of each hit. I prayed that they would have the guts to finish me with their swords and that I would have the strength for one last blow so that I could at least take one of them with me.

"Maybe you should try a nursery rhyme, Grant," Semyaza taunted me. That was how I'd defied him in our battle atop the Emerald Plaza tower.

I was on all fours now. My sword lay on the ground beneath me. The blade was as black as Semyaza's sword.

I hung my head in shame. Of course it was. Why wouldn't it be? I had become just like them. I hated them as much as they hated me. I wanted to hurt them. Kill them. I wasn't fighting evil, I was becoming evil. My sword was proof of it.

Sweat dropped from my face, splatting in the red dust.

Sue Ling's voice sounded in my mind. *I love that you're noble, Grant.*

I was glad she wasn't here to see me now. I was glad none of them were here. Sue Ling. Jana. Christina. The professor—oh, the professor, how disappointed in me he would be. And Abdiel. He'd scoff and say he wasn't surprised that I'd failed to learn the truth about the spiritual world.

I love that you're noble.

Noble men don't have black swords.

Think on these things, Grant.

Abdiel's last words to me. Why would I think of them now?

Noble. Think on these things.

The comments seemed to have a natural pairing. *Noble.*
Think on these things.

Then I remembered.

It was from a list. At the time I thought Abdiel was caution-
ing me to think twice before agreeing to enter Sheol. But he
knew I'd already decided to go. Unlike me, he didn't trust
Belial. He knew I'd be facing opposition. Abdiel wasn't questioning my judgment, he was instructing me on how to defend
myself in Sheol!

Think on these things, Grant.

The list was from the book of Philippians.

Whatever is true, whatever is noble, whatever is pure, whatever is
lovely, whatever is admirable, think on these things.

Three darts hit me in quick succession. One on the side of
my face. One on my hip. The third on my wounded leg. That's
the one that brought me down. I slumped to one side, covering
my head with my hands and arms. My face was inches from my
sword. My black-bladed sword.

It was a witness to my downfall. I wanted to shove it away,
to disassociate myself from it.

No—on second thought, I wanted to change it. Before I
died I wanted it to be silver again. If I was going to be found
dead in Sheol, I didn't want to be lying next to a black sword.

I remembered how Abdiel described the Divine Warrior
doing battle against Lucifer and the forces of evil in the world.
He was aggressively good in the face of wickedness. He gave
sight to a people blinded by Lucifer's lies. He gave hope to the
hopeless. Slapped and whipped, He did not strike back in
return. A victim of power politics, He chose not to defend himself, but to sacrifice Himself for those who hurt Him and deserted Him.

I wanted to be like Him. Not like Semyaza. Not like Belial

or any of the black-sworded beings assembled here. I wanted to be like the Divine Warrior.

Think, Grant. Think!

Under a barrage of fiery darts, my teeth clenched against the pain, my eyes clamped shut, I sided with the truth—that regardless of what happened to me, Lucifer's efforts were doomed. I sided with nobility. Forsaking my anger, I admitted the futility of revenge. With all sincerity, I thanked the Father for putting the professor and Sue Ling into my life. I even thanked Him for Abdiel.

When I opened my eyes, my sword was silver once again.

There was one last thing to do. Show it to my enemies, that they might know that they could kill me, they could make a demon of me, but they had not conquered me. They had not succeeded in fashioning me in their image.

With blood streaming down my brow, running into my eyes, streaking my cheeks and arms and hands, I summoned as much strength as I could find.

The fusillade of darts stopped.

The crowd hushed and became silent.

My legs trembled. With sword in hand I maneuvered my feet underneath me and pushed myself up.

"That old shtick, Grant?" Semyaza bawled. "This isn't like on the towers. A desperate act of defiance will impress no one."

I wasn't listening to him. I was on my feet, a miracle in itself. My shoulders were slumped. I pulled them back. My head was bowed. I raised it. The only thing left for me to do was to lift my sword.

"Do you realize how pathetic you look?" Semyaza said. "Do you really think you can stand against the assembled forces of hell?"

I gripped and regripped my sword. There was no strength

left in my arm. My vision was blurred with blood and sweat. My lungs were on fire. At any moment I could swoon. The sword in my hand was as heavy as an anvil. Yet, somehow, I managed to lift it. My chest burning from the effort, all that was needed to raise it over my head was one final—

"Take him," Semyaza ordered.

At his signal, thousands of demons dropped from above like a swarm of bats so thick I could not see the crowd through them.

They hit me with force, slapping the sword from my hand, pelting every square inch of me, knocking me off my feet and onto my back. They penetrated my chest and head and arms and legs, screaming obscenities in my mind, tearing at my insides, clawing at my soul, as though they were trying to rip it from my body.

I couldn't fight them. I had no strength left. They crammed my mind so full of their shrieks and taunts and obscenities there wasn't room for a single noble thought. Unable to resist even on a mental level, I surrendered to my fate.

But Semyaza wasn't ready for me to die.

I felt myself lifted by invisible hands, suspended above the pillar, my arms and legs stretched out at my sides, pulled by Semyaza on one side and Belial on the other, hanged on an invisible cross.

As he had in the high school office on the day I'd learned my longtime nemesis was an undercover angel, Semyaza burst into brilliance. Belial, likewise, lit up. It was as though I'd been caught in the gravity fields between two suns.

The effect was tantalizing torture. Ripples of pleasure emanated from them, flowing over me like honey, while thousands of demons scrabbled for it like ravenous dogs, scrapping over every morsel. Each delicious sensation ended with a snarl and a bite.

Then the brilliance reversed itself. Instead of shedding glory, Semyaza and Belial fed off me, sucking all color, all joy, all light, every pleasant and happy thought or memory from me, leaving behind a bottomless chasm of hopelessness, a black pit into which the demons descended, making room for more of them to possess me. Upon hearing New Testament accounts of possession, I'd wondered how a legion of demons could occupy a single human soul. I wondered no longer.

There comes a point in a man's life when fight and stubbornness and craftiness give way to reality, when the realization dawns upon him that there are forces in this universe far greater than any one man. Bravery, perseverance, and resourcefulness have nothing to do with it. One man cannot stop a tsunami.

I'd reached that point. All I wanted now was for it to end. For the pain to stop. But it wouldn't stop. I knew it would never stop. Pain was my destiny. I was condemned forever to dwell in misery. There was no exit. For me, eternal life was a curse. The sweet relief of nothingness was but a dream.

And at that moment, I understood.

I understood.

But it was too late. Understanding had come too late.

Just then the flash of a flaming sword severed the tether Belial had on me; a second flash, and my connection to Semyaza was broken. He was hurled aside like a rag doll, howling like an animal at the disruption.

Strong, gentle hands lowered me onto the pedestal. The radiance of the one who cradled me was such that I could not look at him, neither could I make out his features. But there was great tenderness in the way he held me.

"Abdiel," I said weakly. "I didn't know you cared."

My rescuer spoke and I knew it wasn't Abdiel. His voice was

the sound of many waters. He spoke not to me but to the demons within me.

"Leave him," He said.

Such frantic skittering you have never seen. The demons stampeded wildly to get out of me. They did not ask the identity of the one giving the order, neither did they question His authority over them. They'd obviously encountered this voice before. Within seconds they were gone, and the silence within me was deliciously sweet.

My rescuer turned and placed Himself between me and my torturers. His robes were spotless, white, and radiant with glory. The light of His presence fell on the encompassing crowd, revealing them for what they were. Their faces were wrinkled with sin. Haughty eyes bulged. Their garments were stained with the blood of men.

Towering over me, my rescuer stood, valiant and mighty, with the unmistakable air of royalty. How could any of us have mistaken Belial, that comic impostor, for this Divine Warrior, the Son of the Almighty God?

He lifted His sword in challenge. Its blade as pure as crystal flashed with the colors of the rainbow.

Thousands stood against Him, yet none dared accept His challenge.

By this time Semyaza had gathered His wits. "Grant Austin is ours!" he protested. "He surrendered the mark of favor of his own volition."

"That is true," the Divine Warrior said. "But as usual, Semyaza, your interpretation of the facts is self-serving. You knew that the Father would not permit him to enter Sheol with the mark of favor."

"It was his choice."

"You lured him."

"He willingly entered Sheol as a warrior."

"That is true."

Semyaza seized on this. "Everything Grant has suffered, he has suffered as a warrior."

"Again, true."

I didn't like the direction of this argument. Semyaza had regained his swagger.

He said, "Then allow us to conclude what we have begun here."

There was a pause. Too long a pause for my taste.

"Need I remind you," the Divine Warrior said, "that Grant Austin has pledged his allegiance to the Father? As a warrior, he fights under the Father's banner. And we have a sacred tradition in the Father's army. We don't leave our fallen soldiers behind."

An army of angels appeared, numbering thousands upon thousands, ten thousand upon ten thousand, each one with a silver sword that flashed gloriously in the light. They encircled the company of rebel angels.

Semyaza and his crowd loved spectacles. The Divine Warrior was giving them one.

Surrounded, the crowd fidgeted. I'm no expert on angel transport, but from the nervous expressions on their faces it appeared all the exits were cut off. Semyaza was growing increasingly uncomfortable as more and more of the Father's warriors appeared. Maybe he was thinking about how the last battle in Sheol turned out.

"Our work is finished here," he announced.

"On the contrary," the Divine Warrior said. "We have yet to hear from our guest of honor. The one who has brought us together for this occasion."

All eyes turned to me.

I sure didn't want to appear ungrateful, but right now I wanted to get out of here as badly as Semyaza.

"It was thoughtful of you to provide him this forum," the Divine Warrior said. "Grant has something he wants to share with this assembly."

That was news to me. I was no more than a lump on the ground with barely enough strength to lift my head. Besides, there was nothing I wanted to say to those who had put me through this. At least nothing that could be said in the presence of Deity and the heavenly host.

The Divine Warrior turned to me and for the first time I saw His face. Knowing, compassionate eyes looked upon me with a gaze that penetrated deep into my soul. When He looked at me I was known in a way I'd never been known before, yet I felt no condemnation.

"A revelation," He said, prompting me.

It took me a moment before I knew to what He was referring. Maybe it wasn't too late after all.

With the task came the strength. Surprising myself, I managed to get to my feet. I must have looked a sight. My flesh and clothes were tattered and coated with dust. I was covered with red slashes. My face was swollen. I was probably the strangest after-torture speaker Sheol had ever seen.

The first words out of my mouth were raspy and choked, the aftermath of being trampled upon by demons. I swallowed and tried again.

"I came to Sheol, hoping to make passage to heaven and present a petition to the Father," I said.

Laughter filtered through the assembled rebel angels despite their situation.

"Yeah, the joke's on me," I said.

I made the mistake of looking around. This whole situation

was surreal. I was standing on a pedestal in Sheol, addressing the assembled force of Satan and the host of heaven with the Son of God serving as moderator.

"As . . . as many of you know—" I cleared my throat. "Um— one of the archangels . . . Abdiel . . . has been teaching me your history, including what it was like for you before the . . . the . . . insurrection."

"It was a revolution!" one of the rebels yelled.

"We have legitimate grievances!" exclaimed another.

The Divine Warrior made no attempt to respond to them, or to help me out. He seemed content to let me stumble along on my own. I'd never been very good at public debate. He knew that, didn't He?

"OK—" I said. "I won't pretend to teach you your own history. It's just that, whenever Abdiel spoke of the time before the hostilities, he always spoke fondly of many of you, especially Lucifer. It's obvious to me he has great respect for Lucifer's abilities as a leader. And I just can't help but wonder why—if Lucifer is such a brilliant commander—why he can't see that this rebellion is doomed to failure. You can't win."

"We stand against injustice!" a voice bellowed. "We *will* win! Concessions, if not reinstatement."

The rebel angels rallied behind their compatriot. It was the confirmation I needed. They didn't know.

"You're being deceived!" I shouted over them.

They didn't want to hear it. But then, deceivers don't take kindly to being deceived. Semyaza was beginning to fidget.

"The throne of judgment awaits," I said. "You have charted a course of disobedience and destruction. The Father's justice is sure. Lucifer knows this. He knows you can't win. Your destiny is eternal torment."

The crowd roared their displeasure. Semyaza's eyes flared.

Belial's jaw clenched. I didn't even want to think what they'd do to me had ten thousand angels and the Divine Warrior not been at my side.

"Do not listen to the ravings of this insignificant worm!" Semyaza cautioned.

I looked at him. He knew. The others didn't, but he did. He knew Lucifer's hidden agenda.

"Lucifer is no fool!" I said. "Knowing he can't win leaves him only one option—to kick the game board over. His only hope is to convince the Father that creation is flawed beyond redemption. All of it. Earth. The cosmos. The heavens. His argument is for annihilation. Blessed nothingness. No torment. No memories. No earth. No hell. No heaven."

The crowed fell to stunned silence.

Semyaza fidgeted.

"I speak from experience," I said. "The prospect of unending torment is . . . is"—my voice faltered at the recent memory—"is unimaginable. Annihilation would be welcomed as a blessed gift."

Sheol was as quiet as a tomb.

"Every evil in the cosmos adds to Lucifer's argument. I thought you should know what you're working for. It's not concessions. It's not reinstatement. It's annihilation. This is Lucifer's agenda. Semyaza knows this to be true. Ask him."

The rebel angels became embroiled with noise. Shouts of dissension called for support of Lucifer. Others called for Semyaza to address my accusation. Many argued among themselves.

Belial drew my attention. He had gone to Semyaza. The two of them stood toe to toe in heated discussion. Others fell in behind Belial, descending upon Semyaza, demanding answers.

I stood atop my pedestal a safe distance away. Battered. Bruised. Bleeding. But alive and demon-free in Sheol.

"Your task here is done," the Divine Warrior said to me. "We will take our leave."

With Semyaza surrounded by angry, shouting rebel angels, Sheol melted away.

CHAPTER
22

Once again the Father had used Lucifer's strategy against him. And to think I'd witnessed it firsthand. My parting memory of Sheol was of a rebel army in complete disarray storming Semyaza, demanding answers. Semyaza had arranged a spectacle and the Divine Warrior stole the show.

We were standing in my living room. *(The Divine Warrior was standing in my living room!)* How we got there from Sheol I didn't know. All I knew was that the passage was painless, and for that I was grateful.

He stood before me, tall and strong. At once fearful, yet approachable and kind.

"You trusted your enemy," the Son said.

"Yes," I said without excuse, not daring to look Him in the eyes. I suppose it was foolish of me to think I'd escape the inevitable lesson and guilt for this colossal blunder.

"You believed your enemy when he promised to help you gain access to the courts of heaven."

It sounded unbelievably naïve in hindsight.

"Yes," I said.

"Even though your previous attempts to cross dimensions had proven painful and unsuccessful."

"Yes."

"And then you made yourself vulnerable by relinquishing the protective mark of the Father."

"That was—yes."

"All because you wanted to present a petition to the Father."

"Yes."

"On behalf of demons who have on more than one occasion possessed and tormented you."

"When you put it like that, it sounds—"

"The Father has received your petition on behalf of the Nephilim, Grant Austin. We are pleased with you. You have acted unselfishly with steadfast courage and self-sacrifice in the highest tradition of heaven's warriors. We will not forget it on the day of judgment. Well done, thou good and faithful servant."

I dared to look up. Kind eyes embraced me.

Then He was gone.

But He left something behind.

A pair of footprints on my carpet.

I stood there for the longest time as the reality of what I'd experienced began to sink in. My shirt and pants and shoes were slashed and splattered with blood, but my wounds were healed. My silver sword was sharp and had a mirror polish. There was no seal on it. No seal indicating salvation. No seal of protection from the Father. My petition had come with a price.

The following Monday Jana reported on the six o'clock news that the conference in Geneva, Switzerland, had adjourned when Belial failed to make an appearance.

> With the mysterious absence of Neo Jesus at the Neo World conference in Geneva, what had promised to be the dawning of a new era for mankind has turned out to be more of the same old bickering. After two days, when it became clear that the star of the show was a no-show, several ill-advised attempts were made by various delegations to write a new conference agenda. Delegates from Korea, Iran, and Argentina accused the major Western powers of luring them to the conference in a thinly disguised prelude to invasion to establish a central world government.

Taped footage showed a large conference room with long, curved rows of desks. The floor was chaos. Delegates were on their feet shouting at each other in different languages. Two men at the podium fought over the gavel.

> Initially the conference split into two separate conferences, one for scientists and the other for politicians. But the scientists proved no more capable of being able to agree on an agenda than the politicians. Fights broke out at the airport as all the delegates swamped the airlines and runways, all of them insisting on diplomatic privilege.

A video clip played, identifying the speaker as a delegate from England. "Was he the Christ? Not likely. But I'll tell you one thing. No matter where he's from, nobody's going to come to our world and tell us how to solve our problems. We made them. We're going to have to solve them ourselves."

> *According to a local expert on angels, Neo Jesus was a rebel angel in league with Satan. He said, "We can no longer pretend we are alone in this universe. The Bible is unapologetic in its portrayal of a universe in which physical beings and spiritual beings coexist. It warns us that we may entertain angels unawares. We need to learn to recognize them when they appear, and to test the spirits. For some are good. Some, however, are evil."*

> *On a lighter note, a baby Panda was born today at the San Diego Zoo . . .*

As the broadcast continued, I reclined on the sofa and smiled. Jana had used my quotation.

An expert on angels. Don't make me laugh.

Belial was history. At least for now. Who knew when and where Semyaza would pop up. But I decided not to worry about it. In spite of ourselves, the good guys had won this round. But then, sometimes God favors the foolish as long as their hearts are in the right place.

Sue Ling answered the door.

"Grant! You look terrible! You look like you've been to hell and back."

"Sheol. It's in the same neighborhood."

My pants were rumpled. My eyes bloodshot. I had a two-day growth of beard. I was exhausted and smelled as if I'd been wearing the same shirt for a week. My unsightly condition wasn't because of Sheol. The airline industry was to blame.

What should have been a four-hour flight turned into a thirty-six-hour marathon wait in three airport lobbies as two of my flights were canceled due to mechanical problems. Leave it to the airlines to make traveling through interdimensional membranes look appealing.

Sue folded her arms, leaned against the doorframe, and laughed at me. "You really preached to an assembly of rebel angels and demons?"

"Who told you? Jana?"

"Abdiel."

That surprised me. I hadn't seen the big angel since he delivered the message that lost me the mark of favor.

"You've seen Abdiel?"

"He popped in to tell me about your preaching tour. Unbelievable. And you actually lived to tell about it."

"Reinforcements came."

"The Divine Warrior. Oh, Grant, what was He like?"

"Once you see Him, you no longer doubt that good will prevail."

"At first I was angry when Abdiel popped in. But you should have seen him, Grant. He was positively giddy."

"That's hard to imagine."

"He is so proud of you, Grant. And so is the professor. Abdiel told me that when the professor heard what you had done, he whooped so loud he startled some angels to flight like a flock of pigeons."

There was no animosity in her voice when she mentioned the professor. Her sword looked good. Stronger than ever.

"Didn't your mother tell you it's not polite to stare at a woman's sword?"

I don't know why it surprised me that she knew exactly what I was doing. She'd always been one step ahead of me.

"Well?" she said. "How does it look?"

"Beautiful."

When I decided to come to Chapel Hill, I told myself that if her sword had not improved, I'd walk away. I also told myself that I was going to be totally honest with her.

"I no longer have the mark," I said.

Whether she knew it already or not, she acted as though she was hearing it for the first time. She became serious.

"You're just like the professor," she said. "You'd misplace your soul if it wasn't attached to you. Have you considered hiring a housekeeper?"

I grinned. "Are you applying for the position?"

She laughed. "You would hire me even though I haven't earned my doctorate?"

"Life's risky. Sometimes you have to take a chance."

She stepped down onto the porch. She put her arms around me.

"Like this?" she said, kissing me.

Some days you wrestle with the devil. Other days you lose yourself in the arms of a beautiful woman. You never know what the day will bring when you live in Tartarus.

EPILOGUE

Two years after my journey to Sheol I sat in the Loaves and Fishes Bookstore in Chapel Hill signing my new book, *The Divine Warrior*. It contained my transcribed notes from Abdiel, including his recollections of the early church martyrs, which I finally got him to agree to share with me. Including their stories in the book was my way of showing how the life of the Divine Warrior inspires others to live courageous and self-sacrificing lives.

I also included the complete text of the Alexandrian manuscript in the appendix. Once the two narratives were put side by side, it became abundantly clear which was the real Jesus and which was the sham.

Speaking of shams. . . . No one has heard from or seen Belial. I like to think I had something to do with his disappearance and the fizzling of the Neo Jesus movement. That world deception had to be put on hold for a time while Lucifer attended to some pressing internal business.

For the most part, no one seems to miss Neo Jesus. Occasionally his name comes up. But people speak of him much as they do any other passing fad, like the miniskirt of the sixties or the hula hoop of the fifties. And of course there was the conspiracy crowd who pieced together a theory that a faction of Tartarans kidnapped Neo Jesus and did away with him Jimmy Hoffa style. According to Sue, it was faddish among physicists to calculate the location of Tartarus and theorize ways to communicate with subatomic civilizations.

Traditional churches have made a comeback. They always do. Jana did a feature on it that was picked up by the networks. She interviewed three people who had accidentally killed someone. A woman who had backed over her son's best friend who was skateboarding belly-side down. A man who was stretching open a barbed-wire fence for his hunting buddy as he'd done a hundred times before, only this time his rifle fell and went off, killing his buddy instantly. And a rest-home attendant who left the coffeepot on and started a fire that burned six residents to death. Without exception, they said their faith in God helped them through the difficult time.

As the hunter said, "When you hurt that bad, you need more than pulpit jokes and Sunday morning good times."

Dr. Sue Ling sat next to me at the book signing, handing me an open book to be autographed for the next person in line.

A thin, leathery man with no-nonsense eyes picked up one of the books from the stack and examined it through wire glasses.

"Is this fiction or nonfiction?" he asked.

"It doesn't get any more real than this," I told him.

He looked over the book at me. "I guess I'll give it a try."

I signed the front of his book with words the professor once said to me: *Seek the truth, find reality.*

ABOUT THE AUTHOR

Those who have read Jack Cavanaugh's fiction before will recognize that the Kingdom Wars series is a significant departure from the historical fiction Jack is best known for. An award-winning, full-time author, Jack has published twenty-five books to date. His nine-volume American Family Portrait series spans the history of our nation from the arrival of the Puritans to the present. He has also written novels about South Africa, the English versions of the Bible, and German Christians who resisted Hitler. He has published with Victor/Chariot-Victor, Moody, Zondervan, Bethany House, Howard Books, and Fleming H. Revell. His books have been translated into six languages.

The Puritans was a Gold Medallion finalist in 1995. It received the San Diego Book Award for Best Historical Novel in 1994, and the Best Book of the Year Award in 1995 by the San Diego Christian Writers' Guild.

The Patriots won the San Diego Christian Writers' Guild Best Fiction award in 1996.

Glimpses of Truth was a Christy Award finalist in International Fiction in 2000.

While Mortals Sleep won the Christy Award for International Fiction in 2002; the Gold Medal in *ForeWord* magazine's Book of the Year contest in 2001; and the Excellence in Media's Silver Angel Award in 2002.

His Watchful Eye was a Christy Award winner in International Fiction in 2003.

Beyond the Sacred Page was a Christy Award finalist in Historical Fiction in 2004.

Jack has been writing full-time since 1993. A student of the novel for a quarter of a century, he takes his craft seriously, continuing to study and teach at Christian writers' conferences. He is the former pastor of three Southern Baptist churches in San Diego County. He draws upon his theological background for the spiritual elements of his books. Jack has three grown children. He and his wife live in Southern California.